THE
HAIRY POTTER
And Other Al Quinn Mystery Stories

RUSS HALL

The Hairy Potter

Renegade Rhino Press

TABLE OF CONTENTS

THE HAIRY POTTER

"PULL OVER HERE. TRY TO get the car snugged up behind the trunks of that biggest pecan tree." Al Quinn pointed, and Fergie slowed her car and steered it off the road onto a crunch of gravel and pecan shells. She followed the two-rut lane until it ended behind the huge bole of a tree.

"You come here parking a lot? Is that how you know about this place?" she asked.

Dark as it was, he caught the dimple in her cheek and didn't answer.

"That would more likely be Maury's thing," Bonnie said from the back seat.

"Am I the only one having second thoughts about what we're going to do here?" Maury's voice revealed a slight tremor.

"It was practically your idea," Bonnie said.

"I don't think so."

"And I'm just along to drive the getaway car," Fergie said. "Although if you get busted for trespassing I wouldn't want to miss that."

"Turn off the dome light." Al waited until Fergie had done so, then he opened his door, got out of the car into the cool night of what had been a hot Texas day. At this hour it had become more tolerable. He looked around. Not much traffic along Nameless Road at this time of night.

1

The lights of a pickup zoomed by, far enough away Al didn't feel the need to duck and hide.

Once the truck was past the night settled back down over them.

"Holy Hanna. It's as dark out as the inside of a cow," Bonnie said.

"Thank you for that graphic tidbit," Fergie said. "But it sure enough is black out."

Even if the night hadn't promised no sign of the moon at all, the thick cloud cover would have obscured even a crescent sliver. Not even a star poked through when Al glanced up. Just what he had wanted.

"Let your eyes adjust to the extent they can. Use your penlights only when you must. Okay? Are we ready?"

"Umpf."

"Maury, wait on us to start or you'll run into something."

"Too late. Big damn tree, though."

The disembodied voices and footsteps seemed unusually loud to Al. That could just be his nerves being strung tight as piano wire.

Al led the way. He'd been here a few times picking up pecans along the roadside. Back in his uniform days he'd stopped a few vehicles along the road and had crunched his way to their passenger windows on the pecan shells. Later he'd come back in jeans and non-uniform shirt to fill a few bags with pecans before the squirrels got them all. He'd never expected to be back here in the dead of night on a silly-assed mission like this.

"You think you being ex-sheriff's department and Fergie being a former city detective will keep us from being arrested if we're caught?" Maury asked.

"When we get closer to the house we're going to have to maintain complete silence, Maury." Al swept the way ahead with the pencil-thin beam of his penlight. He'd put tight cardboard cones on all the lights they held. "Chances are we won't get arrested. It's more likely we could just get shot."

"Really?"

Al started to turn around and bumped into Fergie. "I thought you were going to stay back at the car?"

"And miss this?" Though she held her light low he caught a glitter in her eyes. "Not for the world."

They wove their way through the end of the thick stand of trees near the road, and then crossed a more open field with only a few live oak trees with all their lower limbs eaten off as high as cattle could reach. Stepping around a few cow pies tipped Al off about the function of the pasture. He swept the beam of his light around but didn't see any of the steers.

"Eww."

"Watch your step, Bonnie." Al glanced back. Bonnie had found a stick to scrape at the bottom of her shoe.

Fergie almost bumped into him, gave him a gentle shove with one hand to keep him moving.

Al had been following a route parallel to the lane. Now he could make out the outline of the house, lit by the light coming through the drawn shades on the ground floor rooms and from one second story room.

"The barn," Bonnie whispered.

Al stopped and let them group up into a tight huddle. He flashed his light around to each face. "From here on in we need total quiet. Not a word."

"But I ..." Maury started.

"Shh." Al interrupted. "Bonnie, if he says another word you have my permission to kick him a good one."

"But I ...Ow!"

"Let's go," Al whispered. "You said the dumpster is along the outside of the barn. Lead me there."

He let Bonnie go on point. They tightened their single-file and followed her.

Somewhere off in the night Al heard a bird he couldn't identify making some sort of loud gulping sound in a pattern so repetitive it quickly became irritating. A twig snapped under someone's foot and he almost stopped them again for another caution.

Bonnie turned her head to whisper. "It's just up here."

Al was listening for dogs. He had brought a small steak on a zip-lock bag. If more than one was running loose they were going to have issues. His own dog, Tanner, has seen him slip the wrapped bit of beef into his pocket and had given Al a tilted-head quizzical look.

Bonnie stopped abruptly and Al bumped into her soft rounded body.

"Don't stop," she whispered.

"Shh." Al turned to Maury, and as softly as he could said, "You're up."

"Why is it always me has to do the dumpster diving?"

"Shh." Al lifted the lid, eased it to hang open.

He and Fergie gave Maury a boost.

"Umpf." Maury tumbled inside.

Al wanted to whisper for him to be quiet, but kept it to himself. He glanced toward the dark silhouette of the house. Nothing had changed.

Bonnie stepped closer and passed a white five-gallon plastic bucket to Al, who lifted it over the dumpster rim, felt Maury take it from him. The three of them outside the dumpster turned off their penlights and waited.

Al heard the clicks and clatters as Al filled the bucket. He saw only a glimmer or two of light as Maury moved around inside. Al glanced toward the house again.

This time he thought the configuration of lights looked

different. An additional window on the ground floor had been lit.

"Let's go." Al stepped close to take the bucket Maury held up, which felt heavier now.

Fergie, who at six-two was taller than Al, reached in to help Maury scramble up out of the dumpster.

"What ...?" Al put a hand over Maury's mouth and stopped whatever he was starting to ask.

Al thought he heard steps coming their way across the hard-packed dirt between the house and the barn. He gave Bonnie a shove and she took off at a fast walk, and wisely didn't turn on her light. Fergie and Maury did the same while Al brought up the rear, expecting at any moment to see a bear-like figure clutching a shotgun.

Maury and Bonnie had said the man was furry enough to live up to the bear image they'd painted of him in their description. Al was willing to take their word for it and not meet the man face-to-face.

Bonnie waited until they started back through the pasture before turning on the thin thread of light from her penlight. Al figured she would risk getting spotted over stepping in another cow pie.

He lugged the heavy bucket and stayed within an arm's reach of Fergie. Every few yards he glanced back. *Nothing.* But he didn't take a deep breath again until they were at Fergie's car, had stowed the bucket in the trunk, and she had turned the ignition key.

"What do you think we'll find?" Fergie asked.

"No use speculating until we're home and can comb through the product of Maury's dumpster diving."

"It was a first for me," Maury said. "I was a dumpster virgin until now."

"That's about the only thing that was virgin about you," Bonnie muttered.

"Now, kiddies, play nice. Don't make me stop this car and have to deal with you." But Fergie was chuckling, and continued to do so all the way back to Al's house by the lake.

———◆———

Al spread newspaper across the dining table. The others gathered around and started pulling the pottery shards from the bucket. Some of the pieces were whole, but twisted and deformed, which is why they'd been tossed.

"Hey, this is one of *my* disasters." Bonnie pointed to a piece that looked like she'd been trying to make an ashtray and had failed at that.

"Those aren't the ones that interest us," Al said.

"This one should." Maury lifted a black shard, broken when something had gone wrong in the firing. "Looks like he was going for something like a Santa Clara Pueblo pot here."

"We do nothing like that in the classes." Bonnie reached for the piece. She held it up beside the screen of the laptop in front of her, tapped a few keys, and drew the shard closer to her eye. "Could be a Mata Ortiz Olla pot he was going for."

"Think big dollar signs, folks," Fergie said. "Would a Maria Martinez be worth more?"

Bonnie put the piece down and clicked away at her keyboard.

"I think he was going for something pre-Columbian here." Maury held up a piece. "I've heard the genuine article has a rough feeling bottom, not smooth like so many fakes."

"Ah, here's something." Bonnie held up a piece that had been part of something Asian. "Do any of you read Chinese? I hear that's a booming market. They're buying up all the objects that appear on the market with the money they get from making about everything we use these days. At least that's what I gleaned from an episode or two of *Antiques Roadshow*."

"The whole point is to know the entire pottery market. It doesn't look like our "Papa Bear" Rum Murphy is doing just one thing, and that's smart. Take this bit of a piece that looks like he was going for George Ohr." Maury held up a fragment. One side showed a mottled blue glaze, the other side the fired inside sweeping curve of a bulbous vase.

"Ohr was an Eighteenth Century potter from Biloxi," Bonnie said. "He gets faked a lot because he never made two pieces that were identical, and he signed the pieces sometimes in big block letters."

Fergie's eyes met Al's. One eyebrow arched. Listening to Maury and Bonnie talk about pottery was like hearing them discussing the details of moon exploration.

Al shrugged. He reached for the piece Maury held. Up close he could see a hair inside the baked clay. Then he saw another. He pointed them out to Maury.

"Yeah. It's a wonder Murphy's pieces don't look like Chia pets. He is one furry fellow and gets close to his work. You ought to see him make a vase that's thrown on the pottery wheel. It's like he's embracing the piece, making love to it."

Bonnie giggled. But sobered when she reached for the shard and admired the glaze. "Any Ohr pot would sell in the thousands. One large vase went for eighty-four thousand at a Sotheby's auction."

Maury dug into the bucket. "Hey, here's one of mine. Might be worth a dime someday."

"What went wrong with it?"

"Got away from me on the wheel and I thought I could

7

save it in the kiln. One of those all-around bad ideas that seemed to make sense at the time."

"I still can't believe you and Bonnie picked making pottery as your new hobby." Al shook his head.

"I think they saw that scene from the movie *Ghost* where things around the potting wheel ended up getting sexy," Fergie said.

Bonnie ignored them. "You'll notice that the bits of pottery we're finding are all aimed at the big dollar market, not the mid-range world of Rookwood, Roseville, Weller, or Van Briggle."

"How do you know this stuff?" Al glanced toward Fergie again.

"We do our homework," Maury said, "just like you do when you're investigating a crime. Plus we know things. That Santa Clara shard was probably meant to reflect the handiwork of Margaret Tafoya. Why? Because that's a top dollar name. Same with Maria Martinez."

"You guys could be talking in pig Latin for all I know." Al put the piece he held into the small pile they had set aside.

"And what makes you think a crime is going on here?" Fergie asked.

"We don't see him working on any of this kind of stuff while we members of his class are around," Bonnie said. "He doesn't have any on the shelves in that workshop area of the barn, either. But the big deal was the house."

Bonnie paused. Al just looked at her, gave her the slack she wanted.

"I mean, the guy mentioned having a wife, but we'd never seen her. Not even a picture of her. But he talks about her, calls her "Momma Bear" Ida Murphy. We're out there once a week. You'd think sooner or later he'd introduce us. It's what made me curious."

8

"Nosy," Maury said. He was looking hard at another broken shard of something that looked Chinese.

"So I go to the back door and peek in one time," Bonnie said. "'Bout knocked my socks off. You saw the outside of the house."

"Not very well in the dark," Al said.

"Well, it's rustic. Take my word for it. Looks like Abe Lincoln built it with his own hands, and never got around to painting it."

"Okay. And?" Fergie said.

"The inside was the stone cold opposite. Looks like how you'd picture the lobby of the Waldorf-Astoria. Swanky. Nice. With fancy do-dads all over the place."

"So he secretly spends money. That's all you had?" Al asked.

"Tell him about the box of dirt," Maury said.

Bonnie nodded. "We use a lot of clay. We're making pottery after all. It's not stuff ol' Papa Bear can find and dig up down by a creek, at least most of it. It gets shipped in. Comes in twenty-five or fifty pound blocks."

"So, one day ..." Maury said.

"Let me tell it," Bonnie interrupted. She narrowed her eyes at him until Maury shrugged and looked away. "We went to get a fresh block of clay. Down beneath the other shipping boxes I spotted one with Chinese on it. Imagine getting clay shipped all the way from China."

"Doesn't surprise me," Fergie said. "We get everything else from them these days."

"That wasn't the big deal. The way Papa Bear reacted when he saw what we were looking at is what blew us away. First time I ever saw him angry."

"He's a big ol' Teddy Bear most of the time," Maury said. He shut up when he got a glance from Bonnie.

"His eyes were sure enough throwing sparks when he

snatched up that box that had to weigh fifty pounds and carried it out the door and over to the house, as much stomping his way as I've ever seen him move," Bonnie said. "So Maury and I asked ourselves why a box of dirt, or clay, would set him off like that." She nodded to Maury that his turn had come.

"We read about how some counterfeiters in Southern China were making two-thousand-year-old pottery soldiers and horses and such by using ancient clay dug out from excavation sites. That way the pottery can pass the carbon dating tests. Experts can usually sort out the fakes, but houses like Sotheby's and Christie's say they're seeing fakes almost daily. But a person can sell them elsewhere and they're hard to spot."

"Especially if they're made of the right clay, old Chinese clay," Bonnie said.

"You take a Han Dynasty piece, and they're regularly faked, it could sell for anywhere from a few thousand up to a hundred and fifty thousand dollars. Any way you stack it, that's buying dirt cheap and selling sky high." Maury couldn't help himself and sniggered at his own joke.

"Sounds like it would take a great deal of talent." Al picked up one of the twisted wrecks of pottery and held it up.

"That's one of mine," Bonnie admitted. "The idea for it looked better in my head."

"I can only imagine." Fergie looked away, but not before Al saw she was trying not to grin outright.

"You still don't have a crime," Al said, "unless you can prove he's making and selling fakes somewhere. This could just be an indulgent hobby of his."

"Explain the inside of his house, then," Bonnie said."

"He may well have an explanation," Al said. "But more to the point, if a crime is being perpetrated here, to use the jargon of our police reports," he glanced toward Fergie, "what do you want to do about it? Have him arrested? You do know that would mean the end of your weekly pottery lessons."

"You always said to do the right thing, what's fair and just, Al. That's especially true if people are being duped and hurt by what Murphy is doing." Maury stared down at the pieces spread across the table. He looked up slowly. "We just want to do the right thing."

Al stayed almost a block back as he tailed the beat-up, fading blue Subaru through traffic. "Well, he didn't blow all the money he's made on a posh vehicle."

When they drove right past a post office Al glanced over at Fergie. She shrugged.

Six blocks later the Subaru swung into the parking lot at a small strip mall.

Al pulled into a parking place as far as he could get from the car he'd tailed. As soon as he turned off the engine he popped out his door and took off at a near trot, then slowed as he fell in behind Murphy, who carried two different sized brown cardboard boxes.

Murphy hadn't met Al, so at the door, Al said, "Here, let me get that for you." He swung the door open and got a quick peek at the address label and return address. A big arm covered in stiff black hairs partially obscured what Al was after. He didn't get enough and stayed close to get in line behind Murphy, who certainly lived up to Bonnie and Maury's description.

The man looked more ape than bear from the back. He was a large, hulkish man with slightly slumped shoulders. He'd had his head cropped to a near buzz cut. Al could see thick black hair everywhere outside the coveralls and

11

rolled-up sleeves of a blue and white checked flannel shirt. Those hirsute sausage fingers didn't look like they belonged to a master craftsman, but Al had learned long ago to discount appearances. Murphy was a big fellow, though, towering half a head over Al, and as furry as they get. No wonder the potters in his class called him Papa Bear.

Al leaned closer to peer at the smaller top package of the two. He was committing the addresses to his memory when Murphy turned to stare at him.

"Heck of a day out there," Al said. "Gonna be a scorcher before it's over. I don't know how you can stand to wear flannel on a day like this."

The man's stare quivered, then broke into a broad grin. White teeth showed through the full black beard. "I keep it cool at home and don't get out much."

"I don't blame you. That sun gets going it can melt off your eyebrows."

Al had to wait in line for Murphy to send his packages. But he did get a glance at the second shipping label, which made the wait worth his while. From the return address he'd learned that Murphy listed this shipping store on his return address, along with a different name, Alonzo Griffin. He probably kept a box here, confirmed that when he called the sales clerk by his name.

By the time Al had bought a book of stamps, paying more than he should, and got back out to the parking lot, the Subaru was gone.

Al had left the truck running for the AC, so when he slid into the driver's seat He put the truck in reverse and backed out of the parking space.

"Where to now?" Fergie asked.

"Road trip," Al said. "First stop is Plano. Second stop is a museum in Fort Worth."

"Oh, my. We do get around."

"We're just lucky we don't have to scoot halfway across America."

"Getting from here to Fort Worth and Plano may well feel like it."

Al shrugged. He knew he couldn't let go of a case like this once he'd committed. Fergie knew it as well. He listened to her hum to herself as they worked their way out of the city and headed north.

———◆———

Aaron Detwiler swung the door open wide as soon as Al started to knock. He must have been standing behind the door waiting. He took in Al but fixed on Fergie, who towered over his small frame.

"You're lucky to catch me at home. I'm usually at the office. I'm a stock broker, don't you know, but it's Saturday." He wore a white dress shirt with an open collar over khaki slacks with a knife-edge seam. The light grey tweed jacket seemed a bit much to Al, who checked to see if the jacket had leather elbow patches. *Nope. Thank goodness.*

"I don't often get visitors, especially ones who wish to see my collectibles. I was actually glad to get your call." He fixed on Fergie again. "I was just sitting around waiting for tea time."

Al could imagine the man spent most of his time sitting around alone. His thinning grey hair made it look like his head was growing through it, and he was acquiring the beginnings of jowls along his neck though he might well only be in his fifties. Al figured him for a bachelor as soon as he led them through the house to a side room. He punched in a number while standing in front of the security panel so Al and Fergie couldn't see the code. Al might have told him that a good crook could have memorized the code from the varying sound of each beep.

"This room has its own security system. You'll soon see why." He swung the door open and led the way inside.

Indirect lighting made the white walls bright, and separate small lights fixed beams on items along the walls. Several lights focused on a red, yellow, and blue bowl in the center of the room. While the walls were crammed with shelves filled with pots, ceramics, metal and even jade artifacts, the bowl in the middle was the one Detwiler stared at, and moved between it and his visitors.

"Is that one you got from Alonzo?"

"Yes. Funny story that. I can tell you if you promise not to tell him."

"Of course," Fergie spoke for them. "I've never even met the man, only heard of him."

Detwiler nodded, bursting inside to tell his story.

"You see, I spotted this thing listed for an auction. I knew what I was seeing immediately, had done business with the man before, so I fired off an email and ended up buying the thing before it ever hit the auction floor. Even then there was a risk of someone else spotting what I had. It was listed incorrectly. What you have here," he waved a sweeping hand at the bowl, "is a Han Dynasty gem of a find. That's a couple of hundred years B.C. It should be in a museum. Now it is. In *my* museum."

"You had it carbon dated?" Fergie asked.

"Of course I did. It's as genuine as you and I standing here."

"I don't know about all that, "Al said, "but it sure is a pretty bowl."

"It's a beaut," Detwiler agreed.

———◆———

Al took the time to stop at a Cooper's BBQ branch in Fort Worth for lunch before he and Fergie rolled into the parking lot of a museum that stood alone on a lot, looking far smaller than the Amon Carter, Sid Richardson or any of the dozen other larger museums in town. The building looked solid, made of stone and showing a cornerstone that declared it had long ago been a Masonic Hall.

The day had begun to heat up in earnest as Al stepped out of the truck. He patted his stomach, glad he hadn't overdone a good thing as was so easy to do at Cooper's.

When they stepped inside the museum their heels clicked on a granite floor. They were the only ones there beside a fellow on the far side of the displays coming their way.

"Always this busy?" Al asked.

If Al expected a "Ha, ha" he would have to wait a long while for it. The museum curator twisted his mouth in a way that said he wasn't much of a kidder on his best days, and this wasn't one of them.

"I'm glad you called ahead. On slow days, as you have surely observed this is one, I often work in the back preparing new dioramas." He held out a hand to Fergie first. "Marvin Whipple, museum curator, at your disposal. Is this about some sort of investigation?"

Al knew Fergie had been careful about her word selection during the call, but she had left room for the curator to think they were two active cops instead of two retired ones.

"As she said on the phone, we wanted to know of you'd purchased any artifacts from an Alonzo Griffin. You said you had." Al knew the museum got boxes from Murphy's alias. He'd seen one at the shipping store and figured it wasn't the first.

This time a smile oozed onto Whipple's face that Al could only call a smarmy smirk.

"Yes. Indeed I have." He nearly worked himself up to a chuckle.

"Were you satisfied with what you bought from him?"

"Whatever do you mean?"

"I mean was it the real thing?"

Whipple suppressed a near snort. He led them to a display of Chinese objects along one wall. Near the center, Al saw a bowl that was a near ringer to the one he'd just seen in Aaron Detwiler's collection.

Whipple waved to it.

"Well, of course I know this to be a fake. Remarkable job, but not the real thing. Nevertheless, a tour de force of an imitation. But I knew immediately." He tapped the side of his nose. I paid a tenth of what I would have paid for the genuine article."

"Why didn't you complain when you found out?"

"Because I bought it knowing it probably wasn't real. We had one just like it that was. So our real one is in the vault now, and if someone steals or breaks this one we're out for a whole lot less, and we've protected a real treasure. All curators have been on their toes since some nut with a hammer attacked Michelangelo's David in that Florence museum."

"So when you see an artifact that matches something valuable in your collection offered at a lower than likely price, you just scoop it up?" Fergie asked.

"There's nothing anomalistic about the practice. Other museums do it as well. Sometimes they stumble across a piece that is real. I haven't been so fortunate."

"Didn't the low price send any kind of signal?" Al said. He noticed the heightened vocabulary that to his ear had taken on a sententious tone.

"The seller sought to play on my cupidity, but I outfoxed his perfidious intentions."

"How do you know it's a he?"

"You should see how the objects are packed. I hesitate to censure by gender, but really. My word."

"You've bought more than the one item from this seller?"

"Yes.

"Does anyone in the public ever catch on that you have stand-in stunt objects in places instead of the real thing?"

"Look around you. Does your eye detect what is real and what is fake, detective?"

As soon as they were outside the building, walking back toward Al's truck, Fergie said, "That detecting quip of his was a cheap shot, wasn't it?"

"Lightly taken from the likes of him." Al said. "I do think that fellow sat on a thesaurus."

"The first thing folks look for on the job description of museum curator, at least in this instance, is that he be a pedantic twit."

"But a happy one since he got the best end of the deal."

"Or so he thinks."

———❖———

Al watched for the exit sign he wanted on the outskirts of Austin when Fergie asked, "What are we going to do about Murphy?"

"It's a conundrum."

"What he's doing is fraud, and though we didn't find it, some people may get hurt when they find the thing they bought doesn't have the value they thought it did."

"I suppose what we do next depends on our esteemed non-paying clients. If they want to make the formal complaint we could see that he gets brought in for what's illegal here."

Fergie dug her cell phone out of her small purse and made the call, turning on the speaker so Al could be part of the conversation.

"Where are you guys?" Fergie asked Maury when he answered.

"Out at Murphy's place. It's pottery class day."

Al listened while Fergie caught Maury up on the results of their road trip.

"So you're saying nothing illegal is going on?" Maury said.

"No. We're not saying that at all," Al said. "It's just that the people we met who are buying the items are pleased with them. Some, like this Aaron Detwiler, we visited even asked for and got a certificate of authenticity."

"That was a nice touch." Fergie said.

"I thought so." Maury said.

Al frowned. Maury had clearly missed her sarcasm.

"Another went to a museum." Al slowed the truck and pulled over. Even though he wasn't the person holding the phone he didn't want to allow a distraction. "They used it in their display so the real one could be kept in a vault. The curator knows it's a fake and is okay with that. Plus he got a good deal, feels a little clever about that."

"Not as clever as that smug Detwiler feels," Fergie said.

"So what are you saying? Should we just let this drop? Surely some people are going to get hurt by this."

"I suppose we could talk to the guy." Al checked the road and pulled back into traffic.

"Well he's not here. He got a call and shot out the door with a couple of brown boxes. We're left to our own devices here and I've got to tell you it looks like everything we're making is going to turn into ashtrays."

While Fergie put away her phone Al glanced at his watch and stepped on the gas. "I think I know where we can find him."

"I had the same notion," Fergie said. "That shipping store is probably still open."

Al was just pulling into the strip mall's parking lot when he saw Murphy climbing out of his battered old Subaru. Hard to miss a hulking bear like him. Even harder to miss the guy running across the parking lot toward him who was waving his arms.

Murphy lowered the boxes he held to the asphalt. The man ran up to him and swung a hard right fist to Murphy's stomach. Murphy stood there, didn't strike back. He seemed to be saying something. The smaller man swung at him again. Murphy lifted a thick arm to fend the blow away from his face, but again didn't punch back.

Al pulled the truck into a parking space, put it in park, and shot out his door, leaving it open behind him.

He got to the two of them just as the man swung for Murphy's face again. Al caught the moving right arm and held it still. The man's head snapped toward him. His face was flushed red. "Leave us alone. This is between us."

Al tugged the man backward until he stood out of reach from Murphy. He tried to get around Al, but Fergie came up to them and stood in front of Murphy.

The man struggled, but Al had him by both wrists he held pinned to the man's sides. "Why don't you tell us what's going on here? Can't you see he could swat you like a fly if he wanted to, but he's not fighting back."

"He cheated me, sold me a fraud."

"Who? This guy?" Al gave a head nod toward Murphy.

" Yeah. Alonzo Griffin. He's the one. I never met him, but the clerk inside pointed him out when he got here."

"I offered to give him back his money," Murphy said. "He got a thirty-thousand dollar vase for three thousand. I told him I'd write him a check right here."

"I don't want the money. I want satisfaction. No one cheats Edgar Hecht."

Al guessed that was the man's name, though it always made him twitch when anyone spoke of himself in the third person. And, of course, it had to be Edgar and not just Ed. "Can I ask you something ... if you'll calm down for a moment?" Edgar still struggled to break free, but Al held Edgar's wrists tightly to his sides.

"I want ..."

"Go ahead and ask him, Al," Fergie interrupted.

Al could see the shipping store clerk looking out the front window at them. Closing time had to be near and seeing the hubbub in the parking lot clearly outweighed tending to the needs of the one or two customers still in the store.

"How did you find out?" Al asked.

Edgar sputtered. He tried and failed again to break free. "I'm a huge, huge George Ohr fan, enough so I drove all the way over to Biloxi, Mississippi. And do you know what I found in the Ohr-O'Keefe Museum of Art there?"

"I can guess, but why don't you tell me."

"I found the exact same piece I'd bought. It was there on display, even had the same cursive signature. An Ohr piece is supposed to be a one-of-a-kind. So, what the hell?"

"Why don't you just take the man's check and be done with it?" Fergie said.

"It's a matter of pride."

"If it were a mere matter of pride any one of us might square off against you and handle you easily," Al said. "Take the man's check."

Edgar's face grew even redder, and he struggled harder, but got nowhere. He glared at each of them, Murphy, then Al, finally landing on Fergie who glared back with eyes narrowed and nostrils flared. He suddenly stopped and let out a long breath. "Okay. Okay."

Murphy got out his check book and wrote out the check,

signed it as Alonzo Griffin, and handed it to Al, who held it out to Edgar.

As soon as Al let go of him Edgar started to rush around Al, but Fergie stepped forward to block his way. The man glared up at her. Al didn't favor Edgar's chances of winning that staring match. Finally he reached out and snatched the check from Al's hand. He crumpled it as he shoved it into his pocket, then turned and stalked away with whatever he probably thought was left of his pride.

"Another satisfied customer?" Al asked Murphy.

"I don't know what you think is going on here, but that was just an unfortunate business transaction gone wrong. Nothing to fret over." Murphy had a low voice, but it was soft, unthreatening, and reflected the way he had just stood there while Edgar was swinging away at first.

"I think you know," Al said. He glanced toward the shipping store, where the clerk was flipped the OPEN sign around to read CLOSED.

Murphy sighed and lifted his boxes from the ground and put them back in his vehicle.

He turned back to Al. "Are you Maury's brother, the ex-cop?"

"She's the ex-cop," Al nodded toward Fergie. I'm ex-sheriff's department."

"Same thing. Right?"

"It's a difference, as well as a distinction," Al said. "But you're right. It doesn't matter a whole hell of a lot. Do many people get riled over their pottery purchases that way?"

Al glanced to where Edgar had pulled out of the parking lot with an irritated chirp of tire rubber.

Murphy seemed to be thinking over what to say.

"We met some of your customers," Fergie said, "or should I say Alonzo Griffin's. *They* seemed okay with what you sold them."

"Looks like you're going to need to move your business to another shipping store, though," Al said, "if the staff of this one gave you up so easily. Do you have to change them often?"

Murphy still seemed to struggle with his thoughts. He finally said, "This is the third one. Yeah, I can always shift that." He hesitated. "Look, most of the stuff will hold up to the closest scrutiny."

"That's not the point now, is it?" Al waited for a response, got none, so he added, "And no it wouldn't in the long run. That Fort Worth curator knows, and even the people doing carbon dating aren't going to be fooled all the time by some old Chinese dirt. Do you know why?"

Murphy's eyes opened wide at "old Chinese dirt." He shook his head.

"You may have noticed that you're furrier than the average bear." Al held up his arm beside Murphy's. He could barely see skin beneath all the thick black hair on Murphy's arm.

"How's that ...?"

"You are leaving hairs in the pottery you make. It would probably be hard not to unless you wore some kind of rubber suit. So you're not only embedding the pieces with a far more recent carbon imprint, you're giving any really good investigator some of your DNA."

Al knew this was true of some semi-burnt bones he'd had to work with in previous cases, was less sure any hairs could survive the extreme heat of a kiln. He did know that in black burnt bones the DNA was highly degraded and in some cases no nuclear DNA was left, leaving mitochondrial DNA analysis as an option. He didn't go into any of that, didn't need to do so. He was after an effect, which he got. Big as he was, Murphy rocked back half an inch. That information had hit him harder than any of Edgar's punches.

He stood speechless, might have even quivered for a second or two. He finally managed, "What …What are you going to do?"

"Tell you the truth, we haven't decided yet." Al glanced toward Fergie.

"Can I ask a favor of you?" His was a very weak voice coming from such a big man.

"What?"

"Can you come out to my place for just a quick visit before you decide? Bonnie and Maury are probably still there with my other students."

"Okay."

Al and Fergie got back into his truck and followed Murphy's Subaru out to the house and barn where not too far back in the past they had both been burglars in the night.

———◆———

While Al parked the truck he saw Murphy waiting by the house. Bonnie and Maury had come out of the barn and stood near him, but none of them looked like they knew what to say.

As Al and Fergie walked up to them, Murphy said, "You probably want to know why I do what I do. Right?"

Al nodded.

"I'll show you." Murphy turned and swung the front door open for them.

Al had heard Bonnie's description of the interior of "Poppa Bear" Rum Murphy's house. He expected to see some pretty luxurious digs. Instead the inside of the house matched the outside in rustic décor. A lone overstuffed chair sat across from an older style television. The floor was worn bare wood. One folding TV tray nestled up against the chair.

Along the far wall stretched a couch that looked dusty enough it hadn't been used in years.

"Is Momma Bear Murphy here?" Bonnie asked in a tiny voice.

Al was guessing she was adjusting to what she had seen compared to what she was seeing now, perhaps wondering if that had all been a dream. Al believed her, but also believed his eyes.

"Momma Bear passed away seven years ago," Murphy said, fought a hitch in his throat as he said it.

"What about ...?"

It was as far as Al got before Murphy made a tired wave with one hand for them to follow. The back of the room separated the rest of the house from the front by a pair of wooden sliding doors. Murphy slid one side open and led the way into the back.

Now this was what Bonnie had described. Someone had spent a lot of time, and money, making this room look like the inside of a palace.

Fergie gasped.

Murphy held up a finger to his lips. The back wall of this room had a huge picture window that looked out over the back yard and into the stand of woods that ran along the property behind the barn.

In front of the window a wheel chair sat pointing out to the lawn.

"She likes to watch the deer and the squirrels, so I put out food for them to come and play," Murphy whispered.

They all moved up closer behind him. Al could see the small figure of a girl with wispy fine blond hair, who leaned to one side, asleep with a red fleece blanket across her legs.

Murphy gestured toward the front room. When they were all back in it he slid the door shut and turned to them.

"She has Down Syndrome, and her legs haven't worked

well enough to get around without a wheelchair since she was three. She's eleven now, and she's my little princess. She asked for just the one thing, and that was to live like a princess in a castle, so I did that for her, made it happen."

Again the burr of emotion showed in his voice. Al looked to Bonnie and Fergie. Neither of them looked able to speak at all.

"Well, dammit, Al," Maury said.

"Yeah, I know." Al shook his head.

"If you have to have me arrested or anything, can you just give me time so I can arrange for someone to take care of Cynthia Mae. She's all I have, and I promised I'd take care of her. I may have crossed a line, but ... but ..."

"Well, dammit, Al," Maury said again.

Al held up a hand. "Give me a second here." He glanced in the direction the barn would be if he could see outside. The dusty venetian blinds were shut and only horizontal slivers of light poked through.

"Let me ask. If you can make pottery of the quality able to pass as genuine or near genuine, can't you makes some original pieces good enough to sell?"

"Don't think I haven't tried. I made a ton of stuff. Still have most of it. And, yeah, it was good, damned good. But with all the time it takes tending to my little princess I haven't been able to get to the street festivals, or shops and galleries to market my own stuff the way I should. I need to have a platform to get my stuff moving. So I had to resort to doing stuff that could almost sell itself. It's why I decided to give the pottery classes. I could be close to Cynthia Mae and make a small bit of money there. I was very fair about the prices on the fake stuff, don't you think? Almost everybody that grabbed up what I put out there thought they got the best of me in the deal."

"Well, that should probably stop," Al said.

"But what ..."

"What if some else could take your stuff to a few street festivals, hustle around and get your pottery into a few craft stores, as your pieces, in your name?" Al said. "Would that start some momentum rolling for you?"

"It sure would. But who ..."

Al nodded toward Bonnie and Maury. "I have a couple of people in mind."

Bonnie nodded right away. Maury glanced her way, then nodded too.

"And it would still be okay for them to come here and get their pottery lessons?" Fergie asked.

"It sure would." Murphy stepped close and drew Bonnie and Maury to him in a gentle bear hug. Maury looked with wide eyes toward Al over the furry arm that gripped him.

Outside, they stood together by their vehicles. Murphy had tip-toed into the back room as they had left.

Bonnie rubbed at her eyes. "Allergies," she said.

Fergie still hadn't spoken.

"Well, this is sure not how I expected this to come out," Maury said.

"You're okay with helping him out?"

"Sure, I guess." He glanced back toward the house. "I think it'll be work, but might even be more fun than it sounds."

"I guess we've got no kick coming," Bonnie managed, "'cause we sure enough dug this one ourselves."

"That's the thing." Al chuckled. "It's like when you dig a deep hole, there's always more dirt than will go back into the hole."

IT'S RAINING MONEY

FERGIE DROVE DOWN THE NARROW two-lane country road with Maury and Bonnie in the back seat cuddling and babbling like two teenagers on a prom date when a green Chrysler Town & Country minivan rolled right through a stop sign and pulled out in front of her. She had to slam on the brake hard to keep from hitting the intruder to her lane.

Loose gravel on the road kept her tires from gripping the way they should. Her car slid to the right. She wrenched her steering wheel into the skid. As soon as the wheels touched the grass, she hit the gas and steered herself away from a ditch and bounced back up onto the road.

Her car rocked into place as she got back into her lane. The minivan ahead of her was pulling away, but swaying from side-to-side as well, whether from its brisk turn onto the road or from shocks that could use some attention. *Shocks*, Fergie figured. She still felt a warm burn of anger inside. She started to press down on the gas and catch up, but made herself stop.

"Hey, what the hell?" Maury said. "Slow down, Fergie."

"Why? I'm only going the ..."

"It's not that. Look to the right shoulder. See it? Looks like a dollar to me. And there's another, just settling down beside it."

Fergie glanced in the rearview mirror. No one was

coming. They were alone on the road for the moment, except for the minivan that was slipping out of sight ahead as it went around a bend.

She eased over into a stretch of gravel by a lane and mail box that gave the mail carrier room to get off the road.

Maury popped out the back door. Bonnie sat there a moment, then said, "I guess I'd best get going too."

Fergie was slower getting out. All she was supposed to be doing was picking them up after their pottery class, and here was Maury running around like a kid on an Easter egg hunt.

"Hey. Hey. Check this out." He came jogging up to her. He extended his right hand that held the green bills of currency. "They're hundreds. Can you believe it?"

Bonnie bent over the ditch on the other side of the road, picking away.

Maury took off in a run.

Fergie looked around. It took her only a couple of moments to find one as well. A hundred dollar bill lay tucked in the folds of a buffalo gourd vine along the side of the road. She found another sitting on top of a green clump of bunch grass, and spotted yet another at the base of a mountain cedar.

She started to feel some of the same fever Maury had shown. She looked up the road. The minivan was out of sight and probably far away by now. It didn't seem to be coming back this way.

<hr>

Al was using the weed wacker to trim away growth around the base of his house when Fergie's car pulled up. The three of them piled out, waving something in their hands. He couldn't hear what they were yelling over the sound of the machine. He hit the kill switch and let the little two-cycle engine wind down to a stop.

"We found money," Maury yelled. "Hundreds."

"Twenty-seven hundred in all," Fergie said, "and we may have missed a few, even though we went up and down the road a ways."

"We think it came out of a Chrysler Town & Country minivan," Maury said, his voice settling down from his yelling. "A green one."

Al glanced toward Fergie. She'd done police work too. Her mouth had a set to it.

"Why don't we go inside and talk this over?" he said. "I just made a fresh pot of coffee."

His dog Tanner came rushing up to him, wagging his tail and nuzzling Al's legs as he patted the dog's back. Maury and Fergie put all the bills together in one stack on the dining table while Bonnie brought over four mugs and the thermos of coffee.

Once they all held warm mugs of coffee, Al said, "Now tell me about the minivan."

"It was green, like I said." Maury stared down at the pile of money.

"Not new, but not real, real old either, Fergie said. "I can't always tell a Ford from a Chevy, but it was one of the two, if it wasn't a Dodge."

"That's narrowing it down," Al said.

"I said it was a Chrysler." Maury raised his eyebrows at Fergie.

"Thanks ever so much." Fergie let the sarcasm drip. She turned back to Al. "I don't think we have a very good chance of finding out who was in the minivan or where it went."

"Oh, I don't know about that." Al was looking at Bonnie, whose head had stayed lowered as she stared into her mug. "Perhaps you haven't noticed the one irregular thing here. Bonnie hasn't said a word so far. How often does that happen?"

Maury and Fergie's heads both spun to Bonnie.

She kept her head down.

"Bonnie? Anything you want to share with us?"

Tick. Tick. Tick.

"Bonnie?"

Tick. Tick. Tick.

"Yeah, come on, Bonnie. What the hell?" Maury said.

"Don't push her," Fergie said.

Bonnie's head lifted and she looked around at them, one-by-one. "I have an idea. I think I know who it was, but I didn't want to say. Don't make me say it."

Fergie drove her car, so they could all ride along. Al looked out the passenger window at some parts of the county he remembered all too well. When she turned into the trailer court, he said, "We busted a meth lab or two in this very place."

"I can't believe Grannie Boo Smitner has been reduced to living in a place like this," Bonnie said from the back seat.

"I can't believe it was her driving a vehicle spitting out hundreds," Maury said. Then, "Umpf," when Bonnie caught him in the ribs with her elbow.

"You're sure it was her minivan?" Al asked.

"Regrettably, yes."

"She's in our pottery class, but Bonnie knew Grannie Boo from way back when they were both nurses at the same hospital," Maury said.

"Does she live near the back of the trailer court?" Al asked.

"Why?" Bonnie sat up closer and stared ahead.

A large black van with ICE SWAT in block letters on its side had pulled up snug to the front of a trailer.

"Yep. That's her place," Bonnie said.

"Good gracious. I'll bet she's sure the talk of the neighborhood about now," Fergie said.

As she pulled closer a man in the black SWAT team gear stepped out to hold up the flat of one hand and indicate with the other that they should turn around.

"I don't think whatever we were going to talk to her about is going to surprise her now," Al said.

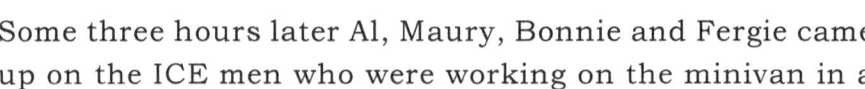

Some three hours later Al, Maury, Bonnie and Fergie came up on the ICE men who were working on the minivan in a garage across the road from the Travis County Correctional complex in Del Valle, where Al had spent many an hour.

The guard at the garage entrance stopped them, but someone from the back yelled, "It's okay. Let them through."

As Al got closer he could see his friend Jaime Avila, who ran most of the ICE operations in the area. They had both taken turns saving each other's lives. Al was trying to reckon in his head who owed who. He guessed Avila had been ahead once but still owed Al now.

Mechanics used long handled crowbars to pry open the dash and other cavities in the minivan. It was going to be pretty much scrap by the time they got done, but they didn't seem to care. They put each bundle of money they found into one bin and tossed left over car parts in a pile to the side.

Jaime pointed to one bundle of hundreds he'd set aside. The corner was torn open. When Al leaned in closer he could see it looked chewed.

"Mice," Jaime said. "At least that's what we figure. From the looks of that trailer court it could have been rats."

Al dug in his pocket and came up with the $2,700 the others had found. He held it out to Jaime, who started to shrug it off, then reached out and took it. He shoved it into the hole in the corner of the damaged bundle.

Each bundle of bills had been wrapped in thick clear plastic so the denomination showed through. All were hundreds.

"Any idea how much you have so far?" Al asked.

"My guess is two-point-two million and climbing. You know, minivans like this are the equivalent of a stealth jet to police officers. You get a soccer mom or a grannie behind the wheel, Caucasian if possible, and the damn things are nearly invisible. Drugs can come into the states and cash goes out. Some folks fill them with kids and see that they're all asleep and shouldn't be disturbed at the border crossing. Throw in the scent of a spoiled diaper or two and not even a drug smelling dog wants to linger long there."

"Grannies?" Bonnie said.

"Yeah. They were using underage kids for a while, since even if they got caught they'd be tried as a juvenile. But that's all changing. One Arizona county is trying them all as adults, whether seventeen or not. It's sending a message, so the cartels are back to little old white-haired grannies."

"Any idea which cartel is behind this?" Al stayed fixed on the men finding bundle after bundle of money.

"My guess would be the Sinaloa Cartel. They specialize in coke and heroine coming in and, of course, money going out. Your grannie was just fixing to go back down across the border."

"Did she confess?" Al asked.

"No. She said she was innocent, didn't know a thing. They all say that."

"It's okay for us to see her, have a few words?" Fergie asked.

"Yeah. I've cleared the way for you four. We've certainly been through enough together before, and Al knows his way around the jail as well as anyone."

"Did she say why she makes as many trips to Mexico as she does?" Al asked. "Is it for some sort of health care she can't get in the states?"

"I'll let her tell you herself. Give her my best. Her vehicle is certainly coughing up *her* best." Jaime turned back to the chore at hand, rendering Grannie Boo's vehicle into scrap metal.

Al, Maury, Fergie and Bonnie turned and headed back out of the garage. When Al glanced back the crew was still prying away, looking for more hidden caches of cash.

⫷⬥⫸

Al knew it was unusual for a posse such as his to be allowed in, all-at-once, to speak with someone in holding, but with his being a former sheriff's department detective, along with Jaime Avila's even more massive clout, they were let into a room to speak with Grannie Boo Smitner.

She sat at a steel table surrounded by steel chairs and looked up at them as they came in.

Bonnie rushed to her and Grannie Boo stood so they could hug, Bonnie's arms going around the wide horizontal black and white stripes of the older woman's prison togs.

After Bonnie introduced Al and Fergie to Grannie Boo, they all sat down, making the usual squeaking clangs of metal chairs on a quite hard floor.

"They are finding an awfully lot of money in your vehicle. Are you sure you know nothing about that."

"Absolutely not. I'm still as stunned by all this as anyone. I'm as innocent as the day is long, and longer. I can't believe this is happening."

"Why do you think those ICE people swooped in on you?"

"They said they got a tip. I don't know from whom. Maybe it's because I don't have a big house of stone." She rubbed the sleeve of her striped shirt under one eye that had begun to tear up. "People say we're trailer trash, think we all have electric company spools as picnic tables. But if you looked there were flowers around my trailer's base. And fresh paint. There wasn't a lot of clutter. It was as nice as I could keep it until those SWAT men stomped and crashed around all through it."

"You're not gonna like what they've done to your vehicle either," Maury said. He got a "hush-up" look from Bonnie and closed his mouth.

"Do you make a lot of trips to and from Mexico?" Al asked.

"Oh, dozens. I've gone every year since I've been retired, sometimes twice a year when I can afford it."

"Why?"

"Are you getting some kind of special medical help down there?" Bonnie asked.

Grannie Boo shook her head. "I go down to do volunteer work in poor communities with my Baptist mission group. Since I was a nurse I have skills that assist a doctor who cares for those too poor to afford medical help."

"That sounds noble enough. Yet there's no doubt that ICE is pulling a lot of money from your vehicle right now," Fergie said.

"Late car," Maury said.

Fergie gave him a quick glare. "Have you any idea how it got in there?"

"Not an iota." She looked down at the table, then back up at him. "Don't you think I'd have used the money for good works if I'd known it was in there?"

"That's not a new vehicle. Is it any kind of a problem driving it all the way down to Mexico and back?" Al asked.

"Not really. The church sees to that. I get check-ups before and after each trip."

"That sounds like a good idea," Al said. "You must surely know that drugs must have been smuggled to the states from Mexico a number of times as well."

"How can I know that? I didn't know about any money. I darn well don't know about any drugs. Hell, those border people went over my car any number of times. They used those little mirrors to look under it and even let their drug-sniffing dog have a go several times. Nothing. I can't believe for a moment I'm a part of anything like it. And now look at me." She waved a hand down across the prison outfit. "I look like some kind of fat zebra. I'm innocent I tell you."

———◆———

As soon as they climbed back into Fergie's car, Bonnie leaned forward from the back seat and grabbed Al's shoulder. "I think she's innocent, and I'd like to hire you to prove it."

"And pay me with what? I'm the one still paying you to nurse Maury back to health."

"Doesn't he just look rosy as a new peach?" Bonnie said. "But really, why are you still paying me? It's clear Maury and I have progressed beyond nurse and patient."

"Don't forget you still give me sponge baths," Maury said.

"And you can't just find money at the side of the road," Fergie said. "Oh, wait. You can ... sometimes."

"I'm going to dump you two off first."

"Why?" Maury whined.

"Because if a cartel is on one end of this, whatever's on the other end could be just as dangerous if we uncover what they're up to."

"Something like that might just get you killed. Right, Al?" Bonnie said.

"Correct."

"Well, we want to be along," Bonnie said, "and share the risk. It's my friend and Maury's pottery classmate. We can help and even stay out of the way."

"We'll see how this first stop goes. If done right it should be harmless enough."

"Where to?" Fergie asked.

"Easy Bill's Auto. It's the second nearest mechanic shop to where Smitner lived."

"Is this a hunch, Al?" Fergie glanced toward him.

"Not really. While Avila's men were reducing her vehicle to rubble, and were tearing out the dashboard, I eased close and got a peek at the windshield. I saw one of those oil change stickers garages use."

"The sticker was for Easy Bill's?"

"Yes, indeedy."

"Now, you two stay in the car," Al said when he and Fergie got out in the parking lot of Easy Bill's. The place looked like most other auto repair and maintenance garages. Four doors, three of them open with vehicles up on hydraulic lifts, the end door closed and padlocked.

No one appeared to be in the office. Al leaned his head into one of the work area bays. A man in blue coveralls with an orange rag hanging out of his back pocket stood over by an open toolbox, the big red kind with many drawers. It sat on a silver cart that had been rolled close to the open hood of a white pickup.

Another mechanic was just popping the wheel off a Toyota sedan, probably to get to the brakes since new brakes shoes lay at the man's feet.

It appeared to be just another not particularly noteworthy day at an auto shop.

"Pardon me," Al said.

The man by the toolbox snapped his head around. The embroidered label on his coveralls said: "Easy Bill's Auto Repair." He had one of those long heads shaped like a bullet, and in his case his pale scalp was shooting out the top of his thinning grey hair as a pointy dome. Fergie was six-two, and this man was three or four inches taller.

"A friend of ours, Grannie Boo Smitner said this is a trustworthy garage, that you go to her church."

"You could say that." The tall man with a deep bass voice grinned. "I'm Deacon Earl Wilson. That's Bobby yonder. Why do you ask?"

Bobby tried to grin, which would have worked better if he had more teeth. Both of the mechanics looked like hard cases cleaned up to Al, not the sort he pictured sitting on a pew with an open hymnal on Sunday morning. Maybe everyone in their church looked like a few miles of bad road, though Grannie Boo hadn't. She looked as advertised, like a retired nurse who was a grandmother to happy, squealing children.

All the while he was talking Al looked around inside the garage. He didn't know what he expected to find, but not so much of a big fat nothing as he was seeing.

"You keep that old Chrysler of hers running?"

"As best we can. She needed it for the missions."

"The ones in Mexico?"

"That's just some of what we do. But, yeah, that's where

she goes most often, to help heal people too poor to care for themselves."

All the while Deacon Wilson spoke he rubbed his hands on the orange rag that had once hung from his pocket. Bobby had somewhere in the exchange picked up a tire iron, which he held down alongside his leg.

"You service her before and after her trips?"

"Yeah? Why you askin'? Do you have a car you want to bring in?"

Al figured he was teetering right on the edge of going too far. He glanced to Fergie, who picked up the cue.

"We'd better get going, honey. This sounds like a fine place to bring the car."

Al almost got turned and headed for the door.

A voice boomed from the open garage door. "Hey, I foun' these two outside pokin' 'roun'"

The Latino speaker wore blue jeans, a blue denim shirt, and held a gun pointed at the backs of Maury and Bonnie. Maury held both hands up. Bonnie had her arms crossed on her chest and wore a look of disgust.

"Wha' you wan' me to do?"

"Well, we weren't going to do *anything*. But now it looks like we have to, Jorge." The deacon reached to his tool box and took out a large gun that looked like an Army Colt .45 to Al. He didn't see those too often these days, and he sure didn't welcome seeing one now. The hole at the end of the barrel looked big enough to crawl into.

"Hey, I jus' see them poking. Wha' you wan' me to do?" He held up a cell phone he'd taken from Bonnie. "I don' thin' she call yet." He threw it to the cement floor as hard as he could. It shattered into far too many pieces to ever take or send a call again.

"We'll have to put them into the room ... for now." Deacon Wilson waved his gun and steered his four

<figure>38</figure>

hostages toward the back, and then toward the bay at the end that Al had seen closed and padlocked. He was getting a pretty darn good feeling that Wilson was no kind of Baptist deacon, though he might have played the role as it suited his needs.

Al kept his eyes open for any opportunity to break free or turn the tables, but the two women and Maury kept him from doing anything rash. The gun barrels didn't waver and he didn't want to make them trigger happy. At least, so far, everyone was alive.

These guys had done something like this before, Al figured. They took Fergie in alone first, then came back for Bonnie. By the time Al was led into the room, the others were on the floor, backs to the wall with their ankles tied together and their wrists behind their backs. The other walls were piled high with boxes Al knew they probably didn't contains treats for any church outing. That Al and the others had seen this told him each of them were living their last moments. If these men didn't kill them now they certainly would later. Bobby stood waiting with two pieces of rope in his hands.

Al caught the looks in the eyes of Maury, Bonnie, and Fergie. Maury looked sad and desperate, maybe a little resigned. Bonnie and Fergie were just plain angry, as mad as he had ever seen them. But risking the lives of the others had kept them from struggling. Soon it would be too late for all of them.

Al dropped to the floor as if he'd just stepped into a trapdoor. As soon as his hands touched the dirty floor he swung his legs around and hit the back of Wilson's knees. The thing about a guy that tall is that a fall has so far to go. Wilson's head hit the cement floor with the sound a melon makes when dropped.

The rope in Bobby's hands didn't worry him as much

as the gun Jorge held and was now swinging toward Al's head.

The Colt .45 Wilson had been holding clattered to the floor. Al didn't have time to pick it up and aim it. He scooped it up and hurled it at Jorge's face. While Jorge was ducking to one side Al grabbed Jorge's ankles and stood up. Jorge flipped backward, the gun falling from his hands as he landed hard on his hind quarters.

Before Al could take a step he felt a length of rope tighten across his throat. Bobby was pulling at both ends from behind Al, and his knee pressed hard in the middle of Al's back.

Al dropped into a sudden low crouch. Bobby's head naturally followed. Al reached up, put both hands behind Bobby's neck, then stood up as fast as he could. Bobby sailed over Al's head and landed hard on the floor.

Both Jorge and Bobby scrambled for the fallen guns. Al had to depend on them not shooting the hostages but coming after him.

He leaped over the deacon, who didn't look like he was going to move soon, and he ran for the light streaming in through the nearest open bay door. As soon as he was through the opening he whirled and tucked himself tight against the side of the building. He listened for the sound of the running boot steps, knew he had his hands full with two against one.

A hand in a black glove tapped his shoulder. He spun to see a man in black combat gear. His heart sank until he noticed the big block letters on the hat and bulletproof vest: ICE.

Jorge and Bobby came flying out the door, pistols waving in their hands. Half a dozen men in black formed a half circle facing them, and with automatic weapons fixed on them.

Bobby and Jorge looked at each other and lowered their pistols to the ground. The men in black swarmed in on them, and in seconds had them stretched on the ground, handcuffed and ready to be hauled away.

"Ha. Ha. Ha."

Al spun to see Jaime Avila coming toward him. He wore the same gear as the others.

"Let me borrow your knife, Jaime."

"Don't worry. I sent one of my men in to cut your pals free, and a couple more to haul out that tall timber of a man who's still as out of it as the fashion of the seventies."

"How much of this did you know?" Al asked. He felt the hard edge to his words.

"Hell, I was still piecing it all together. You're always half a step ahead of me, Al." He slapped a hard hand onto Al's shoulder that nearly jarred him sideways.

"There was no tip, was there? You got what you had from the Mexican end of this, didn't you?"

"Again, Al, my hat would be off to you, if I was wearing one. But I had only fragments, and my goal was, as always, to get all the way back to the cartels. Jorge there will help. He's one of them. The others hiding under the shelter of a Christian mission would have been harder to figure out. But you did, somehow."

"You'd have gotten it too, in time," Al said, "that Grannie Boo was just a blind mule here."

Maury, Bonnie, and Fergie came out the garage's nearest bay door, each rubbing their wrists.

"Well, we have certainly had a day of it. My hairdresser is going to kill me," Bonnie said. She patted her curls back into position.

Fergie shook her head, still irritated, but no longer flushed with raw rage. "Somebody owes Grannie Boo a new car."

"She'll get one," Jaime said. "Brand new and better than ever. We can spend confiscated money on something like that."

"Fix her trailer too?" Al asked.

"Hell, we'll buy her a stone house like she was going on about."

"Oh, and I need a cell phone," Bonnie said. "mine's in a zillion pieces back there.

"Done. I'll get one of those smart ass phone for you."

"It better be," Bonnie said, "or we won't have much in common. And make is sassy too, if possible. Thanks."

"Thank the cartels. It's their money coming back to do some good for a change. We just use it as best we can."

"That's right," Al shook his head. "With you guys it's always raining money."

THE RELUCTANT BRIDE

BRETHEL LEANED CLOSER, WHISPERED, "SEE what I mean?" His breath, warm on Al Quinn's ear, smelled of the short nip of single malt scotch Al had seen him take from the passed-around flask as well as the mint he'd popped in a failed attempt to mask it.

Al had to admit Brethel's niece Verlina looked ready to bolt toward an exit at any second. Normally he dodged weddings, when he could. He lumped them along with funerals and root canal at the dentist. In the past he'd seen brides, grooms, bridesmaids, and even the best man go knee-wobbly and faint. She had the same pasty pallor, but the bird-like jerking of her head and flicker of eyes from left to right said she wished she'd worn her Nike running shoes.

The whole Hanson clan sat in the pews left of the aisle as she had paraded up on the arm of her father, old Skeld Hanson. His mouth looked clenched, keeping him from biting or howling. Al wasn't sure which. Skeld's eyes were red-rimmed and darted in a glare mostly to the right side of the aisle, the groom's side. It had been his flask that had been passed around, and Al suspected he'd finished it.

The ceremony dragged on, as if the pastor didn't have other congregation members needing attention, or just wanted to hear himself talk while torturing those present.

Al watched the patina of light sweat form on the bride's brow. She wore her long blond hair in braids hanging down from both sides of her head. Her dress was white, with enough flowers to make her look like a Swedish dairy maid about to go milk the herd. But she didn't look happy about it, not happy at all.

At last the pastor either wore himself out or took pity and dismissed them. The cameraman swooped in for a few stills. The rest of those attending crowded out through the front door in a surge.

Outside, Brethel stood with the others, some clutching handfuls of bird seed, not having heard that was as bad as rice. A few grackles had gathered close, not minding at all, having been to a wedding or two before. The Texas sun was at least giving the crowd a break by hiding behind a thick bruise of clouds.

"What do you think?" Brethel nodded toward the door.

Al leaned closer. People were crowded around them. "I don't think anything yet. Does she have money?"

"No. Skeld has his original dime, but it hasn't turned into a big dime, farmland being what it is these days. His fields are mostly in hay."

"Does Verlina have any children?"

His head snapped toward Al's, his pale blue eyes throwing sparks of anger. "I've held her in my arms as a babe, watched her grow since she was knee high to a horned frog, if you'll excuse the cliché. I think I'd know if she'd had a child."

"Let me ask you this, then. Did you notice anyone in your family missing today?"

He thought about that for a moment, tilted his head and took a mental inventory. "No. Nope. Where're you going with this?"

"I'm trying to determine if there's any leverage someone might have to make her do something against her will."

"You think someone might kidnap one of ours just to force her into this?"

"Like I said, I don't think anything yet. I'm exploring possibilities. Any thoughts?"

"I can't think of anything."

"The two families aren't feuding? You know, like the McCoys and Hatfields."

"Nope."

The couple emerged from the church door and bird seed began to pelt them from several directions. The groom shared a sheepish grin, the bride a near snarl.

Al wasn't the only one who noticed. Several of the women in the crowd had their heads together and were murmuring low among themselves.

"Given what you've told me, it's a head-scratcher so far. Do you have any ideas yourself?"

"Nope. But you saw her up there trembling, looking ready to faint."

"I see that at lots of weddings. What is it you want from me?"

The couple was getting into their car for the short hop to where a reception was to be held.

"Look, Al, I know you're retired. But you used to be a detective, for the sheriff's department. Can't you nose around a bit, see if she needs some kind of help but just isn't able to ask for it?"

"You should know I don't usually even carry a gun these days."

"I'm hoping there ain't nobody needs shooting."

Al was watching the groom. Like the others in the crowd, Al had known the Hansons for years, as well as the groom, Joey Canfield, and his family. If he had to make a snap judgment he'd say Joey was a good boy. He'd never seen him help little old ladies across the street or anything, but Joey had always seemed a straight shooter, even all the way through high school when so many of his classmates were like the cowboy who hopped on his horse and rode off in all directions, sniffing, snorting, and smoking all the way.

He was, as his own mother put it, "no rocker scientist," but then the whole family leaned more toward being kind than being genius. This marriage thing was new. Al hadn't known that Joey and Verlina were even dating. Then boom. Here they were.

Joey was a big old strapping Texas boy who'd even baled hay on Skeld's spread, tossing about the fifty-pound bales Skeld favored with ease. Of course he'd played football, a boy that size, and it wasn't like a number of blows to the head were going to rob the world of later breakthroughs in physics or medicine. Yet in all that time Al had never known him to show any interest in Skeld's daughter.

An hour later Al sat in his truck outside the reception hall, a VFW building where once he'd heard a barmaid tell a patron, "If shooting starts up, get behind the piano."

Marriage was a delicate subject for Al. His brother Maury was best man at his, and Al recalled noticing his black socks had white letters that said: "sex, sex, sex." Maury would later try to live up to that best man business with Abbie, which led to Al's divorce and twenty years of Maury and Al not speaking. Old news now, but not without the quality of a scab to pick at when he was left alone to think too much. Like now.

He was almost glad when Verlina and Joey were ushered outside to their waiting car by a crowd that hadn't bothered to paint up the aging white Ford 150's windows or tie cans to the back bumper. The enthusiasm for that seemed to be missing, and the couple themselves looked far from cheerful. Al had been to wakes that had more pep.

They pulled away from the curb without so much as a chirp from the tires. No caravan of honking cars followed. Al waited a minute, then pulled his truck out too, sped up until he could see them in the distance ahead. He eased up on the gas and kept them in sight.

The ripple of gossip through the crowd had been that they didn't expect the couple to go far for their honeymoon. Joey didn't have much money. Al thought Joey had been saving all he could from what little he made as a farm hand to go to college.

Just short of the county line Al eased the truck over and kept it running but got out. From behind a stand of mesquite and mountain cedar Fergie emerged, pushing the borrowed Harley.

If Joey had gone the other direction Maury was waiting there with Fergie's car. In either case they shouldn't be able to glance back and spot a tail.

He hopped onto the Harley and reached for the helmet she held. Before she let me have it she leaned in close and kissed him on the lips. "Don't do anything stupid."

"Me?" He put on the helmet, turned on the motor, and headed off after the couple.

The day still had a grey pallor. This was the time of year, near enough Easter where people went out to take sunny family pictures in the wildflowers, their faces full of all kinds of joy, and hope.

Not today, though. The sky looked like a storm could happen at any moment. Or those bulging, bruised-looking clouds could just hang there and threaten with ominous rumbles.

Ahead, the white pickup pulled into the gravel lot of the Sage & Bluebonnet Motel, a bare hop over the county line.

Joey by-passed the motel office and pulled up in front of a first-floor room on the end beside a black Mustang. Verlina was out of the truck and running for the door almost as soon as the truck stopped. Joey was slower getting out. She didn't wait to be carried over the threshold but opened the door and shot inside. Joey lumbered after her.

Al decided to park the bike around back so his stopping there wouldn't be conspicuous. Once there, he pulled the bike into a clump of thick brush along the base of a hill behind the motel. A strip of open gravel lot for additional parking stretched out between him and the back of the motel.

He didn't know what he expected to accomplish, lurking outside the back of their room like some heartbroken stalker. While he stood there mulling it over he heard the roar of a pickup's engine, then the sliding rasp of it pulling into the gravel on the front side of the motel.

The sliding back window to the motel room opened and out climbed a large man, who Al at first thought had to be Joey. As his feet hit the ground he turned and Al saw the face of a young black man, Brandeis Johnson, the running back on Joey's football team.

Next came Verlina, out of her wedding dress and changed into jeans and a white blouse. Brandeis helped her down. Then Joey started to climb out the window. It was like a damned clown car. Al started to wonder who was going to climb out next.

That thought was punctuated by a shot. Al saw a chunk of pink stucco fly off the back wall of the motel. Then, in a blur from the left, came the running figure of a man in a white shirt, who smacked into Verline and knocked her and Brandeis to the ground. He reached out and got hold of Joey by the ankle and big as he was pulled him to the ground as well.

Al was running. He heard another shot. More stucco flew off the wall from around the dot the bullet made, lower this time.

He could see Brandeis struggling to get to his feet. Brandeis had been tackled before, on football fields, but this had to be new. He was halfway to his feet before he was yanked down again, just as another shot came from a ways to Al's right.

Quite a scuffle was going on, with the two young fellows in a tangle that included Verlina trying to get free from the guy in the white shirt. Al jumped in, on his knees and reaching into the thrashing mess, not sure whether he was helping or getting in the way. He didn't know when he'd been part of a more confusing tangle. He finally got hold of the fellow in the white shirt holding onto Verlina and Brandeis, spun him by the shoulder, and his head rocked back when he saw who it was. Old Skeld himself glared at him. "You'd best get down," he hissed, "lest you want to take a bullet yourself."

A bullet slapped into the gravel not far from them, and Al didn't need any more convincing than that. He piled on. Verlina and Brandeis squirmed beneath him. He was hoping Brandeis didn't get the chance to act on some of the threats he was mumbling.

"Who's that shooting at us?" Al asked Skeld.

"It's her Mama, Erin Swanfest Hanson, most bigoted woman I ever knew to draw breath around here. I was hoping she wouldn't get wind of this until the young'ns were hightailed out of here."

Al wanted to ask, "Get wind of what?" But the next shot was a foot away from them and threw a spray of gravel across them.

"The whole dern wedding was to give Verlina a chance

to get a start. We couldn't even so much as tell Brethel and the others. Hell, they should'a just eloped."

Another shot slapped the side of the motel. No one had adventured out to see what was going on, though Al could make out one or two faces against the glass.

Skeld pressed down on Brandeis, who still struggled to rise. "Thank the heavens she was never much of a shot."

"You ever ride a Harley?" Al asked Brandeis. The snarl left his face. He nodded. Al handed him the key. "Over behind that brush."

Skeld rolled to one side and the couple sprang to their feet and ran at a surprising pace, Verlina keeping up with Brandeis, who Al knew to be capable of a 4.35 in a 40-yard dash.

Another shot threw up gravel behind their heels.

"Let me guess," Al said. "A lever action .30-30."

"Yep, and she shouldn't be putting rounds through it. Winchester 94 Lone Star model that was mint, until now."

Al heard the Harley start. Brandeis, on it, shot out from the thicket. Verlina wore the helmet and clung to his broad back.

"Is she pregnant?" Al asked.

"Hasn't started to show yet." The shooting had stopped. Skeld got slowly to his feet, brushed bits of gravel and grey dust off his elbows and knees. Joey stood as well, blinking in the direction the shots had come from. "Did they get away?"

"For now," Skeld said.

A pickup's engine started and pulled out onto the road in a screech.

"Blasted woman will ruin a good truck too before this is over." He shook his head. "I doubt she can catch them, especially since she turned the wrong way."

"You did all this to help your friend, even went through

a wedding?" Al asked Joey, who blushed and lowered his head.

"I 'spect Erin will settle down after a spell," Skeld said. "We probably shouldn't of kept it from her. But you can see how she took it."

Skeld grabbed Al by the hand and pulled him to his feet. He had the grip of a vise. But he was grinning now, enough for Al to think some of that single malt was still square-dancing away in his veins.

"You think you can calm her down after this?" Al asked.

Skeld had torn a hole in one knee of his suit pants and his white shirt was a mess, rumpled and sporting smears of dirt and dust.

"I'll have to remind her of her father being dead set against me for being a protestant. It's why *we* eloped. She might be forgetting that. I love her for her passion but it's a flame sometimes. She wants grandkids, and I doubt she'll mind as much as she thinks no matter how milk chocolate they are. Her daughter, bless her, is just as bullheaded as her ma, and as full of spirit about doing things her own way. Sure, I guess they'll sort it all out fine in time."

Al shook his head. Joey looked at him, as confused and rattled as any groom he'd ever come across.

Old Skeld started to laugh, until Al wasn't sure he was going to be able to stop. He slapped his thigh. "Ain't love grand," he said when he could speak again. Then he started to laugh again, even harder than before.

NOT TO THE SWIFTEST

"**W**HAT ARE YOU TRYING TO prove, that you can kill yourself while dressed as badly as possible?"

Al Quinn took in the outfit Maury was wearing, a fluorescent yellow tank top over tiny black running shorts. He'd picked up a new pair of running shoes the last time Bonnie had taken him to town, bright blue, fragile enough to weigh an ounce each, and he wore them with white socks pulled up almost to the tops of his shins.

"You remember Mark Shiner, went to the same school as us, now calls himself Frank?"

"Yeah. Of course I do. We weren't what you'd call friends, but I knew of him. He was in your grade, wasn't he?"

"He sure was. He's the one who ratted me out to Bessy Hinkle and Alisson Anne Beckett for dating them both at the same time."

"They'd have found out in time."

"But he accelerated their little epiphanies, and called me a cheating skunk in the bargain. Damn near got me beat up by Bessy's hulk of a big brother."

"The fact is, you *were* a little fast back then, and a cheat." They were skating close to a subject they'd agreed to avoid, Maury and Al's wife. Old news. Painful news. Al still wasn't all the way over that. He had to struggle to shrug it off. "What brings up his name?"

"He's won the county half-marathon for seniors three years in a row."

"So? A bunch of sixty-year-olds clacking along to the sound of popping knees. You want to be a part of that?"

"There's no way he can be winning. I raced him when we were kids and beat him every time. He was a turtle, a chubby lizard. In fact, that was my nickname for him, *obese el lagartijo.*"

"And you want to race and beat him now. Do you really think you can?"

"I know I can, if he plays fair. That's what I want to find out."

"You're not just wanting to do this because of him making you play fair way back in the stone ages of high school are you?"

"It's about integrity. Today. Maybe mine as well as his." Hard to believe Maury could sound as huffy as all this given his imperfect past.

"I think this may be the single dumbest idea you ever had."

"Bonnie says I could do with more exercise, and I want to prove you aren't the only detective around here."

"Running a half-marathon might just finish you off. And I'm a *retired* detective, emphasis on the retired. Why doesn't anybody ever get or respect that, or leave me alone to my fishing and a chance to catch up on my reading?" He turned to Bonnie. "Did you really tell him to get more exercise? You know he had a heart attack."

She shrugged her round shoulders and her blond curls jiggled. "I had in mind short walks instead of loafing about so much. I didn't mention Mount Everest or running half-marathons. We might well have to bury him by the path."

"I don't intend to do the whole thing. That's the point." Maury tugged at the bottoms of his running shorts that were showing way more of his pale white thighs than Al had seen in many a moon.

"Don't forget. I was a detective for the city's police department," Fergie said. "If no one else has uncovered anything, what makes you think you can? But if you're stuck on this idea, you know I'd be willing to help."

"I'd just as soon do it on my own ...if, if you two don't mind."

"Bonnie? Do you have an inkling?"

"I'm sworn to silence by the pillow-talk code."

That's as far as Al cared to go with that. Maury in a monogamous relationship was a big enough leap of faith for Al, given the horn dog Maury had once been. He didn't want or need anything like a clear picture of what went on between Maury and Bonnie behind their closed door.

"All I can say is that it must mean a lot to you to go out into public looking like that."

"You think my legs are a little thin?" Maury stood next to Bonnie, whose build was more along the lines of a muffin according to him. They made a real Jack Sprat and his wife team.

"You look fine," Fergie said. "Just remember to run so fast no one can see you for very long."

* * *

The skies looked gloomy and dark on the day of the race, clouds damp and lumpy, as if ready to wring themselves out at any second. The air smelled of earthworms and watermelon to Al, always a sign of a big rain or even a tornado coming. He could do without either.

"Here he comes." Fergie lowered her field glasses and pointed.

Hard to miss Maury's outfit. "Is that Mark Shiner he's running behind?" Al asked.

"Frank," Bonnie said, "and yes. He said Frank likes to distance himself from the pack, ahead of them if he can, but lagging a bit behind if they have some real movers. A lump of them just went by, so there must be some pretty peppy seniors in today's race."

"If that isn't an oxymoron I don't know what is," Fergie muttered.

Al was watching Maury. He didn't know his brother could go that fast. Even in his woman-chasing days he doubted if Maury hit this pace. He reached for Fergie's field glasses and brought them into focus. Maury's face was a bright pink and his breathing sure was labored. He still had some five or six miles to go.

Frank looked leaner these days. While Al was fixed on the two of them, he saw Frank glance back. No one was right behind them after the short curve that led onto the wooden bridge that spanned a stretch of the lake where a feeder creek bled in. Usually families were below along the shorelines feeding the ducks or turtles that dotted the water, but not today.

Frank slowed enough until Maury was beside him. He made an abrupt rush to the right and pushed Maury off the side of the bridge.

"Did you see that," Bonnie shouted. She reached for the field glasses and yanked them away from Al.

Frank kept running, never looking back. Even from this far up the hill Al figured the water must not be deep and had a muddy bottom because Maury's legs stuck up out of the water, blue shoes flailing. Turtles took off in several directions. A couple of ducks along the shore also took squawking umbrage to someone usurping their pool. They sputtered along the shore, flapping their wings against the water, and took off in flight.

"You'd better go see if you can help Jacques Cousteau

there, Bonnie." Al took off down the hill to pick up Frank's tail. Fergie ran beside him, effortlessly. At six-foot-two she was mostly legs and jogged regularly. Al was huffing as he ran, and started to get the notion it would have been better to have Fergie in the race with Frank, in which case it wouldn't be Maury's running shoes wiggling in the air over the dank water.

They were just in time to see Frank glance back at the running trail behind him before veering off the trail to his left. The course was winding down a gentle slope so there had to be stretches where a lone runner couldn't be seen from front or back. Frank seemed to have chosen such a spot to make his "exit stage left."

Al and Fergie were already in the shadows of the canopy above the woods made up on live oaks, old pecans, and heavy brush running down in thick mats covering the hillsides. Al couldn't imagine how Frank intended to wade through that, some of it thorny chaparral.

At the base of a big pecan tree Frank reached up and in a second was soaring away down the hill, feet tucked and arms above his head.

"I'll be damned. A zip line," Fergie said.

Al pulled up beside her. She wasn't even breathing hard. He went up to the base of the tree, reached up to the steel cable. There was no way he could follow without one of the trolleys with handles Frank had used. This one had been placed well so it ran down the slope and came out at a spot the front runners would not reach for another minute or so.

All the advantage you need in a close race is a minute or so, and Frank had just trimmed a mile or mile-and-a-half off his run and put himself in front of the lead runners.

Al looked around. Unless they wanted to cut themselves to ribbons going down that thorn-infested hill they would have to go around. Fergie had already started back toward the running trail to the spot where Frank had veered off into the woods.

They pushed out of the brush into the clear of the road just in time for Maury to come running around the bend and spot them. "How did you two get down here?" The upper half of him was still covered in mud, but Bonnie had gotten most of it off his face, except for what had caked in his hair, which stuck out in spikes going several directions. He looked like just about the saddest clown Al had ever seen.

Maury didn't slow, but kept running right past them. "Come on along. Let's catch up with that bastard."

Al could hear other runners who were soon visible and coming along on the trail behind them.

Al and Fergie broke into a run and pulled up beside Maury. For the first time Al was glad he'd worn sneakers instead of his usual boots. Fergie ran easily, and Maury made a whole lot better time than Al expected. In a short while, Al was fighting against a stitch under his lower left ribs. But he kept his mouth shut and ran as best he could to stay with them.

He couldn't imagine round little Bonnie keeping up with them. After another mile he was mostly surprised he was keeping up himself.

At last the trail opened up into a straight approach and they could see people lined along the sides yelling encouragement to the runners.

A handful of the runners had already crossed the finish line by the time they got there. Al and Fergie peeled off before crossing the line, not wanting to throw the officials off. One of the officials stood with a timer and clip board at the finish line. They all wore white shirts and black pants and had bright red stickers above their shirt pockets. One sat at a table with what looked like a record-keeping log in front of him. A couple of the other officials bent close to the table talking with him.

Al recognized the seated man, Shorty McGlonklin, who ran a retail lumber company by weekday. Al had met him a couple of times while investigating building material thefts that eventually tracked back to a local contractor trying to enhance his profit margin. Al went up to the table. The two men talking to Shorty looked up, saw him, and eased away from the table.

"Are you the head official, Shorty?"

"It's called race director, Al. But yes. Did you run in this race wearing those clothes?"

"No. I always sweat a lot this time of year." Al mopped at his brow with the back of his left hand. "How would I go about reporting an irregularity in the race?"

"Let me guess. It's about Frank Shiner."

"What makes you say that?"

"In some of these races the competitors are required to wear a timing chip to ensure their race times are accurate. Frank managed to lose his in three such races. It's cast a bit of a cloud over him."

"What about this race?"

"A few of the runners asked, but it wasn't in the budget. Not that Frank couldn't conveniently lose his again."

"And how did this race go?" Al said. "I'm guessing Frank came in first."

"We've already had a beef from Mitch Kenner who claims he was in the lead and never saw Frank pass him."

"I can show you how he did it," Al said.

Shorty's eye narrowed and he glanced over to the tables where those runners already finished were helping themselves to drinks and snacks. Frank was among them.

"Wait until all the runners are in and I'll let you do just that."

———◆———

Shorty drove a golf cart up the path until Al indicated the spot where Frank had cut into the brush. Fergie sat in the back seat. Bonnie had driven Maury back to Al's place. He had smelled like the bottom of a pond, and with good reason. As much as he wanted to stay, Al had gone along with the group vote for him to hit a much-needed shower and hit it hard.

"Right here," Fergie said.

Shorty stopped the cart.

Al led the way through the brush and stopped when he came to the right tree. His mouth opened an inch when he looked up.

"It was right here," Fergie insisted.

"Well, I sure don't see anything like a zip line," Shorty said.

Al stepped close to the tree's trunk. "Here. There's the hole where it was attached."

Shorty moved closer and took a look. "All you've got is a hole, Al. That's pretty thin. How could he get back up here and take down a zip line while he was down at the bottom in plain sight?"

Al shook his head. He didn't have a quick answer either.

"Looks like I'm gonna have to let the results stand, no matter how much grousing I get from the number two and three runners."

———◆———

Back at the house, Maury still wore a bath robe and his hair was wet, but he looked cleaner. He sat on the couch.

"Well, that beats all. How do you suppose he got away with it?" He lifted the towel he held on his lap and began rubbing at his hair again.

Al shook his head.

"Well, we'll always have that moment to cherish of your legs waving in the air," Fergie said. "No one can take that away from us." She was trying hard not to chuckle and almost succeeding.

"What about that church thing you talk about sometimes, Al? Have you tried that?" Bonnie came out of the kitchen carrying a steaming mug with a tea bag's tag hanging at its side. She handed it to Maury.

"Do you mean *cherchez la femme*?" Al glanced toward Fergie.

"I always thought that was a pretty sexist thing for the French to say," Fergie said. "Look for the woman. But, you know, this time Bonnie makes a point, a pretty good one."

———◆———

Al ran his truck around through the cul de sac where Frank lived. Then he looped back and parked half a block up the street where he and Fergie could watch the front door.

The neighborhood looked to be a typical suburban hodge-podge of middle class homes, many of which had variations of the same floor plan. Al glanced at the house up the slight hill behind Frank's. He saw a venetian blind settle back into place. "Give me a minute," he said.

Fergie saw where he was looking. "I want to go too."

The two of them went around to the front of the house up the hill. Al knocked on the door, then saw the pearl button in a brass setting. He pressed it as well, reminding himself of the redundancy of men who wear belts and suspenders at the same time. He heard footsteps approaching the door from inside. "Bruiser! The couch."

The door swung open and woman stood there who could be forty or sixty. He looked down at her. She was tiny and wore an apron over a housedress. Al was trying to think of the last time he saw anyone wear an apron around the house. He guessed Bonnie did from time to time.

"If you're selling anything ..."

Al held up his open black leather badge holder. Even though he was retired, Clayton had insisted he hold onto his badge in case the sheriff needed to call on him, which he did, more often than Al liked.

The woman looked up at Fergie, way up at her. "Oh, come in. What's this about?" Up close the topography of the wrinkles on her face fixed her age at closer to sixty than forty.

"We have a question or two about your neighbor, Frank Shiner."

"Mark. I still call him Mark. Knew him as a boy. Odd how we came to be living near each other. Settle yourselves."

Bruiser, it turned out, was a tiny brown Chihuahua who quivered in one corner of the couch with wide-open dark eyes. "Ignore him," the woman said.

She sat down in an overstuffed power chair in the corner that faced the television. It had a reading light behind it, and a stack of crossword puzzle books on its side table. She just about disappeared into it, but seemed cozy. Good. He wanted her comfortable.

Fergie sat on one end of the couch, opposite the dog. Al eased down into a green corduroy wing chair by a fireplace that had never had a fire in it.

"I wonder if you could tell us if Frank, Mark rather, had a girlfriend. We know he never married."

RUSS HALL

"Oh. Oh my. I can see where you'd go wrong about a thing like that."

Al glanced toward Fergie. One of her eyebrows lifted.

"Care to explain?"

"He parks about where your vehicle is right now. Goes around and slips in the back way. "They're both on, how do you say it these days, the down and the low."

"He?"

"The significant other. I believe I have that right. It's so hard to stay hip these days. If it wasn't for the television and the grandkids I don't know how I would flounder along. They keep me up to the date."

Al had harbored a suspicion that this neighbor up the hill kept track of pretty much everything that happened in the neighborhood. He had been right.

———◆———

Al drove Fergie's car back to their spot after a trip home and a stop at a convenience store. He pulled farther up the street but where he could still keep an eye on where he'd parked before near Frank Shiner's back door. Maury and Bonnie sat in the back seat. They'd insisted on coming along.

"Now this is what a stakeout should be like." Fergie reached for one of the packs of chips. Al was opening the beef jerky, and they had enough diet sodas they were going to have to think about a spot in the bushes later if they weren't careful about pacing themselves.

"It's like a double date," Bonnie said, chuckling to herself. "Been a long time since I did anything like that."

"Ah, the days of the drive-in movies and four in a car." Maury sighed. "I remember one time I was in the back seat and heard a sound. It was the keys swinging back and

62

forth hitting the dash. The couple in the front seat were on the far sides of their seat. So it was ..."

"Let's keep some of these memories of your less-than-pleasant days to yourself," Bonnie said. "Okay, honey?"

She must have reached and grabbed him someplace soft firmly. Al heard the sharp intake of air and then got nothing but silence from Maury for a bit.

As it turned out, their wait wasn't long.

The older PT Cruiser eased into the spot as soon as it had glided around the corner. A thin man got out slowly, looking up and down the street. Al and Fergie slid low in their seats. The man's sweep of the area barely paused on Al's truck.

"You want the front or back?" Al asked.

"Better go with the front," Fergie said. "You're more that fellow's back door type." She winked as she clambered out of her side of the truck.

Al waited until he heard knocking at Frank's front door. He glanced up the hill, saw the blinds there pretty blatantly pulled open at one side. He climbed over the waist-high chain link fence the way the visitor had and eased up to the back door.

If it was him in there he would just hunker down and wait them out. But that man had looked antsier than that. Al was right. A moment later Al stood to one side when he heard the back door opening.

The man stepped out while looking back over his shoulder. Al stepped close and tapped on the man's upper arm. The guy shot a foot into the air. His head snapped around, eyes wide open and fixed on Al.

"Let's say we go inside," Al said, "and talk." He waved to Bonnie and Maury, who had crept close enough to peek around a fence corner. They stepped out and came toward the house.

The man didn't ask the question about whether Al had a right to come in. He just turned and led the way. He seemed to be thinking it over by the time they all were in the kitchen. Al reached out and grabbed him at the elbow, more firmly than needed. "What's your name?"

"J-J-Jason." He looked about fifty, was slender as a stick.

"Open the front door, Jason, so Fergie can come in and join us."

She was still knocking.

In a moment she was inside. Al took in the living room, mostly that square Swedish sort of minimalist thing he usually found a little stark. He didn't comment on the chance that Jason had been the one to pick out the furnishings. The only things not bought at a store were the good-sized trophies in a line across the mantle.

"Are you married?" Fergie asked. She stood close and hadn't sat yet. He had to look up at her.

Jason bowed his head. "Yes, but you know how that ..." He looked up. "Is that what you want to talk to me about?" His voice grew more confident, but his pale cheeks flushed pinker.

"No. We want to talk about the race," Al said. "The marathon where you were yesterday."

"How did you ...I didn't see you there."

"I doubt you did scampering through the woods to take down that zip line before we could come back to it," Al said. He looked to Fergie. "He's more of a woodsman than you'd think."

Before he could respond, Fergie said, "All we want to know is why?"

"Why what?"

"Why cheat? Why does Frank do that? And why do you help him," Al said.

They stood there in a tight circle. There were chairs and a squarish looking sofa, but no one seemed inclined to sit. Maury and Bonnie stood close enough together to hold hands. They didn't take their eyes off Jason.

"It's okay not to answer," Al said, "but, if you don't, this is going to turn into those very public things. You know, newspaper stories, media folk calling your house."

Jason seemed to think about it, picture it in his head. "I can't. You know. Well, I won't."

"Okay, have it your way. You'll be exposed as well as everything about Frank. I imagine the zip line gear is in the garage. At the very least its sales record can be traced. Come along, you guys." Al nodded to Fergie, Maury, and Bonnie.

It took only two or three of Al's steps for Jason to respond.

"Wait. Wait. What is it you want?"

"Like the lady said. We want to know why? You're as much a part of the cheat as Frank. Why would you do that?"

Jason's shoulders slumped. He sagged into a chair. "Why don't you sit?"

They stayed standing, looking down at him.

"I don't think ...Look you'd better talk to Frank."

"He's here?"

Jason nodded. "It's all he has." He stared across the room at the trophies. "You have to understand. Frank spent a lifetime as a loser, a second-place man. When he found out, this was the one thing he wanted."

"When he found out what?"

"That ...that he has cancer. Maybe not quite a year to live. Even now his strength is starting to go. He just ... He just ..." Tears were welling up in Jason's eyes. He put his face down in his hands. His shoulders shook. "That's where he was until now, at the hospital." His voice was a mumble from behind his hands, but he didn't lift his head to look at them. "They're starting the treatments. Not that they can save him at this point, just ...just make the ending easier." A sob escaped from the hands that tightened on his own face.

"I'll get him. He's lying down, resting." He rose and almost ran out of the room. When he came back into the room, Frank was right behind him.

Frank looked like he couldn't decide to be angry and assertive or embarrassed. If he was going to try anger, he should have led with that. It was too late now. Hard to tell which flustered him more, being caught at cheating during the races or that he had a male lover, one married to someone else, a woman.

He was about the same height and weight as Maury, but looked a little more solid. Probably had two-percent body fat. Something like that. He wore a white short-sleeved shirt and khaki slacks. His burgundy loafers he wore without socks.

Up close Al could see the beginnings of the end in Frank's skin tone and the way it strained him to force himself to stay upright. Cancer gnaws at a person from inside, and its effects had already begun to show.

He had to be wondering what came next. The newspaper stories. Committees coming to take back his trophies. His friends, neighbors finding out. For a second his head bowed under the weight of it, then he forced himself to look up at Maury then Al, as eager as Hermann Göring at Nuremberg. "You have something to say to me?"

"You understand that it's not right to cheat. Right? Both of you." Al's head swung from Frank to Jason.

Jason lifted his red face toward Al. "I ...I know. It's just ..."

"Just nothing. It never is." Al didn't say anything about people who try to cheat death. He didn't need to. He didn't feel preachy or judgmental at all, just a little tired.

"What ...what are you going to do?" Frank asked Al.

Fergie was looking at Al.

Al turned to Maury. "This is your case. You're the client as well as chief operative. And whatever is gnawing inside you is driving this. You decide."

Maury bent his head, thought a moment, then slowly looked right at Frank.

It all came down to this. Al watched Maury closely. It was a lot to ask of anyone, especially with Maury's past.

"It ends," Maury said. "It ends now and doesn't happen again. Do you understand?"

"You're not going to expose him?" Bonnie said.

"Not if it stops. Are we clear?"

Frank looked to Jason, then back to Maury. "Y-yes. Clear."

Al didn't say anything as he went across to the door, or even in the walk back to the vehicle. Fergie walked along beside him. He got in. She did as well. Maury and Bonnie climbed into the back seat. He was pleased, and proud of Maury. But it was the kind of thing you don't talk about. Still, it tickled him to the toes of his boots.

None of them spoke until they were almost back to their house.

"Maury? I thought you were going to be a little upset about getting so muddy for nothing." Fergie looked out her window while she spoke.

"It wasn't nothing," Maury said. "I accomplished what I wanted. That's more than most people do some days. Besides, the mud was probably good for my skin."

"We'll keep an eye on that, see if it improves," Al said.

Al pulled in front of his house, the car's wheels crunching on gravel.

"Let's just do." Bonnie put an arm around Maury's shoulders and squeezed, grinning and doing her best not to laugh out loud. "Let's do just that."

THE LAST FIRST TIME

A L QUINN FELT THE SPRAY of water splash across his face as he swept his bass boat around Windy Point. He backed the big motor off and turned the key. The engine died as the boat rocked to a stop. He drifted into the wide cove and let the boat glide into the spot where he'd been fishing yesterday.

The water around him was in the lee of the wind, so he could see farther into the partially clear water. He saw a bluegill or two take off in little zips as the wake of his boat subsided. Al caught a glimpse again, the lip of a metal barrel, grown fuzzy with rust and underwater plant life.

He stood, leaned out to look down closer. The water had gone down another inch during the night as the lake succumbed to the drought that had been going on for three months now. The heat of the sun beat down on him. He reached up to lift his hat and rub the moisture from his brow. In a few days he wouldn't even be able to get the boat in the water, so he'd been getting out on the water every chance he got.

As the boat settled and calmed, and the waves from his wake that had echoed back from the shore to slap against his hull subsided, he could see better. Yep. He could see it clearer than he'd been able to see the day before. Al sighed, reached for his phone, and tapped in a familiar number.

"Sheriff's Department."

"Hey, Betty Lou. It's Al. Can to get me the big guy?"

She put him on hold without responding. The big guy was Sheriff Clayton. Few people could get quick access to him, but he and Al had a history.

"Yeah. What is it?" The voice grumbled, as usual like a bear being prodded prematurely from its hibernation.

"Bones in a barrel. I'm on Lake Travis."

"You sure?"

"I wasn't yesterday, but am today. I'm on the lee side of Windy Point."

"I'll get the department boat right out there." Clayton paused. "I thought you were retired."

"Well, like a cashiered bloodhound, I guess the nose still works."

"I have my days," the sheriff sighed, "when I wish it didn't." He hung up.

Nothing to do now but sit and wait. Al didn't reach for one of the bass rods held in place in the bow by bungee cords. He went up to the front, lowered the electric motor, sat in the front seat and just kept the boat in place until they came. It shouldn't be too long. He would rather be fishing, but there you have it. Some days you just have to sit and wait. Al looked around at the receding shoreline, some boat docks were already stranded. Central Texas around Austin sure as hell needed some rain.

Water. Being on it, or in it, was the basic first part of it for him, whether salty or fresh. Smelling it. Seeing its sun-silvered skin glisten in waves, or pausing to stare when it lay still as a mirror to look into his own soul.

The fish mattered as much. It had been that way for him since as a small boy he'd lost his father. His grandfather had stepped in to take him fishing more. Gramps had most often used a fly rod, while Al progressed from cane pole to the casting reels and rods he favored now, whether after bass in a lake like the one he lived on, or when after redfish off the gulf shores of Texas. Or triggerfish, barracuda, grouper, even tuna on those dashes he should be making more often to the Bahamas now that he was a retired detective with the sheriff's department.

Each time he'd cast, his mind's eye could see the lure as it fluttered downward, sometimes catch the flash of a silver side as the fish struck. He could feel the eager thump of the hit, the living slab of muscle fighting beneath the surface across which his line sliced.

That was what drew him out onto the water. The tingle of the chase, the suspense of the hunt rewarded with the surge of blood through his heart each time he set the hook. And the fight. He used as light a line as he dared and played each fish through its runs, dives, and frantic leaps out of the water. To bring it in at last to the boat, and then let it go, making sure the fish was fit to return to its haunts, all made him hum with joy inside.

This was the hardest part to explain, but the easiest to understand. That's the way with a passion, how things feel when they run deep through every vein of you, and throb in excitement when you are on the water, and urge you to get there when you are not. He knew that. He had it, and had it bad, which was good.

People had asked him, mostly one or two of them, why he fished. Did it hurt the fishes? Did he feel a bigger man for hauling something out of its environment only to put it back again?

He had wrestled with all aspects of it, but in the end he let the unconscious side of his brain decide. He did it because fishing was one of the things that kept him feeling alive, maybe the main thing.

He heard the sound of a big motor coming. That would

be the department's dive boat. Al made out the fluttering red flags with white slashes as it came around the point. They certainly had scrambled and wasted little time.

He sure hoped this didn't turn out to be deer bones, or some such. But he knew enough about anatomy and had been at enough crime scenes to think not, or he wouldn't have roused the bear. He knew a human tibia when he saw it.

Al stood up and waved to the boat as it approached.

———◆———

Fergie came out the back door carrying two glasses, ice rattling, wedge of lime and sprig of mint in each. Her long red hair swept back in a gust of wind from the lake. She was the same age as Al, but sure didn't look it. She'd been in the sun recently and the tan on her face suited her. She handed one glass to Bonnie, who was stirring a large bowl of potato salad. The other glass she put on the stand beside where Maury spread BBQ sauce on the pieces of chicken before flipping them to the other side.

"Let me know how the experiment works," Fergie said. She'd attempted to make mojitos with tequila instead of rum. They'd had the tequila and mint, or *yerba buena.*

"Spot on." Bonnie held up her glass after a hearty sip. "We'll see if it stirs Maury into a mood to do some salsa dancing."

Fergie pointed to the bottle of amber Dos Equis beer Al held. He shook his head. He'd been nursing this one until it had become warm.

She came over and sat in the matching Adirondack chair beside him, both facing the lake. Before she had a chance to say anything, a deep voice boomed from behind them.

"Hey."

Al turned his head, saw Sheriff Harold Clayton coming around the corner of the house. Al's lakeside place had two floors, the upper opening to where his truck was parked, the lower to the flagstone patio where they sat. Clayton walked down the hill from the front. Al hadn't heard the truck pull up to the house. He didn't know what to make of Clayton's expression either. Looked like he'd just gulped down a rotten quince.

"Got a moment, Al?" He nodded to the others. "Howdy, y'all. I recall Al telling me once he was fine with living alone. Now if this don't beat all. It's getting to be a regular Woodstock around here."

Bonnie held up her half-finished beverage. "Want something for your whistle?"

Clayton shook his head. He and Al ambled down the hill and out onto the fishing dock next to the boat shed where Al's bass boat was hoisted up above the water on its electric winch.

Once on the dock Clayton glanced back up toward Al's house where the others were chattering. "For a fellow who once told me he'd be fine living alone when the time came, you've certainly gathered a flock about you."

Al shrugged. They both knew how Al had had to put aside twenty years of having nothing to do with Maury to step in and save his life when he was threatened. How Maury's nurse, the buxom blond Bonnie, and Al's high school classmate Fergie came to be staying here was all part of a long, tangled story. "What's on your mind?" Al asked.

"It's about those bones you found in a can. I'd like you to run with that."

"You've got plenty of good active detectives. I'm retired. Happily retired."

"Which is exactly why I'd like you to be the one on point for this."

Al asked the question with his eyes.

"You'll know why when you get into it," Clayton said. "The bones and other effects are still with the M.E. You might start there."

"You sure you don't want the regular staff handling this?"

"Very sure. I'm asking the favor, Al."

Al nodded. "Okay. Just so long as I'm not stepping on anyone's toes."

"Oh, there'll be plenty of that." Clayton held out a hand and shook before turning and heading back up around the house. Al thought he heard an enigmatic chuckle, though it could have just been a bear-like grumble.

Fergie came over to stand beside him as he watched Clayton walk away. "You know, you don't always have to do these little chores he asks you to do, just because he's an old friend. A couple of them have darn near gotten you killed."

"He asked the favor this time."

"Oh, my. This must be a big one, a very big one indeed."

———◆———

Al always found the lights in the M.E.'s lab too bright. The whole ceiling seemed made of fluorescent lights. He guessed they didn't want to miss the least speck of anything. Clive Barnes, the medical examiner, stood by the steel table on which lay the steel drum on its side that Al had last seen hugging the bottom of Lake Travis. Clive's assistant Teddy was arranging small objects on trays. She glanced up, startled at first, then relaxed when she recognized Al. Her touch of autism made her wary of most people, but may have contributed to how good she was at her job and how devoted she was to Clive, who treated her like anyone else. She was short, stocky, had blond curly hair, and looked like she might well be a relative of Bonnie. She sneaked glances and shared a rare quick grin with Al, who was one of the few people she had come to trust.

"What have you got that's worth knowing, Clive?" Al came up to the table.

"The body's over there." Clive nodded to the steel drawers along one wall. "I should say, both of them."

Al felt his eyebrows rise.

"Yep. She was pregnant. First glance said the woman was twenty-five to thirty years old, maybe four-foot-nine to five feet tall, and Hispanic. Death was probably instantaneous, caused by blunt force trauma to her head, and that did it for the seventeen-inch fetus as well."

"I guess we'll play hob finding out who she was or where she came from." Al reached out and touched the rim of the barrel. Years of being under water had corroded any markings from its sides. "How long ago did she wind up being down there?"

"I've got it down to about 18 years ago. We're talking about a fifty-five gallon metal drum, barrel if you will, that weighed three-hundred, maybe three-fifty with her, some scrap granite rock for ballast, and everything else in it. All that weight is what held her to the bottom so long."

Al shook his head. He felt the cold door of impossibility closing on this investigation.

"We were able to salvage a few other objects." Clive pointed to the tray where Teddy was arranging things in order by size. "She had two rings, and a locket. One ring has the initials A.P.M. inside, her initials."

"How do you know that?"

"Because of an address book, sealed in a plastic bag,

75

pretty damaged anyway, but I was able to dry it out and forensics got some information from it under an infrared light. They got one or two names of friends from the book as well."

Al waited. Teddy had her head down, moving the items on the tray with one finger.

"Her name was Angélica Patricia Mejía. She was originally from El Salvador. Her alien card number on the first page was about all we had to go on. But that did help us with the timetable. She went missing eighteen years ago."

Al nodded. "And the fetus? Will you be able to get a DNA sample from that?"

"Of course we will, Al. Of course we will."

—◆—

Al stepped out into the growing sun that was soon going to be a scorcher. A big man, with a big belly, blocked his way. He looked up. The last time he'd seen Rubin "Hoss" Hodgkins it had been an amiable enough meeting at work when they were both still on the job. Now Hoss's bulldog-like face looked ready to growl, or bite.

"I thought you were retired," The man boomed. Street clothes and all he acted like he was still Chief Deputy, a cut even above the majors and captains on a force as big as this county needed.

"I thought you were too, Hoss."

"You know I'm running for sheriff."

"Until you win it you're as retired as I am." Al made note of Hoss's presence just outside the M.E.'s office, but he sure didn't have a handle on the why of it yet, though he got his usual nervous itch about it.

"Well, just you wait. And what is it you're up to here

that has you scrabbling around like some crab minion doing Clayton's bidding?"

Al still had no idea why Hoss was stepping into him, but he suspected he would find out soon enough, and he expected the worst. "Maybe I'm on my own here. Why?"

"Just remember, I make a better friend than an enemy."

Al recalled Hoss was prone to clichés. "Are you threatening me?"

"Why not? Neither of us is official anymore. We could mix it up right here." Hoss stepped forward until his bulging belly nearly touched Al.

"There are witnesses, plenty of them, who will see you start it."

"Well, don't forget. I know where you live, and those pals of yours in that frat life style you've taken on."

"Really? You'd hurt my brother and friends?"

"Just remember, there's a first time for everything." That was Hoss's favorite gag, his catch phrase he wore out at every opportunity. He winked slowly, the kind of wink he used to show when sharing a joke not suitable for all ears. Only this time Al saw no glitter or fun to those eyes, only malice and perhaps raw threat. Al could recall Hoss as a jovial man, for the most part. That was sure not his mood today.

"I know where you live too," Al said. And he did, had envied the place for years. That's what comes of inheriting old money. Hoss had a lakeside 7,000-acre spread that sprawled along two-and-a-half miles of shoreline. He raised black-tail deer and sold the venison, had all kinds exotic game, and a friend of his had used the place for a reception when he thought of running for governor. Hoss's son, Kyle Luke, still lived there and managed the ranch side of it. He was quite a specimen of a human being who had flunked out of three prep schools and had taken the bar exam a dozen times and had still never managed to pass.

———————⊷◆⊷———————

"Why didn't you tell me what you thought up front?" Al sat across from Clayton's desk. Clayton pushed aside a pile of files and went to the door to his office, closed it, and locked it.

"Because I didn't ... couldn't think anything then. Still can't." He walked back across the room and plopped into his leather chair. "It's why I didn't want anyone from the department handling this. Politically, this couldn't have happened at a worse, or better time. Why don't you just tell me what you have?"

"I have a hunch not much of this is going to surprise you."

"Try me."

"You know the name of the victim and where she was from. She's listed as a missing person. You probably know where she was working when she disappeared."

Clayton nodded. "You tell it."

"At the time she went missing, eighteen years ago, she was working as a nanny then as a maid for Rubin 'Hoss' Hodgkins after he lost his wife in that car accident. This, as you know all too well, is a man who was until not too long ago your Chief Deputy and who is currently running against you in the coming election."

"You see the delicate part?"

"I dealt with Hoss a lot in my day. He always seemed a straight shooter to me. Have you discussed this with him?"

"There was a bit of a kerfuffle when he retired ...early."

In all of Al's twenty years in the department, much of it working closely with Clayton, he'd never heard the man use the word. It sounded, coming from his cautious lips, like the coarsest profanity.

"Well, that aside, I liked the man."

"So did I," Clayton said. "So did I. Yet you said he even mentioned your family. He was always touchy and protective about his own. How'd you feel when he turned on you and yours, snapping away like he did?"

"I felt bad, like a puppy that had been kicked. Threatening and hostility were so unlike him."

"That's how I felt when I first heard he was running against me. Came out of the blue. But it made sense when I thought about it. He was suited for it, and I still liked the guy. Couldn't help but like him."

"Yeah, I know what you mean. He was always laughing, joshing, getting along with everyone. But there's no getting around he was pretty confrontational when I met him this time," Al said.

"I suspect he'll be more so when you approach him the next time."

"Yeah, I need to get a DNA sample from him."

"Try asking the first time."

"I don't fancy my chances at that."

"Asking would be a courtesy. I worked with the man for years."

"And you never had an inkling?"

"I *still* know nothing until the hard facts are in. Savvy?"

<hr>

The drive out to Hoss's spread was a pretty one. The wildflowers lining the two-lane road were just turning into waves of swaying yellow and orange blooms after the earlier splashes of bluebonnets everywhere. They didn't help Al's mood. A few pecans still clung from last fall to the branches of towering trees as he got to the pink granite beside the closed steel gates.

The bell was the kind where the visitor had to get out of the car to press the button, in rain or blazing sunshine. When he pressed the button, Al heard a buzz then a chime. A voice came over the speaker a minute later. "Wait there." The voice had a high-pitched country sound that never sounded all that manly to Al, like Glen Campbell in that movie *True Grit* trying to act the part of a Texas Ranger but sounding more like a screech owl.

Al looked up on the top of the granite pillar where a metal fake yucca with a green patina sat beside a security lens that stared down at him. The opposing pink granite pillar had a matching yucca and camera. It always baffled him when people paid serious money for a copy of a plant that grew everywhere out here and was practically indestructible.

In the nearby open pasture stood a kudu, along with some much smaller dik-diks, and what looked like a couple of springboks grazing under the broad limbs of a live oak, as natural as if they were native to Texas. Hoss had once long ago shared a comment about the dik-diks being smaller in Africa. But that had been before Internal Affairs had started cracking down on just that sort of banter in the workplace.

A black pickup truck with four back tires and four spotlights across the top came slowly up the drive and stopped inside the gate. The gate didn't open. The door to the truck opened and out climbed Kyle Luke Hodgkins, the son. Prodigal, Al might say, but he was running a ranch.

Down far along the fence line Al could make out an open jeep with three Hispanics in it riding the trail along the inside of the fence, checking it for any breeches.

"What the pluperfect hell do you want?"

Al flinched at the high notes. Kyle was thirty-six now, would have been eighteen back when Angelica was a maid here at this same ranch house. Al had heard the place had two swimming pools, with a waterfall running down from one to the other. He'd never seen it himself, but the tales about Hoss's spread were many.

"Just want to see your dad for a moment or two." Al held up a DNA swab kit. "Won't take any longer than that." Al was thinking about a time The University of North Texas Health Science Center at Fort Worth took nine months to make a DNA match in a similar barrel case because they said they had 430 cases pending. He was sure Clayton knew someone he could give a hot foot to do better than that this time.

"You can eat burnt biscuits." Kyle was the same height and had the same build as his father. They probably hit the same BBQ joints together, often. Hoss, though, had a deep, full voice. The son, not so much.

"What?"

"I said if you want anything like that, come back with a warrant."

"He told you to say that?"

"I can think for myself. But, yeah, he said it."

Al had a problem with young people who had grown up feeling entitled, perhaps because he'd grown up poor. Or maybe he respected the idea that everyone should earn their way to their successes. He knew it to be a prejudice, and he kicked himself in the seat of his blue jeans mentally for thinking like that, but that didn't make it go away.

"As you wish." Al said. He climbed back into his truck and pulled away with Kyle glaring at him from behind the steel bars of the gate.

While rolling along, Al used his cell phone to call in the request for a court-order warrant. Since he was to hell and gone out on this side of the lake he headed for the address of the only living friend to turn up from Angélica's distressed address book.

Catrina Chávez sat on a rocker in front of a double-wide trailer mounted on a cement slab. A slight hill ran around the residence. Flowers bright and swaying in the wind had been planted in a ring around the home's base. The front door was open, the inside too dark for Al to see anything but a black rectangle. A tired looked dog of mixed and questionable heritage came out the doorway, glanced at him, and went back inside without so much as a wag of its tail.

"I should a known. I get named Catrina after the Lady of the Dead and sooner or later I get this news of my friend Angélica." She stayed seated as Al walked up to where she sat. She waved to a green plastic chair beside her.

Al turned the chair so he could see her and not just sit beside her. He eased gingerly into the chair, expecting it to explode beneath him. It held, but wobbled as he shifted in his seat. He sought to stay still.

On a small table to her side she had a pitcher and two glasses. One already filled with an amber fluid, the other with just ice. "You wan' sweet tea?"

"Yes. Please." He'd learned the hard way to accept what others offer. Years ago he'd thought it polite to refuse. Now he knew that accepting drew others closer. He took the glass she held out to him. She had deep lines to the tan of her face, as if the years had scratched themselves across her. They emphasized every emotion she had however she might try to suppress them.

"It's funny you called, 'cause I waz just thinking about her." The "k" was so soft in thinking it came out more like "thinning." Al had spent his whole career listening to variations of the same accent, so it gave him no problem. He did hope she didn't shift into Spanish. It always embarrassed him to know so little after working among a good mix of Latino population for so long.

He nodded. Let her speak. She had apparently been sitting here a spell and picking her words with care.

"Angélica, she have a beautiful personality. She come to America, want to become a citizen. She love her family, but only leave El Salvador when she find her husband has lover who is going to have his child."

"Did she ever say anything about her relations with the Hodgkins family?"

"By relations, wha' you mean?"

"Make of it what you will."

"She admit once that she have, how you say, the affair with her boss. She thought she would marry, then maybe she say she still have husband, or he find out. Then he angry and she was afraid he would kill her."

"She said as much?"

"Yes. She tole me so."

"Did you know she was pregnant?"

She looked down, then back up at him. "Yes. I know."

———◆———

"Did you get the warrant?" Al asked Clayton over the phone.

"Yeah. I'm on the way there myself with it."

"I thought you wanted me on point with this."

"You still are, but I'm coming, and I'm bringing Clive with me."

"Why Clive?" Before Clayton could answer, Al said, "Oh."

The gates were open wide when he got back to the

Hodgkins' spread. A cruiser sat outside and Deputy Bob Leroy waved him on.

Inside, two other deputies waited in the den, a room lined with books, a pool table along one set of shelves, and floor-to-ceiling glass windows that looked out over the two pools, one flowing in a waterfall down to the other. Al had doubted if he would ever see that in person, and now he had. It didn't thrill him the way he had hoped, given the circumstances.

Hoss was in the red burgundy leather reading chair. True to the style of a man who liked his share of clichés, he had eaten his gun—put his automatic into his mouth until the barrel rested against the roof of his mouth, then he'd pulled the trigger. Never very pretty. Lots of cops talk about eating their gun one day, but Hoss, so full of life and even toughness, was about the last person Al would have ever expected to do it.

Al went over and took a look at the body, how the gun had fallen, even checked the trigger finger. He'd been on a suicide once where the trigger finger was broken. Hard to do that yourself. Then there's always the classic where the gun falls from the right hand of a left-handed man. But everything looked authentic here. His instincts were good that the GSR probably looked just the way it should, not a product of someone holding the gun in his hand and squeezing one off into a pillow or the wall when he was already dead. Still, this was Hoss, and that alone made the least sense of all, even given the cold, cold case Al had turned up when he found the barrel.

"You bastards. You drove him to this." The son, Kyle, stood off to one side by a fireplace, as he had been directed. His hands were clenched into fists at his side."

"We didn't drive him to do a damn thing," Clayton

grumbled. "Whatever was gnawing away inside him brought about this."

"I still think it's on *your* heads." Kyle might have had a drink or two before the crime scene crew arrived. His face was flushed red and he quivered like a man who could use another. "I'm calling our lawyers and I'm going to sue you until ..." His mouth was spraying a little spittle with each word.

"You would like a phrase our FBI friends are fond of," Al interrupted. "It goes: 'deny everything, admit nothing, begin counter-allegations.' It's not going to work in your case. The hard science is going to defeat you and however many lawyers you want to bring to the fray. Do you want to know why?"

Kyle had sputtered to a stop. He glanced from Al to Clayton. "What the hell are you saying?"

"I think you know." Al glanced toward Clayton, who stood there like a stone.

"No. No I don't." Kyle started to take a step toward what was left of his father. It should be a hard thing for any son to see and go through, but he seemed to be focused on himself. Al couldn't imagine how he'd feel if he was seeing his own father looking like that, especially when he had one moment been a prominent public figure running for office and the next ... well, nothing close to a pretty picture.

"I think you should close your mouth and sit down. This is still a crime scene we're processing." Clayton looked toward Al. "Why don't you explain it to him, and in small words even someone who's failed the bar exam often can understand."

"Do you think Hoss knew there'd be DNA from the fetus?" Al asked Clayton.

"He knew," Clayton said. He looked sad. Of course he

was. He'd worked with Hoss for years, and Hoss had been his number two man.

"Are you saying my father knocked up that maid and killed her way back when?" Kyle was shouting now. Again he started to move to his father, where Clive was bent close, absorbing every detail he could, probably coming to the same conclusion Al had. Teddy stayed close to Clive's side, glancing at Al or Clayton now and then but keeping her head down around the others. The messy ending didn't bother her as much as the proximity to people she didn't know well. They got some help from the deputies getting him up onto the gurney. Teddy covered him with a sheet with the same loving care she might show one of her dolls.

"I told you to sit down and shut up." To underscore, Clayton gave Kyle his Miranda rights.

"I can't believe it. How dare you think you can arrest me. For what?" Kyle sought to sound assertive, but a crackle of uncertainty crept into his words. For the first time, Al thought the son seemed remotely human.

"I doubt you've had time to get the results on the DNA of Angélica's fetus back yet," Al said to Clayton.

"No. Not yet." Clayton spoke through clenched teeth. "And that's even after considerable pushing and a little shouting."

"You see. You see. You have nothing!" Kyle shouted.

"I said shut up. Go on, Al." Clayton's face was nearly as red as Kyle's.

"While the sheriff never speculates, and I rarely do, I will go out on a limb here and tell you what I think the DNA of the fetus will show. It'll be close to Hoss's, but not a perfect fit. It'll be more like someone in Hoss's family, like a son."

"You have nothing! Nothing!" Kyle screamed. A deputy

pushed him down onto one end of the leather couch and held him in place with one hand.

"Remember what I said about having your lawyer present and shutting up until then," Clayton said in a low rumble.

"You see, the real problem is that we knew Hoss too well," Al said. "He was a family man above everything. Why else would he indulge, spoil, and tolerate a turd like you all these years?" Al paused. "I got my first indication of where this might go when he threatened *my* family, as surprised as I am to have one these days. Neither the sheriff nor I can see Hoss doing himself in for anything less than to protect you. He was someone who lived life with a passion and who would be reluctant to leave it, especially this way. Still, it failed, and didn't draw all the attention away and onto himself like he thought it might. We now have his DNA, and will soon have yours, and the rest is a matter of due process."

"You have nothing to hold me on. It's just your stinking word." Kyle struggled to stand upright, but the deputy standing behind him, who was smaller, had no difficulty in holding him in place. Kyle looked up at him with more surprise than hate.

"We have plenty enough to hold you," Clayton said. "Tell him, Al."

"How heavy did you say that barrel had to be, Clive?" Al asked.

"Like I said, three-hundred, maybe three-fifty with all the granite rock in it as well. Why?"

"Because it had to take at least two men, big men, to get that barrel into a lake," Al said. He watched Kyle.

"Are you trying to point to me as an accomplice ...?" Kyle started to say.

"Don't even bother," Al said. "That's the least of your

worries. We have enough to take you in, Kyle, and get all the DNA samples we want from you."

Kyle looked ready to bluster some more. As suddenly, all the air went out of him. "It's a shame. All a damned shame," he said. "Dad would have made a good sheriff."

"I think so too, son." Clayton nodded to the deputies. Another came up behind Kyle and the two of them started putting on the cuffs, got no resistance from him.

Before they took him away, Clayton stepped closer and said, "I liked old Hoss, enough I gave hard thought to just stepping aside and letting him have a clean shot to run the department. He was a lot younger, and I never had any reason to dislike or mistrust him, until now. Even his last act was for someone else, a son who hardly deserves it."

"It's too bad it didn't work. I liked the old Hoss too," Al said.

"He said he'd never sacrifice himself for me, ever." Kyle stared at the covered shape on the gurney.

"There's always a first time for everything." Clayton shook his head, turned, and walked away.

MAGICAL ME

"**W**HY ARE PENN AND TELLER like a married couple?" Maury stood behind the red satin skirting of a makeshift table on the far side of the living room.

"Why?" Bonnie said. She wore what Al could only describe as a princess outfit that was two or three sizes too small for her.

"Because only one of them gets to talk." Maury held a wand, wore a cloak, and held a black silk top hat in his other hand.

"I don't know if I'm going to allow you to use that one," Bonnie said.

"Okay. I've got lots more," Maury said. "My lovely assistant must be magical, because I've fallen under her spell."

Al had just come in the door, was greeted by his tail-wagging fur pal Tanner, and then took in the scene unfolding in his living room. Fergie sat on a folding chair facing the two ad hoc performers. Al eased up to her, leaned down close, and whispered, "What's going on here?" Tanner climbed up onto Fergie's lap, where he'd probably been before Al arrived.

"Maury got roped into doing a magic act on the local community theater stage. A woman who bought pottery from their potting mentor, "Papa Bear" Rum Murphy, talked Maury into this."

"She must've bought a helluva lot of pottery."

"She did. It's a charity show put on by Florence Stanton Beckerman. And you know what it means when a woman like that has three names."

"That her husband's the one who married into money."

"And he's a doctor, a surgeon." Al glanced toward the stage area. Maury had stopped, crossed his arms, and was tapping one foot. "From what I've seen of where they live, it's way above what even a surgeon makes," Al finished.

"You'd best sit down before he tries to make you disappear," Fergie said.

"Ahem. If I may be allowed to continue," Maury said once Al had dragged a chair over beside Fergie's and sat. Tanner leaned across Fergie to lick Al's hand.

"Where'd you get all this stuff?" Al waved a hand at the table of props."

"Magic store," Maury said. "Express shipping. I would have loved to do a dove act, but they're harder to ship and too unpredictable unless you've spent hours with them, and they're not as cheap as you'd think."

"No sawing anybody in half either," Bonnie said.

Maury nodded. "I saw one instance where an amateur magician used a chain saw for that trick and accidently cut the throat of his twenty-eight year old wife. She couldn't get her head tucked into the middle compartment and tried to scream and wave her arms to warn him. But he couldn't hear her over the chain saw."

"Thanks for that bit of nightmare soup," Fergie said.

"I believe that so-called mistake was part of the act," Al said. "The woman's just fine."

"Well, I still say, no!" Fergie said. "I quite agree with Bonnie. Nothing like that sort of act."

"That's why he's using his funny bone instead and going with humor," Bonnie said.

Maury took the cue. "Do you know what's it called when you get something for a penny at the magic store?"

"No."

"A cheap trick."

"Do I groan now, or do you have someone lined up to do rim shots?"

"Give him a break, Al," Bonnie said. "He realizes he's not gonna be good, given the time to learn, so he's using humor so he isn't boring."

Al started to say something, but Fergie squeezed his arm, encouraging him to keep silent.

Maury went through his ring trick routine, a silk handkerchief number, and a card number using Fergie as his audience participant, a trick that he got right on the third try. Al managed not to yawn. He'd been to these charity shows before, and Maury was neither better nor worse than what Al had seen then. The jokes were pretty stale, though. "Did you hear about the angry magician who pulled his hare out?"

Al could tell the big finale was coming up when Maury swept away the skirting to reveal a coffin arranged on sawhorses horizontally and at an angle. When he lifted the lid off and set it aside his audience of two could see that the silk-lined inside of the coffin was empty.

"You can tell when you've got a cold when you're a coffin." Maury put the lid back in place and waved the skirting like a cape, in a way that nearly concealed Bonnie climbing up a small stepladder, lifting the lid, and getting into the coffin.

"There will be a black velvet sheet hiding that during the show," Maury said in an aside to his audience, of whom only Tanner seemed to be enjoying himself, and that was because Fergie was scratching him behind his ears.

Maury whisked the red satin away from the coffin, all ready for his "ta da" moment. But the lid rested half a foot above the coffin with Bonnie's hands holding it in place.

"Pull the lid down closed," Maury stage-whispered.

"I can't. Some of me's in the way."

Maury tried to press on the top.

"Ow."

He stopped. The lid slid off and landed on the carpet.

Bonnie sat up, tears running down her cheeks. "I'm too big. You need a limber skinny girl who can bend herself into a pretzel and fit into a damn coffin."

"It's okay. It's okay." Maury glanced toward Al and Fergie, his eyes wide.

Bonnie climbed out, got down the ladder, her shoulders shaking as she sobbed. "I'm just too roly-poly big."

She ran from the living room, her crying getting louder instead of fading.

"I'll rent a bigger coffin!" Maury ran after her. "I like rubbing your round little Buddha belly."

"I could have lived the rest of my days happy to have never heard that said out loud," Al said.

"A woman at the grocery once asked her if she was pregnant. She's sensitive about her little belly."

"I think it's cute," Al said.

"So does Maury, but he's going to have his hands full getting her to accept that." Fergie sighed and nudged Tanner off her lap. The magic act was over.

———— ⊰⊱ ————

Al sat in the audience wearing a suit jacket and open collar white shirt, a concession on his part. Fergie wore a green sweeping gown that set off her long red hair.

So far the crowd had been pretty kind toward Maury's lame attempt at humor. The gags were bad enough the audience seemed to think the act was kitschy and he was doing it on purpose. Maybe he was.

"I'm glad they patched up their differences," she whispered.

"Is that what that was? I thought a cat got stuck in the washing machine."

"The worst of it was that Maury was the one making most of the noise." The corner of Fergie's mouth twisted into her sarcastic grin. She seemed happy for the opportunity to dress up and sit in a dimly-lit theater looking up at a stage.

Al felt happiest because Maury was just coming to his coffin bit, so Al knew the act was almost over, approaching its climax. He'd seen Maury practice the bit enough he could tell when Bonnie would be slipping around behind to clamber up the stairs and climb into the coffin. Give them credit, he couldn't see where any of that was to happen now, thanks to the black velvet.

But Al could hear a blood-curdling up and down the scale scream from Bonnie.

Maury spun, dropping the red satin cloth, and gaped wide-eyed at Bonnie. She stood on the ladder staring down into the coffin. "There's a body already in there."

———❖———

Maury and Bonnie came up to Al and Fergie in the parking lot. Maury still looked dapper in his tux. Bonnie was oozing out of part of her costume. Neither looked happy.

Flashing blue and red lights swirled across the outside of the community theater building.

"I suppose you've heard who it was in that coffin," Maury said once he was up to them.

"Yep. Florence Stanton Beckerman herself. You couldn't have dropped a bigger bomb on this event," Al said.

"We had nothing to do with it, though we're having one heck of a time convincing your former colleagues of that. Speaking of which ..." Maury nodded toward two approaching men, one a deputy in uniform, the other in plain clothes. Al knew the detective in plain clothes, Victor Kahlon."

"Evening, Al. Fergie," Kahlon said.

"Howdy, Vic. Sorry to meet again in such circumstances."

"No worry. You know I gotta take your brother in, his magic assistant too. You can follow along if you like."

Al nodded, knew it was a courtesy Vic didn't have to extend. But they'd always gotten along. "I appreciate that."

<hr>

When detective Kahlon came out two hours later to where Al and Fergie sat waiting in the lobby of the sheriff's department office, Al asked him, "Well, Vic, do you know now that Maury didn't have anything to do with it?"

Vic shook his head, "I don't know anything for sure right now. But I have enough on these two to keep them here. They were closest to the victim."

"Are you sure?" Al glanced to Fergie. "Bonnie was on stage the whole time until she had to slip into that coffin. Anyone there can tell you her screaming showed genuine surprise. Didn't anyone back stage notice anything?"

"We've brought in the stage hands too," Vic said. "They claim innocence, same as your brother. You know I gotta go through the steps, Al, unlikely as your brother may be. They have the best opportunity."

"But you have squat for motive."

"Right."

"And, as for means, you don't even know cause of death yet, do you?"

"Nope."

"Any way I can just take Maury and Bonnie home?"

"Nope." Vic shrugged. "Even if Clayton were here at this time of day I doubt he'd clear that. But we can keep them here, not send them down to the correctional complex."

Al sighed. Maury and Bonnie had looked tuckered to their bones and ready to go home when Al had last seen them, but it looked like they had a longer night ahead of them. He knew the drill. It's not like they were going to get fingerprinted and have to wear those black and white striped pajamas. But they would be uncomfortable and inconvenienced nevertheless.

Vic lowered himself down into a chair across from Al. "Look. In any other circumstance we'd have a real candidate."

"Her husband, Doctor Beckerman?"

Vic nodded. "We've been to domestic disturbances at their place countless times lately. Heck of a big place, a mansion really."

"What kind of abuse?"

"Every kind, from verbal to him knocking her around that big place like a handball. But they had one of those kind of relationships where she owned the house but kept letting him come back into it. She never once got a restraining order. It's an old story."

"Yep. One I've unfortunately heard before."

"But this one has a slightly different spin. She was apparently showing the early stages of dementia and was being treated for it."

"You think she forgot to report him knocking her around?"

"Like I said, I'm not really thinking anything yet."

"Yet you're not bringing the husband in, Doctor Punching-bag?"

"I would if he was within a hundred miles of here. He's all the way over to Houston giving a talk to other surgeons. Something like two hundred witnesses saw him there and can vouch for him not being anywhere near here."

Al stood and Fergie and Vic did as well. They shook hands all around.

"Look, Al, no hard feelings here, okay? I know you, more by rep than getting to work with you that much. You'll go poking around in this, and for the most part I can't stop you, wouldn't if I could. But if you do get a better handle on this than I have, will you at least share it with me?"

"That, Vic, I'm very pleased to agree to do."

Al and Fergie turned to leave.

"Wait," Vic called out.

Al turned his head.

"I will give you one crumb," Vic said. "The two stage hands said they were back stage a full half hour before Maury was doing his act. They said they didn't see a single other person back there."

"Thanks," Al said. "Thanks a lot. That might just be something that helps."

Al was all set to swing his truck out of the sheriff's department lot when he spotted a silver Volvo station wagon parked down at the far end of the main building. He turned that way and drove down to park beside it.

"Not going home yet?" Fergie asked.

"Nope. The night is young, for some people."

Fergie didn't even glance at her watch, just followed along in her glistening green gown.

Clive Barnes, the M.E., looked up from a row of test tubes at a lab along one wall. His stocky sidekick and assistant Teddy, who had a touch of autism, wasn't present, so Clive must have come in on his own during off hours, as he often did.

"Oh, my. I didn't know tonight was formal or I'd have brought along my cummerbund. I've never seen you so spiffy. Were you out styling, Al?"

"You should have seen my brother Maury in a tux. He absolutely looked like the little man on top of the wedding cake."

"And you, Fergie, stunning." Clive's eyes swept over her. "I wish Teddy were here to see you in that. She has a thing for princesses."

"I hardly feel like a princess just now. I'm starting to feel like the last chapter of 'What's the Use.' But I'll bet Al has other topics to discuss."

"Did you get anything yet?"

"Nothing I'm willing to announce just yet. But it looks to me like she has the equivalent of five to six codeine pills inside her."

"That isn't anything she should be taking for dementia, is it?"

"Of course not. I don't even know how she'd get her hands on this much."

"Her husband's a doctor," Fergie said.

"Is he a suspect?"

"Unfortunately, no. Right now they're holding my brother Maury."

"Then you probably shouldn't be here in the lab, Al."

"Oh, Maury didn't do it. I'm just trying to piece together what really happened and who did do it." Al looked around the room. "Anything else quirky or kinky about this?"

"Not unless you consider a partially empty water bottle as such."

"Really." Al scratched at his chin.

"I see those wheels inside your head whirring around. What is it?" Clive asked.

"There *is* one way to look at this that makes sense when you bring together all the parts of it."

"How's that?"

"Let's say a woman is mad at her husband, in a passive-aggressive sort of way. She's been his kicking stool for years and wants to really put him in a hard spot. She organizes a big charity event and figures out how she can star in it and take him down."

Clive nodded to himself. "She takes the pills and climbs into the coffin. She'd be dead in twenty minutes or so. Maybe she swallowed them once she got in. That would explain the water bottle. And it would mean she could have still been around at the start of the event to greet people and such. Then she has her own starring moment."

"It could be the way it went down," Al said.

"But what about the husband being away, having a hard alibi?"

"Her dementia," Al said. "Maybe she forgot."

"Hmm." Clive was teetering.

"The thing too is that her husband was a violent man, beat her repeatedly," Al said. "He hardly seems the sort to resort to poison."

"If it was him," Clive said.

"If it was him, or someone on his behalf," Al said.

Clive nodded again. "I can go this far. I can say suicide *or* homicide. But I can't go so far as to say suicide outright, just yet anyway."

"That's fine for now." Al gave Clive a pat on the shoulder and tugged Fergie toward the door. "I'll go do some more digging, maybe use some of Maury's magic and see what pops up."

Al and Fergie climbed out of his truck the following afternoon. He'd parked in the circle drive right in front of the main door. He looked up at the house, mansion really. "Man, that is some kind of house. Must be thirty-two rooms."

"And just the two of them live it in," Fergie said. "Crazy."

Al rang the bell, then rapped on the door. He kept at it for five minutes before he finally got a stir. The front door swung open with a snap.

A man stood there in his robe and pajamas, even though it was one in the afternoon. His long, greying hair was tousled, as if he'd barely had time to run his fingers through it.

"I had a long drive back and then had to speak to the police, or sheriff's department, whatever. I didn't get to bed until two. This had better be extraordinarily important to disturb me. I thought it might be someone from law enforcement again."

Al dug out his badge and flashed it, too quick for Dr. Beckerman to gather much from it. Fergie did the same with hers since neither of them were active anymore. But the good doctor couldn't know that.

"Well, what is it?"

"This shouldn't take long, "Al said.

Beckerman glared at him.

"It's about money," Al said.

The doctor's eyes opened wider.

"I've been to your bank and find you don't have much there. As for the house," Al gave it an eye roll, taking it all in, "it's double mortgaged. Even if you sold it you'd owe big."

"What's your point?"

"The thing is, the M.E. is talking about suicide. You realize what that means, don't you?"

"I'm sure you're about to tell me."

"Because her life insurance policy, which you recently increased, was less than two years old, you stand to get back the premiums if it's ruled a suicide, but not the death benefit, which was a pretty whopping amount."

"Is that all you have to say?"

"Is it enough?"

The man slammed his door in Al's face, but Al was grinning as he and Fergie walked back to his truck.

"You kind of stretched it there about what the M.E. was going to say, didn't you?"

"I stayed strictly within the limits of truth. I said he'd mentioned it."

"What did you hope to gain by that?"

"Type A personality like his? We'll see. He could probably scrimp, cut back, and with the money he makes crawl his way back to solvency. But it would take time, a lot of it, and some daily sacrifices that might just be painful to someone like him."

———————⋖⬦⋗———————

Al got the call to come pick up Maury and Bonnie before five that same afternoon.

"Darndest thing," Vic shuffled the release papers on his desk and looked up at Al. "I went to talk again with the good Doctor Beckerman, and don't you know I found him dead in his reading chair. He'd shot himself through the temple. Left a note too. It said, 'I've been a bastard.

I've always been a bastard.' What do you suppose drove him to that?"

"You've got me. "Al shrugged. "I did figure him for more likely to use a gun than poison. At least you can put a lid on this, and in record time."

"It's a head-scratcher. That's for sure. But Sheriff Clayton tells me that used to happen a lot with your cases."

"Just lucky, I guess."

"Yeah. Lucky."

———◆———

Walking to the car, Maury and Bonnie seemed to be dragging their wagons, though they had both had opportunities for a night's sleep on hard steel bunks barely covered by thin mattresses. Al felt just as tired as they looked, and a glance toward Fergie confirmed they were one pooped posse ready for a few days of idle rest.

"That sheriff's department detective was very apologetic. Is he a little bit afraid of you Al?" Bonnie asked.

"No. He's probably a little twitchy about the department getting sued if he makes a wrong step. He's new. That'll wear off."

"He said you parsed it out right way quicker than he did," Maury said. "That the woman used us as dupes to set the stage for making her own disappearance act."

"Yet it'll be your performance the public long remembers, Maury."

"Hers was an act of desperation. A wife-beating husband drove her to it," Fergie said.

"The detective told us all about it," Maury said. "She did what she did to point the blame at him, not us. The poor thing just didn't remember he was going to be elsewhere."

"He killed her all the same," Bonnie said. "His abuse

led her to this. She died at much at his hand as if he'd shot her with a gun."

"What made him crumble, though? I figure a rough guy like that, even a doctor, would stand up to any kind of questioning." Maury said.

"Al had a chat with him," Fergie said. "He can be persuasive. Her suicide sure fixed him with the insurance people. The future probably started to look bleak and maybe he was even capable of regretting his past."

"I wouldn't give him that much credit," Al said. "He was one of those people who use money way too fast, and even with a surgeon's income his prospects looked grim ... to him. There aren't many redeeming qualities to him, if you ask me, unless you count how he bowed out. And that was probably for selfish reasons."

"Did you intend for him to do himself in after you spoke to him?" Maury asked.

"No. I had no way of seeing that coming. I was just seeking some wiggle room to get you two turned free. His end was his own choice, a fortunate one for us as it turned out."

"Well, I guess he found a way to make himself disappear, sort of." Maury said.

Al and the others snapped their heads to Maury, but no humor showed on his face, and Al figured this was pretty much the end of his magical days as well.

GONE FISHING

AL CARRIED THREE BASS FISHING rods down to the boat and put them in beside his tackle bag. He heard steps behind him and turned. Fergie came walking down the path to the dock in his back yard. She wore a white blouse and the shortest red shorts he'd ever seen her wear. The contrast made her legs look long and starkly pale. The shorts didn't clash with her long swaying red hair.

"Do you mind if I go with you?"

"Well, um ... Okay, I guess, if you promise not to give away all my favorites holes."

"I know all about your favorite holes."

"Well ...okay, then." He looked away toward the lake. A light breeze gave the silvery-blue surface a ripple.

Fishing was his time to get away, think, and sometimes just bob around on the water and not think at all. But he guessed just this once he'd live.

She eased all six-foot-two of herself into the passenger seat.

"Do you want me to get one of the spinning rigs in case these casting reels aren't what you need?"

"I don't want to fish, just ride along. I don't even have a license."

Al glanced up the hill to the house. He wondered what the others were doing. Then he saw Maury standing at the corner of the house, peeking around, looking down at him. He wore a convenience store t-shirt Al had gotten him that read: "If you hear banjos, paddle faster." *Where is Burt Reynolds when you need him?* Maury looked like he wanted to come too, but hung back, had probably been instructed to do so by Fergie.

Al looked up to see if any clouds were bunching in the distance for a storm. "Ready?" he said.

She nodded.

Just before he fired up the big engine a mockingbird began to chatter and babble high on a sycamore limb. "Yeah, have your fun," Al muttered under his breath.

On the way out through the center of the lake, their wake splitting into two white waves behind them, Fergie's hair swept out behind her as she smiled and looked around.

Maybe this won't be so bad after all. He did enjoy having someone on board when he caught a fish worth seeing.

Twenty minutes later, he sat in the front fishing seat using the electric motor to edge the boat inside the mouth of Cow Creek when he felt a thump. The rod bent in his hands as he set the hook. He glanced toward Fergie, who smiled with her mouth this time but not her eyes. He reeled in a five pound largemouth and held it up for her to see before releasing it.

"Was that a nice one?" she asked.

"It was ... okay." He fought hard not to bite the words. He'd gone days before without catching anything so nice. He'd caught ten pounders before but, darn it, the one he'd just caught had been a good fighting fish, and a handsome one at that. The defensive grouch he felt swelling up inside him came from not wanting to have to explain, as well as knowing she had some other reason for being along for the ride.

"What is it?" he said. "What do you really want to talk about?"

"I didn't mean to make you grumpy by being along."

"That's not it. Well, a little bit."

"We are all quite aware of how twitchy you get sometimes just by having people in your home, Al. It's why you take off onto the lake and rarely bring back a mess of fish for dinner."

"I turn bass loose because they're over-fished." Al looked to his lure, slid the chartreuse grub closer to the jig head.

"Not the point, and you know it." Fergie paused, looked off to her right along the shore where two turtles slipped off a log into the water as the boat drifted closer. "We try to respect your ... call it twitchiness. But it makes me wonder if you'll ever let down the barriers, or relax them, enough to be close to someone again, really close."

Al swallowed. She might not have heard it, but it sounded like a thump on a bass drum to his ear.

"Well, anyway, that's not really the conversation I wanted to have with you out here. That topic just happened to come up."

Al felt relief sweep through him, but it came with a twinge of confusion, which he chose to ignore.

"The thing is, Al, I need your help."

"With what?"

Fergie's face had shifted to a level of intensity where she didn't blink. The wind tugged at her long red hair that hung down along her cheeks. She ignored the breeze. "My best friend's daughter is in fix, a legal one."

"What'd she do?"

"Drugs, the cops say."

"What's her mother say?"

"My best friend is dead. It's up to me to step in."

Al let out a long breath. At least this was something he was more comfortable discussing. What do you know so far?"

"Alicia pulls up to the West Middleford Elementary School, the way she does every day to pick up her son Jimmy. She's a PTA mom, so she spends a lot of time in or around that place. Anyway, someone taps on her window and she looks up to see a deputy sheriff. Not only that, but another cruiser is pulling up. The first deputy has called for backup."

"That doesn't sound right."

"She's thinking they might be going for a DWI, but she's had nothing stronger than iced tea and is pretty sure she didn't weave around on the road while looking at a cell phone or anything."

"They tell her they've received a call about her, Alicia, specifically her. By name. The caller said she was acting suspiciously, had been driving erratically as she pulled up into the School Zone and that he was pretty sure he saw her hiding drugs behind the driver's seat."

"And?" Al said.

"They ask if they can search her car. She says, 'Sure. Go ahead,' thinking they might find a crumpled hankie or one of Jimmy's toys."

Al saw the boat was drifted too close to shore, so he goosed the foot pedal of the electric motor with his foot and eased them back away. "What'd they find?"

"What makes you think they found anything?"

"Because it's going to turn into a pretty tame story otherwise." He cast ahead to a shadow line along a rocky small cliff face of limestone, the lure dropping into the water with a soft "plop".

Fergie sighed. "Right in the pocket that's behind the driver's side seat they found a little baggie of marijuana, a pot pipe that had been used, and on top of that two unmarked vials of pills, Percocet and Vicodin."

"None of it was hers?"

"Of course not."

"How'd she explain it?"

"She couldn't. That's why she got locked up until her husband Hank sprang for bail. And now her son Jimmy is too traumatized to go back to school."

"And she has no idea how that stuff got there?"

"Oh, she has ideas. But I want you to hear them first hand."

Al nodded.

"Just so we understand," Fergie said, "I want your help, but I don't want you to step in and run the whole thing. Do you understand?"

"Sure. You have the con. Okay if Maury and Bonnie pitch in? They have a restless, hungry look about them for something to do that rattles their comfort zones to the core."

She nodded, and didn't say another thing until he had pulled up beside his place and had helped her off onto the dock.

"Just one more thing," she said, "on that other subject."

"Oh?"

"It's okay for you to let me slip between your sheets, but you need to make a little more room in your heart as well."

"I have."

"That door's only partially open."

"This is especially hard for me."

"You want to talk about hard ..."

Al waved her quiet since Maury and Bonnie were heading down the walkway from the house coming their way.

Al sat in the passenger seat and took in the house as Fergie pulled up in front of it at the end of a quarter-mile driveway. It looked like the sort of country home a PTA mom from West Middleford Elementary School might live in, but he could be projecting some of that, so he made his mind a blank slate ready to hear the woman's story from her own lips. Still he could figure the house itself for about half a million, and with the view of the lake as well as ten or twelve acres of land around it, at triple that. This sprawling ranch home was nobody's shack.

Inside, the perception of a perfect life faded a bit when Al saw Alicia Hamilton. She had been crying and had tried to hide it, with little success. She had taken some time to ensure her strawberry blond hair was in perfect order. But she gave herself away with the puffiness around her eyes and the small jerk of her hand as she waved them through the living area to a small dining table by the kitchen. Big picture windows and sliding glass doors let Al look out into a tree-shadowed back yard where the husband Hank was playing with their son Jimmy by the kidney-shaped stone edged pool. Al couldn't see Hank's expression, but he seemed to be going through the motions, just something to keep Jimmy's mind occupied.

"Hank's taking a few days off from his construction company to help out around here ... until I get my act together," Alicia said.

She poured them each a cup of coffee into bone white cups on matching saucers without asking if they wanted any. She slid the tray of sugar and cream toward them. They both shook their heads, but she was looking out the window toward where Jimmy played in a subdued way for a boy of six.

"I take it you've had a rough week," Al said.

Fergie's head snapped toward him.

"I mean ... Fergie told me what happened. Can you explain it?"

Alicia stood up. They'd barely taken a sip of their coffees. "Do you mind if we walk? I need to move about."

They both nodded, trading quick glances as Alicia slid the glass door open and led them out across a flagstone patio through the back yard. She gave half a limp wave to Hank and Jimmy, kept moving as the flagstone path led in a weave through a stand of trees and down a slope to the lake.

A dock, with a grill and Adirondack chairs, extended out into the lake beside a boat house. Al glanced inside as they went by, saw two jet skis and a Bayliner boat with a bimini top. He doubted they had been on the water in the past few days.

Alicia waved a hand toward the wooden chairs but paced back and forth along the water's edge side of the dock while she talked. "First of all, I don't do drugs. Never have. I think twice before I even take an aspirin. It's what's so devastating about this, and the neighbors just look at me. Forget about me being president of the PTA. I'm strictly *persona non grata* there now."

"If you didn't put the drugs and paraphernalia there, how did they get there?" Al asked.

"Planted. Had to be."

"By whom?"

"I didn't know ... Well, I didn't at first. Then I had time to think about it, in a cell, before Hank bailed me out, which was not cheap, by the way."

"And?"

"It hit me, and then everything was obvious."

Al glanced toward Fergie. Getting this story out of

Alicia was like pulling the hen's teeth of cliché fame. An event of this magnitude, coming out of nowhere like this with such disruptive power, was no doubt a hard tale to tell, and a harder one to live.

The house, their lives within it, had to be a dream that had just made a hard paradigm shift into being a nightmare, especially if she was innocent.

"Well?" Fergie prodded.

"I couldn't for the life of me think at first who could hold this much animus toward me, to plant these things on me, to make the call to get me arrested. Then I remembered. If I hadn't been so upset and discombobulated I would have thought of it right away. Of course. The Adamsons. Biff and Laura Adamson."

"What makes you say that?" Fergie asked.

Al glanced at her. She had snatched away his line of questioning. She gave him a short nod that she understood.

"There was an incident at the school with Laura's son Kyle. He was late coming out of the building. I was helping with pick-ups that day. She was upset because she had to wait twenty minutes. I said, 'I wouldn't worry about it. Kyle's just a little slow.' By that I meant in the physical and literal way. He dawdled. It didn't even hit me at first why she seemed outraged. It turned out she thought I was implying he was retarded or something."

"But it didn't end there, did it?" Al said.

"No. She kind of flipped out. I mean, she and her husband are both lawyers, from top Texas schools. Her degree was from Baylor. He got his at the University of Texas. She went to the principal and demanded that I be removed from my volunteer duties. Demanded."

Alicia sighed, looked out across at small white caps beginning to form on the lake's surface. "When the principal didn't act she claimed I stalked her for a while and even threatened to kill her. That's just plain nuts. Bongo in the Congo." She reached up, patted her head. "I think my hair is starting to fall out. Stress. We don't go out, not even to dinner anymore. We're ashamed the neighbors and our former friends will see us. And let me tell you, after the arrest there were sure a lot of rats leaving the sinking ship."

"I think you're going to like our next stop," Al said as soon as they were back in Fergie's car.

"Oh?"

"To the sheriff's department, Alfred."

"Who are we going to see there?"

"My new friend Detective Victor Kahlon is handling the case, and he's invited me to sit in while he questions a couple of people."

"Really? Let me guess. Biff and Laura Adamson?"

"That was no guess, and you're spot on."

It may have been his imagination, but Al thought she goosed the accelerator a bit as they roared off onto the chase.

Victor was waiting on them as they came into the department lobby. "Al. Fergie." He nodded. "There's something I want you to listen to before we go in. It's the nine-one-one call."

Al and Fergie leaned over the tape player on Victor's desk. He turned up the volume enough they could hear clearly, but the surrounding deputies at work making their daily hubbub around them probably couldn't.

"There is a woman who concerns me veddy much," Al thought the person sounded like someone trying to sound like they were from India. "She was driving all erratic, weaving across the lanes of the road. She worries me veddy much since now she is parked, if you can belief, in front of the West Middleford Elementary School that my daughter attends. I have seen this woman before. I belief her name is Alicia. It worries me greatly that she is on drugs and is a danger to the children. I saw her stuff something behind her driver's seat as she pulled up. She is right in front of the school as I speak."

"They had to respond to that?" Fergie asked.

"Right in front of a school? Hell yes."

"It didn't sound a little bogus to anyone?" Al asked.

"The dispatcher doesn't get to make that call. The procedure is to check it out, and the deputy on the scene and his backup did find drugs."

"But she claimed to be innocent, this Alicia?"

"And cried like a baby. Didn't want her young son to see her with the drugs spread out on the hood of their car. Too late."

Victor turned on a heel and led the way down to one of the interrogation rooms. Outside the door, he turned to Al and Fergie again. "I want you to be mighty tip-toe around these two, Al. They are a couple of real deal hot shot lawyers. I asked them if they'd be willing to submit DNA samples, so I could check against that pot pipe, and they immediately accused me of witch hunting and started to discuss between themselves what they could sue me and the department for."

"I don't believe I've ever met a passive aggressive lawyer," Al said. "And we do live in a pretty litigious society these days."

Victor nodded, still looking like he'd swallowed the sour pill. "Remember what I said. Go real easy here." He pushed the door open and led them inside.

The seated couple sure looked like lawyers to Al. He glanced to Fergie, who had dealt with this sort plenty of times in various courtrooms. She kept a straight face, but he could imagine the eye-roll.

The man wore a three-piece grey pinstriped suit, this on a day when the heat index could hit one hundred outside. Instead of the red aggressive tie he might wear in front of a judge, he had opted for a more demure grey knitted tie.

The woman, with black hair with a tinged hint of dyed red to it, wore a woman's suit and over-sized horn-rimmed glasses that were supposed to make her look more intelligent, but instead made her look like a hostile owl.

Before Victor could speak, the man said, "I'm Biff Adamson, and this is my wife Laura. We would like to go on record from the first moment here that we resent being asked to come and explain ourselves about something of which we have no part."

"We've heard of the woman before," Laura said. "Sounds like she got what was coming to her. What's it have to do with us?"

"You've more than heard of her," Victor said. He spoke to Laura. "You requested a restraining order against her, claiming she was psychotic and unstable, that she'd tried to kill you. A request the judge denied."

"Stupid ass," she muttered. "The judge, I mean." Biff gave her a quick glance.

"This Alicia kept my wife waiting outside the school for nineteen minutes, out of spite, before Laura could pick up our son. There is something wrong with that woman. Now we know what it was."

Victor took over the questioning, in a cautious and routine way, Al thought. He watched the pair, their confidence never shaking, perhaps growing. The word "deniability" kept repeating in his head. It was Alicia's word against theirs, and they had the moral high ground since she'd been caught with drugs, a point they stressed more than once. He kept listening to Biff's voice when he spoke, trying to imagine if he could sound like someone from India on the phone. From the way Biff controlled his inflection on everything he said, Al concluded that Biff was quite capable of sounding like almost anyone if he chose to do so.

After a few minutes of that sort of thing Victor stood and went to the far corner of the room. Fergie and Al crowded close. "Well?" Victor asked.

"Oh, my God. They're impregnable." Fergie glanced over at the two.

"I don't know," Al said, loud enough to make the two at the steel table sit up straight. "I saw something at Hank and Alicia's boathouse that might turn this whole damn thing around."

Victor leaned closer, whispered, "What the hell are you doing, Al?"

"You couldn't get a warrant for the Adamson's could you?" Al whispered. "So you can't check their DNA or cell phones. Right?"

Victor gave a short shake of his head.

"You come out there tomorrow and I'll have all this wrapped up for you," Al said, louder again.

Victor shook his head harder and waved them out of the room.

As Fergie and Al walked away, she asked, "What were you doing just then?"

"Fixing things. Victor should have grounds for a warrant by tomorrow."

"And just how are you going to manage that."

"Did those two strike you as the manipulative, take-control type?"

"Of course they did."

"Just like hungry fish." Al tapped the side of his nose. "Real hungry ones."

"I worry that you're up to something, Al Quinn."

"You should."

———◆———

Al's cell phone rang. He glanced at his watch as he pulled the phone out of his pocket. 2 a.m. "Yeah?"

"The eagle has landed."

"And you guys are okay?" Al glanced toward Fergie on the passenger seat beside him. She was checking her Glock, the same type of pistol she'd used while an active city detective.

"You bet. Come on down."

"Don't let Bonnie shoot anyone."

"She knows she's just here for my protection. Besides, she says they weren't packing heat."

"Packing heat? What're you guys, stuck in the nineteen-eighties?"

"Get down here, Al. I think you're going to enjoy this."

Al turned off the phone and slid it back into his hip pocket. He reached to touch the Sig Sauer in its holster at the small of his back. Then he drove up the lane until he was in front of the house. He got out of his truck while Fergie scrambled out on her side.

The house was dark. He was glad Hank and Alicia had taken Jimmie to a motel for the night as he had suggested.

He led the way around the house and Fergie followed close all the way down to the boathouse. Al could see the beams of flashlights waving around in the night like light sabers.

"Be careful where you step." That was Maury's voice.

Al eased up to the doorway, reached in to flip on the light.

Light flooded the interior. Beside him, Fergie gasped.

Al could make out more of Biff Adamson than Laura. Both had dressed in black. Regular little ninjas. He could make that out in spite of each of them being covered in sticky sheet rat glue traps.

"How many of those did you put down?" Al asked Maury, who stood on a slim bare spot just inside the door.

"Enough to cover the whole floor, except for where the boat and jet skis are docked."

"Took us almost two hours to get them all spread out nice," Bonnie said. "Now look at the mess these two have made of our work."

"Entrapment," Biff yelled with a voice muffled because half his mouth was shut tight by a glue sheet.

Laura seemed unable to speak. Her face and hair were covered, except for one eye that glared out with as much venom as Al could imagine.

"Assault. Look at us." Biff mumbled.

"I'm not the one who suggested you roll all over the place like tomfools while trying to get loose." Maury was having trouble keeping himself from laughing.

"This one here," Bonnie stood on the other side of the boat shed. She held a pistol down along one thigh. With the other hand she pointed to Laura, "couldn't even breathe when I got to her to tear out a nose hole. She should be thankful. I saved her life." She too was grinning, having far too much of a good time.

From the glare and fierce mumbling Al didn't think Laura was any kind of grateful right now.

He took out his cell phone, punched in a number.

"Yeah?" the voice was sleepy.

"You'd better get over here, Victor. I think you'll have enough to get a warrant on the Adamsons now."

"The boat shed?"

"Yeah. I was just doing a little fishing."

"What the hell? I thought you said you'd have this solved by tomorrow."

"It *is* tomorrow, Victor. You'd better get shaking." Al clicked off the phone before he had to listen to some first rate cussing.

———◆———

Fergie looked up from her newspaper and saw Al come in the front door from walking Tanner. He the kind of guy who worried at first that Tanner might pose a threat to the deer who Al fed through the drought times. But Tanner had turned out to be pretty *laissez-faire* where it came to deer, squirrels, and bunny rabbits. Al had a bit of the same attitude, except where it came to someone threatening his friends or family.

Al undid Tanner's lease. The dog raced across the room to leap into Fergie's lap, knocking the newspaper to the carpet.

"I was just catching up on the results of the trial."

"And?" Al came over to sit down on the couch beside her, close enough his thigh was touching hers. He reached to rub Tanner behind the ears. Tanner leaned back into his hand. Sitting on Fergie's lap and getting rubbed by Al. He seemed to be saying, "*Ah, that's heaven.*"

"The judge awarded Alicia five-point seven million." Fergie nodded toward the fallen newspaper.

"Zow."

"She'll play hob getting it. The Adamsons declared bankruptcy before the trial. They had to see this coming once their DNA matched that on the pot pipe, and Victor found all those text messages back and forth on their cell phones. Victor even found that a video surveillance camera captured Biff making the nine-one-one call to the sheriff's department from a business center in a hotel near his business office."

"For someone who got all the credit for breaking the case, your pal Victor didn't seem too appreciative."

"He values his sleep too much. Some people can deal with disruption in their lives, others not so much."

Fergie gave Al's shoulder a light shove. "Something I didn't know," she said, "it turns out Laura had written a novel, one about which the blurb says 'if you knew how to commit the perfect crime, would you do it?' That didn't help her case as a master manipulator."

"I'm surprised Alicia pushed as hard as she did." Al moved his hand to sweep across the soft fur of Tanner's back.

Fergie moved Tanner enough to reach and pick up the newspaper. "Says here that she said, 'We had to do it because we were so bullied. Those people were just plain raw evil.' And I have to agree with her. They, and anyone like them, needed the lesson."

"Even with the hard evidence the case wouldn't have been so easy if the husband hadn't rolled on his wife. Gave her up as the brains of the plan, according to Victor."

Fergie sighed. "I suppose a man like that gives up his wife when he's threatened. Self-preservation, I guess. But whenever I've been threatened you've done the opposite, come to my rescue and stood unflinchingly at my side."

"I might've flinched once or twice."

"But you never spoke of it."

"Who would listen?"

She gave his shoulder a gentle push. "He certainly demonstrated what kind of man he was. I learned something from that. You're demonstrative in your own way. The point is, you showed what you're made of when it counted. There's no need to tell as well."

"I can show you again, if you like."

"I'd like," she said. She lowered Tanner to the floor and reached for Al's hand to lead him across the room to his bedroom. He came along like a fish being pulled from the water.

THE TROLL UNDER
THE BRIDGE

THE DAY HAD ALREADY BEGUN to heat up in earnest. Al had his shirt off while he cleaned his boat and checked its trim, tightening a screw here and there. "Futzing about" Fergie liked to call it. And here she came, leading some fellow down the path to where Al worked. He almost reached for his shirt, then thought, *"To hell with it."*

Tanner lay curled out in the sun on the boards of Al's dock. He lifted his head, gave a low growl, and got up to climb into the boat and curl up at Al's feet.

Hmm. Tanner had proven in the past to be a pretty good judge of character. Al waited.

"There's someone here to see you," Fergie swept a hand toward the man beside her when she came to a stop on the dock. "He says he needs your help."

"*Seeks* your help," the man said, ignoring Fergie's head snap his way for correcting her. He stood about five-six or seven, quite a bit in the shadow of Fergie's six-two. His black hair was thinning and he must have tried to comb over the growing evidence of male pattern baldness, but the wind was playing hob with that, lifting and fluttering the longer strands of hair in energetic waves.

He wore jeans and a long-sleeved blue denim shirt, which in no way made him look more macho, especially with the two half-moon sweat spots showing at his armpits. Al could have pictured the man with the taped glasses and pocket-liner of a college nerd, but he struggled not to judge.

He did think the man's mouth looked weak, but the eyes could either squint into being mean or wince like a dog about to be kicked.

"What I have to say is personal." He glanced toward Fergie. "If you don't mind."

"I don't care, but she will," Al said. "You might as well talk in front of her. I'd have to repeat what you said and I might get it wrong or tangled."

The man sighed. He hadn't been asked into the boat, or to sit on one of the Adirondack chairs, so he stood and looked awkward. "My name is Roy Coddles."

Al nodded.

Roy glanced toward Fergie, who was easing herself into one of the chairs. "The thing is, I've been threatened," Roy said.

Al sought to raise an eyebrow, the way Fergie could, but he wasn't sure he pulled it off, had no way of seeing himself. "I don't do bodyguard work. I'm not even a practicing detective. I'm just a retired dude trying to fill my days with the sort of things that give me joy."

Roy looked out across the lake, finally panned back to Al. "I heard you're good at fixing things, that you can be trusted."

"To my friends, yes."

Roy nodded, seemed to absorb what he could from that. "I don't live far from you. I have a sort of cottage, under the bridge where the highway crosses the lake."

Al glanced at Fergie, then back at Roy. "I know where that is. There's an RV court there."

"I live right next to that." Roy said. "Will it help if I tell you my problem?"

"It couldn't hurt." Al promised nothing. He waved him toward the chair beside Fergie.

Roy eased down into it, cautiously, as if he might fall on through into the lake. He thought of something, just as he got settled, and struggled back up to his feet to come toward Al. He dug in his back pocket, took out a folded sheet of paper, now bent in the shape of his pocket, and handed it to Al. Then he went back to the chair and lowered himself again.

Al opened the paper.

"It's a screen dump," Roy said. "Somebody sent me that message."

Al read the terse note: "Within five days a family member of yours will be killed."

Al looked up. "What family members?"

"A wife, two children, and a dog, who I think of as family." He nodded toward Tanner. "I see you like dogs."

"Do you know who sent it?"

"Of course not."

"And you haven't been able to find out?"

"No. And I have tried very hard. I'm quite good at computer things, but I haven't had any success at this."

"Any idea who might be stirred to write such a thing?"

"No ... Well, maybe." Roy glanced toward Fergie, whose smile was somewhere between Mona Lisa and the cat that just got the bird.

"Why don't you share who you suspect?"

"It's more than one person."

Al waited.

"The thing is ... Do you know those people who lurk around on the internet behind fake names and say horrible things about others? You know, 'This person is fat. That person is gay. Hey, everybody, I bet you didn't know that.' You know, that sort of creep."

"Yeah, I sure do."

"Well, I'm that sort of person."

"Really?" Fergie sat up straighter in her seat.

"I'm not proud of it or anything. I just get my jollies that way. I've always been small, been picked on and such, but on the internet I'm big, and I'm mean."

"You're a bully," Fergie said.

The man's face flushed pink for the first time. "I'll admit to that. I even have a handle. I call myself the Troll Under the Bridge."

Fergie made a noise. Al thought it sounded like she started to snort but swallowed her tongue in the process. She wasn't doing anything to disguise how she felt about Roy. The words "toe jam" crept into Al's mind.

"And you have no idea which of the people you have hurt while you wore a mask might have found out who you are and become enraged enough to try to harm you, or your family?"

"Oh, lord no. There have been hundreds. I made viruses and turned them loose. I wrote awful book reviews. I shamed people for the clothes they wore. I terrorized organizations and both major political parties. For my own amusement I destroyed many a good name. I'm really not a nice person at all."

"You're getting no disagreement from us at all."

"You know the thing that really disturbs me?"

"No. What?"

"*How did this person find out who I was?* I'm supposed to be strictly anonymous."

"You're not now, apparently. There are lots of ways to track down the sender of secret or disguised messages."

"But that's just the thing. I use every firewall

imaginable, go through satellite links, do all I can to stay in the shadows."

"Welcome to the sunlight."

"Can we focus on my family? I know I've done a few lousy things."

"A few?" Fergie made that noise in her throat again, not her most attractive moment, but Al happened to agree with her.

"What is it you hoped to get from me?" Al asked.

"Just help me find who this is so I can plead with him ... or her. I'll grovel, lick boots, anything. I just need to connect so I can protect the ones I love."

"Have you ever hurt anyone else's family?"

"Yeah. A lot. Often." Roy's voice went up an octave. "Look. I admit to everything. Can you just help me? Please? Oh, God. Please?"

"I'll see what I can do," Al said. He watched Fergie's eyes pop open wide.

Roy got up and, head bowed, found his own way back up along the side of Al's house to where his car was parked.

"Why?" Fergie said. "Why on earth would you ever stoop to help someone like that chunk of rotting cabbage?"

Al reached to scratch Tanner behind his ears while looking out across the lake at the small white caps that were beginning to kick up in the breeze. "It's not him I'm helping."

<hr />

"I'll tell you something," Fergie said, as she drove them to Meat Jenkins's place in her car. "I've not been perfect myself. Just last week I got cut off by a truck on my way to the grocery. Then the woman bagging my stuff was putting cold things into the one plain cloth bag I'd brought while all the rest of the bags were the thermal ones specifically for cold items. And the young lady ringing up the purchases dropped a package of lettuce that went everywhere. She offered to have someone get me a new bag, but by then I had grown so grumpy from an accumulation of irritations that I snapped at her that I'd just do without salad. Later I thought about going back to the store to apologize to her. The lettuce bag breaking wasn't her fault. There was no reason for me to hurt her feelings just because of my bad day."

"You know the difference between your story and Roy's?"

She waited.

"You felt guilty. All he felt was scared."

She glanced toward him.

"You're a good person," Al said. "You can't help yourself. He can't help himself either, but it's not in the urge to do good."

"The point is, here is this Roy doing rotten things every day and he doesn't seem inclined to feel sorry about any of it. He's just, as you say, scared because someone has pulled away his mask."

"He's not going to win any humanity prizes," Al said.

"That's for sure." She glanced toward him. "You sure your friend Meat is going to be home?"

"He's got the day off as the department Alpha Geek," Al said. "Of course he'll be home."

"He doesn't mind being called a geek?"

"Hell, he doesn't even mind being called Meat, which is something for a man who casts the kind of serious shadow he does."

"You're not taking him a cheesecake this time?"

"He says he's on a diet. That is if pouring six packets of ranch dressing on a large chef's salad is a being on a diet."

"He's struggling, Al, but at least he thinks he's fighting the good fight."

"Well, it's getting the best of him in three falls so far."

As she pulled up in front of Meat's house, which sat alone in the sun in the middle of a two-acre lot, she sighed.

"I told him we'd come around to the back, maybe share a lemonade at his picnic table."

"Whew. Thanks for that. The smell inside that house was nothing I wanted to wade through again soon."

No trees, no garden, no fence stood around the yellow-sided box of a house with its single-car garage. The house had two bedrooms (one a computer-room/office now) and a single bathroom, out where Al knew the land was cheaper. Meat was no lover of nature or aesthetics. He just needed a roof and a place to eat, though that was probably celery stalks for now.

When they came around the side of the house Meat was just easing out the back door with a pitcher of lemonade and three tall glasses he held with his sausage-like fingers inside each.

Meat was a man who had fought a battle with hair growing everywhere, and lost, had fought a battle with food, and lost. He was young—well, younger than Al. His black hair was a tangle of unregulated curls that shot out in several directions. The black hair extended to his face, long sideburns, mustache, with what looked like flecks of egg on the ends, and a chin and cheeks he'd shaved within a week that had grown back nearly solid black again.

Five-foot-six and a good three-fifty. Sweatpants, sneakers, and a yellow t-shirt enough sizes too small so that a hairy belly-button stuck out exposed beneath the bottom of the shirt. The sweaty smell of the man swept toward them, until Al moved quickly to get on the upwind side of the picnic table that had been bolted to Meat's wooden deck. Here's a man who lived alone out of some self-fulfilling prophecy. Meat grinned, and showed off his white sparkling teeth

He eased into the seat on the other side of the table, which creaked in spite of being bolted down. Meat poured them each a glass of lemonade and slid the glasses across to them.

Al lifted his, looked for the side without a fingerprint on it, and sipped from that. He almost coughed. He'd never tasted lemonade made with that much sugar.

Meat took a big gulp from his glass and smiled, waiting.

Al dug out the paper with the screen dump message. He handed it to Meat.

Meat grinned. With teeth like that he liked to grin. "There's nothing here I can work with. Once you told me who it was I hacked in and checked through the guy's own system. The reason he couldn't find his way back to the sender is because it isn't possible. Not to him. Not to me. I suppose someone in National Security might be able to get past all the encryption, bouncing through satellites, and who knows what else that went into sending the message. But I couldn't chop through the jungle leaves back to him."

"Or her," Fergie said. "This fellow does harm regardless of age or gender."

Meat nodded. His eyes popped wide. For a second Al thought he'd had an insight.

Meat struggled to his feet and started for the house. "Just a minute."

He came back carrying a unopened package of Oreo cookies and a bowl. "Since there's company, I guess we can open these bad boys that were just lurking in the pantry. Don't know how they got there."

He poured the cookies out into the bowl, which he held out to them. They each took a cookie and placed it beside their glasses. Meat took three and shoved them into his mouth, his eyes twinkling as he chewed.

"Okay, you couldn't get to the person who sent the threat," Al said. "Let's ask ourselves something. What are the two distinctive things about such a person?"

"He ... or she," Meat glanced at Fergie, "probably has way above average computer skills, as well as a malicious and vengeful turn of mind."

Al ignored the bits of black and white cookie bits clinging to Meat's teeth, as well as him reaching for another three cookies.

Meat shoved the cookies into his mouth and spoke around them. "Just do a Venn diagram and see who fits in the overlapping spot of anyone smart enough to do that, and with enough animus against Roy to do it."

"I think the haystack is more of a mess than that for finding our needle," Al said. "This Roy has annoyed people near and far, and many of them have computer skills. But your not being able to track backward on this culprit, and I speak of Roy's antagonist when I say that here, gives me hope. He or she must be quite a bit more skilled than your average computer ..."

"You were going to say nerd, or geek," Meat said. He reached for more cookies. He was tucking them away like someone shoveling coal into a steam train's engine.

"Hey," Al said. The thought startled him so much he almost reached for his glass of over-sweet lemonade before he stopped himself. "Maybe I'm trying to play this the way a computer person would. There's a lot more we know about the person who threatened Roy."

"Like what?" Fergie asked.

"Well, he made the connection to Roy as the Troll Under the Bridge. Maybe it's because he knows Roy. He seems to know Roy has a family, one he values enough to get in a do-dah about the possibility of them being harmed."

"That's right." Fergie nodded. "Are you thinking stakeout?"

"Sure, if you don't mind. Maybe we'll end up necking or something."

"Al, not in front of ... your friend."

Meat's chuckling slowed and he leaned forward, serious for the first time. There were only two cookies left in the bowl and he glanced at them before fixing Al with a stare. "If you catch this person, Al, what will you do to him?"

"If the potential victim wasn't a family member, or maybe a pet, and not our troll who was going to be done in I would let this run its course. Roy's no prize at the county fair. But that's not the case. I guess I'll have to wait and see how dangerous this threat is."

"Has the thought crossed your mind this person might also be dangerous to you?"

"It has, Meat. It certainly has."

———⟨◆⟩———

"I'm getting old," Al said. He turned off the key to his truck and let the sound of the engine cooling send its pings and ticks through the darkening night.

"Why do you say that?" Fergie sat in the passenger seat. A cooler of beverages and sandwiches nestled in the extended cab behind them.

"In years past, the first thing I would have done was check to see that Roy actually has a wife and two kids."

"It is kind of hard to imagine some female allowing herself to be wooed by the likes of Roy, but I suppose there's somebody for everyone."

"And now you have the beginnings of a country western

song. But here. Take a look." He handed her the binoculars he'd just used to look down the hill toward Roy's house.

"Ah, a swing set, and a sandbox. That's a good start," Fergie said. "And it looks like the Missus Coddles likes some of her washed things to smell like sunshine. She has a clothesline, and some of the clothes are those of kids."

"We're a swell and clever couple of detectives, aren't we? He said he had a family, and we've proven it."

"Hold on there, Dick Tracy. I can see through the picture window that faces the back yard that the kids are running around in what must be the rec room. Two little ones and one a much bigger girl. A teen maybe."

Al dug the other pair of binoculars out of the glove box and took a look. As the evening darkened he could see into the window more clearly. The three kids seemed to be playing, That's all. He swung his glasses the other way, up the hill behind his truck. "Uh oh."

"What?"

"I don't think we're the only ones watching Roy's house."

She swung her binoculars the way his were pointed. "A large white van with tinted windows. Nothing suspicious about that. My rosy red butt."

"Is that what you want to talk about?"

"Stay focused, Al."

"Oh, I'm focused. This is what I expected, at least hoped to find." He put his binoculars back into the glove box and took out the Sig Sauer. He slipped it inside his belt at the small of his back. "You didn't bring a gun?"

"Of course I did. I'm wearing it. Want to pat me down and find out where?"

"Not right now. Maybe after we find out what's going on in the van. Let's take the wide way around and come in at it from the higher ground up the hill. If he's sitting in there with a sniper scope we don't want to walk right into his path of fire."

He led the way up and around, crossing the road out of sight from where the van was parked along the right shoulder of the road.

Just in case anyone looked around, Al took them through a thick stand of sumac and tall grass before leading them down to the ditch across the road. The whole area behind him was going to be a hospital, or motel at some point in the future, but right now it was a vacant field, home to critters Al could hear moving about in the dark. Possums, raccoons, maybe a fox or two. Something was rustling about in the dried leaves of ground cover. He stayed fixed on the van, a VW now that he was close enough to see it clearly.

They had to duck low when the lights of a pickup or car swept past. The traffic on the road wasn't heavy, except for brief flurries when the traffic light down at the bottom of the hill changed.

At a calm moment Al gave a wave and they scurried across the road, pistols drawn. He'd seen her take a chief special out of an ankle holster. He'd have found it in a search, but wouldn't have gone directly to it. He'd have to pat her all over first.

At the van he swung the driver's side door open while Fergie covered the back and downhill side of the van.

The man spun from looking down the hill at Roy's house through the side glass in the back. He started to raise what he held in his hands. Al dove across the top of the front seat and landed on the guy, knocking away what he held and pressing him to the floor of the van.

Fergie swung open the back door of the van and pointed the beam of her flashlight at them. "I hope I'm not interrupting anything intimate."

The man squirmed under Al, who held him tighter.

She swept her flashlight beam across the floor around where Al and the man pinned. He saw that what had fallen from the man's hands was a camera. He hadn't put up much of a fight, though he looked fit enough, a man in his thirties with long red hair and a matching beard, nicely trimmed. He didn't offer any resistance. Al couldn't tell, but the man's face was wet and he might just be weeping.

Now, the correct thing for the man to have said at this point was, "I can explain everything," which would have included looking down the hill toward a house where three children could be seen playing though the window. Instead, he said, "I want a lawyer."

Al eased up from the man, told Fergie, "Keep him covered." She did, with her small .38.

Al dug out his cell phone and punched in Victor Kahlon's number. When the detective deputy answered, Al said, "You doing anything right now?"

———— ◆ ————

Al and Fergie sat in the sheriff's department lobby, listening to the murmur of the slow beginning to another long night shift. Some people had been brought in, but the hour was too early for the DWIs and most of the domestic craziness that made the shift such a joy to those whose turn it was to work it.

Fergie looked over at Al. He sat slumped in one of the chairs. No magazines were piled on the end tables. She sighed. "This happened fast. I didn't even get a chance to open a soda, much less have a go at those sandwiches Bonnie made up for us."

"You make a good point. Let's not wait in here. I'll leave word for Victor."

In a few moments he led the way outside, took in a deep

breath of the night air, which was still warm from a hot day, but tasted far better to him than the department's stale, overworked AC.

Detective Victor Kahlon came out the front door an hour later and spotted Al and Fergie sitting on the tailgate of his truck with the cooler between them. He started across the mercury vapor lit parking lot toward them.

"Want an egg salad sandwich?" Fergie asked as he got close. "Bonnie did a first rate job making them and of course made far too many."

"I wouldn't mind."

"And a Diet Coke?"

"Perfect."

Al slid the cooler farther into the bed of the truck and Fergie slid over closer to him. Victor sat down on the other side of Fergie. He waited until he had sipped at his soda and a had taken a bite out of his egg salad sandwich before he spoke. "It's no wonder that Bonnie is a roundish little thing. She makes a helluva sandwich. I'll bet all her cooking's good."

"Too good," Al said. "I've been having to go to the gym again. Now, what's going on in there?"

"Have you ever thought of calling me in daylight hours, Al? You know that is my regular shift now that I'm a detective."

"Ah, but who doesn't like to come out when it's dark and make a grab when the real nasties are out and about."

Victor chuckled around a mouth full of the last of his sandwich, which he washed down with some soda. He took a napkin Fergie held out to him and rubbed his mouth. "The guy's name is Erich Mehlesson. We kept him waiting in holding until we could develop the film from his camera in our own dark room. Technically we were allowed to do that since you, as a citizen, turned over the camera to us instead of us violating his rights. Of course, he might sue you for messing with those rights, but I doubt it after what we found."

"What's that?" Fergie asked.

"All his pictures were of kids. Small kids. Some on playgrounds, some taken through windows, and quite a few in various stages of undress."

"Oh, my." Fergie said. "That doesn't sound like what we were expecting at all."

"That raises another burning question I had. Just what were you to up to at that particular spot and at that particular time?"

"Nothing that connects to what you've turned up, Victor. I'll fill you in at another time."

"Okay. I have hands full now with seeing Judge Harper first thing in the morning to get a warrant to search this Mehlesson's house."

"Single fellow is he? Couldn't find anyone his age who interested him?" Fergie asked.

"He's single." Victor crushed the empty soda can and put it beside the cooler. He hopped off the tailgate.

"Can I come with you tomorrow?" Al asked.

"It's probably better you stay as unofficial as possible on this just now. Tell you what I'll do. If I find anything, I'll give you a prompt call. Okay?"

Al nodded.

Victor started to walk back toward the department building, but stopped and looked back. "You're making me look like some kind of rising rock star with these busts, Al. Clayton says to hang onto your shirt tails and I'll be all the way up to lieutenant in the time it takes a pigeon to fart."

"He didn't say that about the pigeon, did he?"

"No. That was mine."

"I thought so," Al said.

———————◆———————

Al didn't get the call to come in until late the following afternoon. A young deputy ushered them back to Victor's desk.

Once they were seated across from him Al glanced toward the retreating deputy. "Are they getting them right out of high school now?"

Victor chuckled. "That's you showing your years. At a certain stage everyone begins to look like that they haven't started to shave yet."

Fergie sat near enough to give Al a gentle elbow in the ribs.

"Well, what did you find?" Al asked.

"Enough to make me look pretty darn good. The guy had his own dark room. You can't believe the stuff we found in there. Enough to send this guy away for having short eyes. That's for sure."

He slid a thick folder over to Al, who opened it to see a pile of photographs, each eight-by-ten. Good clear photos with the same subject, young kids. Some clothed, most not. Al felt his own inner heat rising, glanced toward Fergie and saw her jaw clenched.

He leafed through the photos quickly and set three aside. "Do you mind making me copies of these?"

Victor flipped them over and made a note of the numbers on the back. "You can take those along. I'll have new copies made. I owe you. He wasn't what you were after?"

"Nope. Just a lucky find."

Victor looked down at the photos Al had picked out. "And it wouldn't have happened if you weren't nosing around where you were. Care to tell me what you had going on?"

"Maybe later. We're still too early in it to know much ourselves. I'll let you know, if it's something you can use. This Erich Mehlesson guy was a good bust for you."

"Well it sure enough was. I gotta tell you, Judge Harper doesn't give out warrants lightly. He's what you might call a tough tortilla. But he signed right away once he saw the photos we developed from Mehlesson's camera."

Al slid the three photos he'd selected over to Fergie. She looked down at them. One showed the babysitter running through the house with Roy's two kids, Dusty and Isabella. The other showed Roy and the babysitter outside the house on what must have been a previous night. He was trying to pull her into his embrace and she was twisting to try and get away. The next photo showed her running away and Roy standing there, not going after her.

Fergie looked away, off into a corner of the room. Al thought her jaw was clenching and unclenching enough to chew gum, which he knew she didn't use.

"Did you find anything on the guy's computer?" Al asked.

"Not a thing. Do you know why?"

Al waited.

"The guy didn't even own one. He used to have one, but then he heard about guys like himself being caught in pedophile sting operations. He's enough of a Luddite to not know how the law was coming through computers to nab people, so he got rid of his. But he certainly printed up enough hard evidence to do himself in for a long stretch and get registered as a sex offender when he gets out."

Al gathered up the three photos and stood up.

"Hey, you want to know something funny?" Victor asked.

When Al didn't say anything, Victor said, "He used to be a wedding photographer. But now you know where he works, or did work until now?"

"No."

"At one of those cute little ChuckECheese places."

He was still chuckling as Al and Fergie walked away. Fergie had yet to speak.

———◆———

Back at his house Fergie went to the fridge and took out two Dos Equis amber beers. She held them up by their long necks toward Al. He shook his head. He knew she needed to cool off, but he wanted one of them able to drive.

She shrugged and put them back, went to the range and started to make a fresh pot of coffee.

Al said, "Meat told me that Roy works at one of those refurbishing discount warehouse businesses, where they have parts sitting around in bubble wrap and you can get any device driver you want. They build computers and security systems from the ground up. He's pretty much a whiz. One of the only ways that message, untraceable to him, might have gotten onto his machine is if it was put there by someone right in the house."

"The babysitter?" Fergie said.

"You think she could be the one entering messages on his own computer?"

"From those photos she certainly has the grounds. Meat says that would explain not being able to trace the thread back."

"When did you call Meat?"

"Back while you stomped down to the shore by the dock and kicked the whey out of that poor helpless bush."

"That bush had it coming."

"Someone did, but I doubt the bush ever did you or anyone else any harm."

"It'll grow back. It was full of thorns. It turned out to be more of an even match than I expected." She reached down to rub at one leg.

Al was going to say, "Well, good for it," but thought better of it. Instead he said, "Once you have that coffee made why don't we grab a couple of travel mugs and go try to talk to that babysitter."

Al drove all the way to Roy's house this time. He'd given being subtle a chance and didn't have much to show for it.

Fergie knocked on the door. When it opened, she said, "Are you Roy Coddles's wife?"

"Why? What's this about? Is he hurt?"

"No. Nothing like that at all. Can we come in?"

"Are you cops or something?"

Al and Fergie both flashed their badges. Fergie had managed to filch hers back from the P.D. after she had retired. She had never said how.

"Oh, come in. What *is* this about?"

"We'd like to ask you the name of your babysitter," Fergie said.

Rose Marie spun. They stood there. She hadn't asked them to sit.

"Her name's Nancy Blitzer. Why? Is she in trouble?"

"No, we'd just like to talk to her, briefly. It's about something we're working on," Fergie said. They'd agreed on the way here that she should do most of the talking at first, a woman's touch and all that.

Al thought Rose Marie looked like a lot of women Al had met while working on the sheriff's department. Tough in a worldly wise sort of way. Long fading blond hair, a lean peasant sort of face, a little more makeup than your average housewife, and a tired but far too aware look to her eyes.

"Did you know your husband professionally before you wed?" Al asked.

"I'm a hair dresser."

"I know."

"I thought you were implying I might have been a hooker. I wasn't. I made a lot of bad choices and decisions, but that wasn't one of them."

"I meant did you cut his hair?"

"Oh."

Fergie glanced at him, because that hadn't been what he'd meant at all.

"The babysitter," she reminded Rose Marie. "Where does she live?"

"In the RV court next to us. She's real good with the kids. I hope nothing's wrong."

"We don't think so. We just want to talk. Can you give us the address?"

Rose Marie went out of sight, off into what was probably the kitchen. She came back with the address written on a short piece of paper marked "Grocery List." She let Fergie take it, but spun to Al. "I'd usually be at work. You were lucky to catch me in. I took the afternoon off because the kids are supposed to be home early from school. I promised them ... that we'd do something fun."

"That's fine. We'll leave you to that," Al said. In spite of him giving her a little push she'd bounced back well. He was growing to like her. She seemed like one of those people to whom life had been rough, but she kept bouncing back up on top. Good for her.

On the way back to the truck Fergie asked, "What was that about?"

"I'm just trying to get a feel for the dynamic here. You've got to admit that Roy's the kind of guy who makes your skin crawl."

"Agreed."

"Well, I wanted to get a handle on what kind of woman could manage to live with someone like that."

"It is a head scratcher," she agreed.

They left the truck where it sat and walked across to the RV court, on a path that Nancy had probably taken often enough herself.

When they came to the right RV Al knocked this time. It didn't look like the sort that hit the road rolling often. Permanent looking planters lined each side of the steps up to the door. They showed off thick red and yellow of geraniums and marigolds. Cheerful and bright.

The woman who answered the door wore a baby blue dress with white lace trim at the bodice and hem. It looked like the sort of dress a young girl might wear to a tea party rather than a mom would wear around the house on a week day.

"You're Harriet Blitzer?" Al asked. He'd seen the Ralph and Harriet Blitzer on the wooden sign hung under a front window. He wondered sometimes why people would live in an RV when they clearly looked to be more the cottage-by-the-lake sort. Now Roy, he might need a home on wheels before all this was over.

"We'd like to ask you a quick question or two about your daughter's babysitting. Is that okay with you?" Fergie showed more care and charm than usual.

Harriet's head snapped back an inch for a moment. "Is everything ...?"

"Everything's fine," Al said. It's more about the people for whom she babysits."

"Oh, that. I guess I could see that coming." She hadn't asked if they were cops or anything. Yet she'd expected them.

"What do you mean by that?" Al looked around the living area, saw a glass cabinet that held Hummel figurines. He would be darned if he knew why, but almost every RV he'd even been in had housed at least one collector of one thing or another.

"Well, I thought we had left that bit of unpleasantness behind us. Roy said it was all an accident, a misunderstanding, and he'd doubled her babysitting fees. We said okay as long as nothing like it happened again, and it hasn't."

"Is your daughter handy at all with a computer, ma'am?" Al asked.

"Oh, don't call me ma'am. Harriet is fine." She glanced toward the kitchen. "Do you think I should make tea?"

"No thanks. Is Nancy around where we could talk to her?"

"Heavens no. She's at school. This is her senior year, and give credit where it's due. She's struggled her way all the way through it."

Fergie tilted her head.

"It's no secret. Nancy has autism. Not a real extreme case of it, but bless her heart, it's made everything harder. We thought the babysitting was good for her or we'd have just been done with all that, as long as all that's straightened out. It is straightened out, isn't it?"

"Is your daughter good with computers?" Al asked. When he had found the M.E.'s assistant Teddy was somewhat autistic he'd looked it up and found it happens more often in boys than girls, but as many as one in sixty-eight children have the disorder, which can vary from one individual to another.

"Oh my, no. Her doctor says that a computer can actually make her condition worse. He advised her to stay away from them, and she has."

"Why so?" Fergie asked. "I thought autistic children loved computers, that they thrive on them."

"And that's the danger, at least according to our doctor. And don't think that makes school any easier, what with so many of them using tablets and such in the classrooms, far more than books. That's one reason we're living here, when we could live anywhere. This school hasn't gone digital yet. My husband Ralph is a construction supervisor and could find work just about anywhere. He's such a hard worker. He's the one who wanted to smash Roy in the face."

"About the computers?" Fergie drew Harriet back to the subject.

"Ah. Doctor Botoman says that using a computer engages your mind in a particular kind of manner, that using a data machine makes your brain work in a more linear step-by-step way. What it could do to someone like Nancy is develop an over-reliance on the left side of her brain. She needs to stay as much as possible in the real world, where she can work with the right side of her brain to learn to better interact with others, keep her social skills growing."

"Is this a widely held opinion?" Al asked.

Fergie shook her head at him. "So, long story short, no computers."

Harriet smiled. "Not in this house, I'm proud to say. You should see her with water colors. She *is* a whiz with those."

On the walk back to Al's truck, Fergie said, "I don't like where this is going."

"I think it's already gone there. All we can do is straighten this out, to the extent we can."

Fergie sighed.

Al knocked on the door this time.

Rose Marie swung it open. She started to say something, but the fierce resistance on her face melted away and she turned and headed inside. They followed.

"You might as well know that Roy came to us, told us about the message he got on his computer," Al said.

"Why?" Fergie asked.

Rose Marie turned back to them, waved to a couch and loveseat, both covered in a worn but cheerful yellow and orange cloth. Tears ran down both cheeks, and she shook as she lowered herself into a rocker.

An old dog, a mostly golden lab sort of rescue mutt, maybe ten or eleven years old, came limping out from the kitchen, lowered himself beside her, let her reach down a hand to rub his back, get what comfort she could from that. He must have sensed her mood.

"The threat was empty," she finally managed in a voice that quivered. "I just meant it to sting, enough for him to quit cyber-bullying, and doing things like hitting on our babysitter."

She lowered her head, shoulders shaking with sobs. Fergie stood and went over to put a hand on Rose Marie's back.

"You know," Fergie said, "someone like that, engrained as deeply as he is with his habits and desires, is going to be hard to change."

"I know. I know." She took the Kleenex Fergie held

out to her and rubbed hard at her eyes and cheeks. "But dammit I can try. Sometimes that's the best you can do in a world like this. Just try. All you can do."

———◆———

Al put the phone down six weeks later. "That was Victor."

"And?"

You know that the Coddles moved, to a county just south of here. Roy quit his job. I heard he was working as an auto mechanic. Not a computer in house."

"How's that going for them?"

"Victor just got the word from the Hays County Sheriff's Department. Roy committed suicide."

"What do you suppose drove him to that?"

"I tried all along through that mess not to be judgmental. But I'm surprised he went this way. I didn't think he had the stones to do something like this."

"Maybe he didn't. But *she* was tough enough," Fergie said, "when it came right down to it."

"I suppose."

"Are you going to do anything about it?"

"It's in the hands of the Hays County deputies now, and they seem satisfied."

Fergie didn't say anything.

"Are you sad?" Al asked.

"I'm trying to be ... but sometimes it's darn hard."

DOG NINJA

A**L'S CELL PHONE RANG AND** he lifted his left butt cheek to dig the phone out of his pocket. He saw it was the sheriff himself calling. He hesitated, because sometime Clayton came up with distractions from the life Al led that was already filled with distractions. But he shrugged, winked at Fergie and answered it.

"Is this one of those occasions where you sat on your cell phone and called me by accident."

"No." Clayton's voice was a low humorless rumble.

Fergie kept on fishing. She was using a spinning rod and reel she'd picked out herself when they got her fishing license at Academy, the sporting goods store Al should have bought stock in years ago if he'd known how much he was going to spend there through the years. She had picked out her own lures too, all quite similar to what he used, only different. Where he favored a chartreuse grub, she'd picked out a package of pumpkin seed ones. His plastic worms were black with a yellow tail, while hers were purple with a pink tail. And darned if she wasn't catching more fish than he was so far.

He was secretly pleased she had decided she wanted to go fishing with him more, even if that bit into the last of his alone time. But he hadn't told her that. She knew.

"What is it?" Al asked.

"I've got something unusual going on, so naturally I thought of you."

"Kind of you. You recall I'm retired?"

"This is a retired person sort of a task, if you don't mind. Someone is doing a bit of dog napping."

"Don't you have an animal control person, Hugh Meadows?"

"We do. But Hugh is scratching his head on these too, and a lot of them happened out in your neck of the county."

"What so puzzling about it?"

"The dogs most often stolen across the nation, and I'm reading off a list here, are Yorkshire terriers, Pomeranians, Maltese, Boston terriers, French bulldogs, Chihuahuas, and Labradoodles. The ones being stolen around here include bigger dogs and are a mixed up mess at that."

"And your point?"

"My gad you haven't changed. It's a wonder I put up with you for so long. Anyway, most of the ones disappearing off lawns in the night aren't pure breeds, in fact many are mostly plain mutts. Mixed breeds, a few pit bulls, part-labs, and in general just a hodge-podge of dogs most dog customers wouldn't cross the street to see, much less pay money to adopt them."

"You said lawns."

"Yep. Almost to the dog they were left outside, sometimes chained, other times just fenced in behind some chain link. They'd been through all kinds of weather, and some of them might have even been abused."

"I'm kind of leaning toward the dogs' side already myself. Besides, what you ask is almost impossible."

"I'm asking the favor because I have some fine young detectives coming up through the ranks, but they still think in straight lines. Some of them think you do some kind of voodoo."

"Victor?"

"He's one of them."

"They're never going to learn unless you let them go out there and stumble around a bit."

"I know. Yet I'm reaching out to you. The owners nevertheless have rights, and they're squawking."

"And you have an election coming up."

"And I have an election coming up."

"How do you figure I should go about looking into this?"

"I have no earthly idea, Al. None of my guys think it's even possible in anything like a timely and cost-effective way. But you've always thought so far outside the box I'm sure you could come up with something none of my deputies could figure out in a month of Sundays."

"You're serious about this?"

"Of course I am."

"I'll think about it. Right now I have to get back to fishing."

"Yoo hoo, sheriff," Fergie called out in a high feminine falsetto.

"Hmm. Just be careful what worm you're using." Clayton hung up.

"Well, thanks for that." Al put his phone away and reached for his casting rod. They were drifting toward a towering limestone cliff, so he nudged the foot pedal of the electric motor and backed them away, but not before Fergie hooked a fish from a nice long parallel cast.

"He's always asking you for favors out of your time," she said, "ones that you don't get paid for and sometimes run the risk of getting shot at."

Al reached for the net to help her boat her bass. "Well, we'll see. Maybe this time I won't get halfway killed at all."

"Don't say anything to Maury or Bonnie about this," Al said before he fired up the boat to head back to his dock.

"Why?"

"You're hinting at the possibility of danger got me thinking about the kind of folks who leave their dogs outside in all kinds of weather. Most of them own guns and are fond of using them. Just last month we had one good old boy fire his deer rifle into a bush he saw moving without so much as calling out to ask if anyone was in there. Turned out there was someone in there, his neighbor, who had been looking for his cat. He ended up dead."

"Well, I'm not so encouraged by the idea of *you* tempting fate like that either." She stowed her new rod with his on the deck-top rod holder and stretched a bungee cord over that. "I have no idea where you might start with a thing like this."

"First step will be to find out where the dogs are going. They're not just disappearing. Are they being sold? Where? We can check classified ads and internet lists. Is some pet store handling them? Not likely. These are mostly mutts."

"That's all doable."

"But just a step, and not likely to be a productive one. I suspect Hugh Meadows, Clayton's animal control person, is every bit clever enough to have already checked on any local sales routes." Al looked across the lake. The afternoon breezes across the water were kicking up and white caps appeared in rows.

"Unless he wrote them off as mutts not worth selling," she said. "Still, he might have looked and poked around. It's not like Clayton to hand you something that hasn't already flummoxed his pros from Dover."

"If we find, as I suspect we will, that they don't seem

to be dogs someone is selling, the next step will be to find out what *is* happening to them."

"What do you think?"

"I don't think anything yet. But that's the way most cases start for me. I'll just have to take whatever steps I can and see if I can clear away some of the smoke about this mess."

"Well, good luck with that."

<hr/>

On the drive into town to meet Fergie, three days later, Al gave closer than usual attention to the various dogs along the way. He saw three people walking their dogs on leashes, two letting their dog bound around them without a leash, against the ordinances in some areas, and one lab chasing a tennis ball, over and over. A block later he saw a woman carrying her small white mop of a dog that seemed to have given out while on a walk. Its leash hung in a small loop down beside it. The woman didn't seem unhappy, or mad at the little dog, which after all didn't look that heavy as it looked up at her.

He only saw one dog out by itself in a lawn with a chain that went up to a clothesline. The dog, of mixed and dubious breed but at least part pit bull, had its head on its paws and with its back half in a dog house while it looked across a lawn where not much was happening. Al could see where that might disturb some dog fanciers, especially on a hot or rainy day. But the truck in the drive had a red NRA sticker in the window and a dog-napper would have to think twice about sneaking into that yard at night. Plus there was always the chance the dog would bark and give its rescuer away.

<hr/>

Al didn't see Fergie pull up near the Daily Grind coffee shop an hour-and-a-half later. She just suddenly appeared beside his table where he bent over a map of the county.

"What took you so long?"

"Had to stop and get gas. I'm getting the worst mileage lately."

"Maybe you'd better take the old heap over to Dave's and have them see if you have squirrels sucking up the gas or anything."

"I'm not so sure I'd be comfortable taking my vehicle to one of your good-old-boy pals."

"Dave hasn't been part of things for years. He climbed into a bottle and his ex-wife Melissa runs the shop. She still calls it Dave's because people are reluctant to believe a woman can know as much about cars as she does. She'll be fine with your old heap."

"Okay then." She turned toward him. "My car is two years younger than your truck."

"Which I also call an old heap. Well, hell. I guess I'm a bit of an old heap myself."

"You'll get no argument from me."

"Hey." Al looked up from the map. "You know our complaint department is headed by Helen Waite. So, if you have any complaints take them to Helen Waite."

"Oh, my. That gag's older than you are."

"We're both a couple of fossils. I get it. Why don't you grab a cup of coffee so you have the energy to talk?"

She plopped into the seat in the other side of the outdoor table a few minutes later and looked around. A large green umbrella put most of the surface of their table in the shade. She put her coffee mug down and pointed to the map. "Is that every dog-napping you know about?"

He nodded. "We won't have to go traipsing all over the county. More than half of them are a hop-and-a-skip from my place."

"Well, I got something from my morning spent on the phone."

"You didn't let Maury or Bonnie hear you calling, did you?"

"No. I operated my call campaign down on the boat dock. But I finally did get lucky."

"Good, because I've been driving all over the county, looking everywhere, with little to show for the effort. He reached for his cup, took a sip, even though the coffee was cold.

She leaned over the table, pointed to the county map again. If the red spots denote dog-napping spots, what do the green spots mean?"

"Where I saw dogs tied up outside. You know, the heat index is going to get up to one-twelve today. How'd you do on the phone?"

"First I was able to eliminate the likelihood that the dogs are being sold anywhere, as unlikely as that was anyway given what a mutt bowl they were. So I started on rescue centers."

"And?"

"Bingo. I made calls in a widening circle and I finally came across one two counties from here where dogs keep appearing tied to their front railing. The place gets top marks from reviewers for being a good no-kill kind place to get or surrender dogs, so I figured that made them a desirable spot for a dog dump."

"What else?"

"The dog's tags were removed, which the volunteer I spoke with, Meg, was quite upset about since their rabies shot records went with the tags. But two of the dogs had microchips. Only two, which tells us a little more about the dog's former owners. And, of those two, only one owner came and got the dog. He cussed Meg out plenty good for taking the dog. She said it got dropped off in the night like the others. She didn't get anything like a thanks or a donation from him. The other former dog owner said they were too far away. To just keep the dog, or turn it loose."

"Did the guy who came for his dog fill out any kind of form?"

"Nope. But she did get his name. Luther Boudreaux. His dog was a white and brown girl bulldog, mostly. Her name was Lucifer."

"Really?"

"Such is the *crème de la crème* who think dogs are lawn ornaments."

"And in this heat. But you might have just saved us a ton of time."

"How so?"

"I was going to suggest we split up and try to stake out some of the green spot dogs, in case someone comes for them next."

"What do you think is going on here, Al?"

"I think we have us a dog ninja."

"A what?"

"There was a woman in Moriarty, New Mexico, who finally got caught after stealing up to sixty dogs that had been left tied outside. The sheriff's department called her an 'overzealous animal rescuer turned serial dog-napper.' Her name was Connie Swinnerton, or something. She was about sixty. Got caught when a woman returning home early from work to her trailer court saw Connie loading two pit bulls that had been tied outside a trailer into her Ford Escape. When the woman gave chase Connie let them out at the next intersection, but the woman had her plate number by then. That's a dog ninja. You know, some tree-hugging, animal-rights nut who is probably thinks he or she has the animals' best interests in mind and is trying to take them away from suffering and toward a better life."

"You know anyone like that?"

"I lean that way myself, but having worn a badge before I kinda have to stick to the letter of the law and just groan inwardly as I drive by."

"I'll bet you're a helluva tree-hugger."

"Oh, I've hugged one or two."

"What are you thinking here?"

"Let's pack our cooler. It's time for one of our famous stake-outs."

"And stake out what?"

"I think our dog ninja will realize that Lucifer—oh hell, let's call her Lucy—is back in her yard. And if rescued once ..."

"It sounds a bit of a long shot."

"But better than hopping around at the dozen and a half green spot locations. I'm counting on someone wanting Lucy to have a better life. They rescued her once. I'm betting they'll try to rescue her again. It's not a sure thing, but it may not be the long shot you think."

"Just remind me never to take you with me to Las Vegas if I ever go."

"Where were you until late in the evenings for the past couple of nights?"

"Sitting at a couple of those residences you have marked with the green dots."

"Do any good?"

"Nothing."

"Then let's just try it this once my way, okay?"

<hr>

Al pulled up just far enough from the place he could tuck the truck into a stand of thick brush on one side and a stand of mountain laurel on the other.

"I can see the yard from my seat. Can you?" Fergie whispered.

"Just barely. But I don't want to move us any closer."

Al had packed the cooler with the usual junk food he favored for such stakeouts. Diet cokes, some bottled water, beef jerky, and breakfast bars. He reached in, took out a bottle of water, and took a cautious sip. They could be out here quite a while and he didn't want to be creeping around in the bushes when anyone like Luther Boudreaux stepped out back onto his porch with his weapon of choice. Luther had a sheet for domestic violence and had been in a bar fight where he'd come within a hair's breadth of a manslaughter charge. The fellow he'd knocked across the room into the jukebox had lived, and for one reason or another had decided not to press charges.

If it had been up to Al he would have chosen almost any other house to be watching at this hour. The lights in the house went out, even the pale flickering colors of the television. The night settled into a stretch of profound silence for the next hour or two.

A bank of thick clouds drifted over the sliver of a moon and obscured every star in the sky. Al had a hard time seeing anything through his binoculars.

"You know what Bonnie would say right now." Fergie lowered her glasses. "She'd say it was getting as dark out as the inside of a cow."

"I doubt if she'd say that at all."

"Why?"

"Because that's her scurrying across the back yard toward Lucy."

"What?"

She snapped her binoculars back up. "Oh, my heavens. What *can* she be up to?"

"Take a guess."

"That's Maury too. He's throwing the dog some sort of treats."

"I wonder if it's the sort of treats I've been buying for Tanner that have been disappearing faster than I expected." Al swept his glasses toward the house. They must have come for Lucy once before, he figured, so maybe she would stay quiet and let them get away without a fuss.

But no. Lucy began to bark excitedly, and jump to get into Bonnie's arms while she was undoing a chain and hooking up a leash.

The back door of the house few open so hard the screen banged against the outside wall with a hard slap. "Hey!"

Luther leveled the scoped rifle he held. *Bam. Bam.*

On the run, Bonnie handed Lucy's leash to Maury. Both were going across the back yard as fast as they could and quickly faded into the dark of the brush.

Bam. Luther shot again.

Al could make out Bonnie, popping out from the bushes, raising one arm into the air straight up. *Bam. Bam. Bam. Bam.*

Beside him Fergie had her right arm out her window. She fired straight up into the air. *Bam. Bam. Bam.*

Luther dove for cover, then scrambled on his hands and knees back inside. He slammed the screen shut behind him, then the door inside.

Al turned on his engine. "Time to get the hell out of Dodge."

Fergie was calmly reloading from a box of ammo she'd slid out from under her seat.

"Did you have to do that?"

"Yep. Bonnie needed a bit a ground cover. I think gunfire from two directions calmed Luther's jets a bit."

"I'll bet it did. Probably cured him of constipation as well. That still doesn't make it right."

155

"I know," Fergie said, but she couldn't stop chuckling all the way back to the house.

———◆———

Bonnie and Maury didn't get back home until going on 4:30 a.m. Maury parked Fergie's car and they came sneaking in the front door a few moments later.

Al flipped on a living room light.

The two of them froze like kids caught coming in way after curfew from a date.

"I suppose you've got a perfectly good explanation," Al said.

"And it had better explain why my gas mileage has gone to hell on a roller skate," Fergie said. She sat up from where she'd been dozing on the couch.

"Would you believe ...?"

"Before Maury could finish, Al asked, "What'd you do with the dog?"

Maury glanced to Bonnie.

She shrugged. "You can beat us with your rubber hose, officer, but I'm saying nothing."

"And are those my sweatshirts?" Al pointed to the black hooded one Maury wore. Bonnie's was a dark navy.

"Hey, were you guys there?" Bonnie asked. "How do you know ...?"

"I have a lot to explain to Sheriff Clayton. What have you two got to say for yourselves?"

"He was beating that dog," Bonnie said, a burr of emotion showing in her throat. "I watched him go for his belt a couple of times until I had to turn my head and look away."

"I made her promise this was the last time," Maury said. "There were shots coming from every which way. It was like World War Seven out there. We were lucky to get out alive. Feel my head if you like. I think a bullet grazed me."

"I imagine a limb scraped you. Fergie was shooting into the air."

"Well, that dog's owner wasn't."

"Then you're lucky to be alive. Are you serious that you're done with all this?"

"Last time. Scout's honor," Maury said.

"You were never in the scouts."

"Well, there was this one time with a Brownie ..."

Bonnie popped him in the shoulder with her fist. Then grabbed him by the arm and pulled him downstairs toward their room.

"What're you going to tell Clayton in the morning?" Fergie said as she stood to head for their bedroom.

"I'll tell him I looked into it, but failed to shed any light on it. In a while, when no more dogs are napped, he'll move onto other pressing issues. After all, I'm getting too old for this kind of stuff."

Fergie reached out to take his hand and lead him toward the bedroom. "I don't know about that. I think there might be a trick or two left in the old dog yet."

TOMORROW BECOMES
YOUR YESTERDAY

A L QUINN CAME IN HIS front door and reached down to undo the end of the leash. Tanner shook his floppy grey ears and sprang free, charging across the room to leap up onto his favorite end of the couch, next to where Maury sat, bent over looking into the screen of Bonnie's laptop on the coffee table. Tanner, the small Australian cattle dog Al had rescued from a shelter a day or two before he was to be put down for being older than most folks want to adopt, knew he had a home now and had taken to it like he'd lived in it all his life.

"How'd his rabies shot go?" Maury looked up with the faraway gaze of someone wrested away from deep thought.

"He was very brave and I'd promised him some treats, so I stopped on the way home and got him some beef jerky. At least he wasn't there to be tutored."

"Neutered?"

"Don't say that word out loud. That happened to him a long time ago and there's no need to remind him." Al glanced at the computer in front of Maury. "Since when did you have an interest in computers or the outside world?"

Maury looked up from the screen to fix in an unblinking stare at Al. "Is it possible to get a sample of someone's DNA legally?"

"Where are you going with this, Maury?"

"Humor me."

"Only if you ask the person and he or she says okay."

Maury sighed. "And if the person is in jail?"

"In jail for what?"

"Bigamy?"

"Do you have any reason to believe this person might be your son?"

"What led you to that convoluted logic and wild assertion?"

"It's how my mind works. You have a sudden interest in DNA and are acting as sneaky as a kid caught by nuns while masturbating. A man of your horn dog background couldn't have gone about sowing as many wild oats as you did without getting the occasional backlash, or progeny. Does he look like you?"

Tanner looked up at Al with tilted head. Al went over and patted Tanner's head. While there, he peeked at the computer, but Maury had diminished the screen and all Al saw was a screensaver shot of ocean waves breaking on a white sand beach beneath swaying coconut palm trees.

"More than you can believe." Maury shook his head.

"Really? How old is this possible Maury junior?"

"Older than you'd expect, and don't call him that. So far it's just an idea I have, and a bad one. It's why I wanted the DNA test."

"Let me see a picture."

Maury hesitated, then sighed. He popped a Facebook page back up onto the screen.

Al bent closer. The fellow's name was Bernie Meiyers. "Yeah, I can see it. He has your eyes, and that chin might as well be on your face. But what's a guy with multiple wives doing with a Facebook page?"

"It's what tripped him up. He didn't think the other two

wives were computer fans. Turned out they didn't need to be. Friends of the other wives tipped them off."

"Not too bright of him. Wonder where he got that?"

"Hey." Maury's head rocked back to look at Al. He sighed again. "Probably from his mother."

"Since that side is for sure traceable, who was the mother of this prodigy. From the looks of him he wasn't a recent hatchling."

"Do you remember Mary Ann Hatchaway?"

"From high school?"

"Yeah, from high school."

"You dated her. Didn't she move away before we graduated?"

"According to her, I took her virginity. And, yeah, she moved away. I never knew why. I was off to the next willing face by then and didn't give it much thought."

Al flinched at the ease of the confession. He'd graduated high school a virgin himself. Maury, certainly not. The difference between them would, in time, cost Al his marriage and twenty years of not speaking to Maury.

Maury couldn't leave anyone alone back then, even Abbie. But Maury's recent beginnings of a relationship with Bonnie, his nurse who was barely forty, had been the first hint of hope for him at last, even though he and Al were in their sixties. It had taken a while for the nut that was Maury to crack.

"Why this sudden interest in something that happened forty-five years ago?"

"I don't know. You grow a little older you start thinking about how you're going to spend your final days, knowing you have some thread of family and people around you or end up whiling out your days alone in some rest home with a line of drool running down your crackpot chin."

"What makes you think you'll be alone?" Al asked.

"Yeah. What?" This shout came from the kitchen where Bonnie had stepped around the corner to look into the living room. Her face was pink, scrunching into a red pucker. Tears started down her cheeks and she spun and ran out of sight.

"Uh oh. Looks like once again I have to fix what my stupid mouth has done again." Maury stood and rushed out of the room after her.

"They'll be fine." Al gave Tanner's floppy ears a rub. "Usually she's the iron fist of that pair. He'll try to comfort her and the next thing you know ..."

"What are you telling that dog?"

Al looked up. Fergie had come out of the bedroom and stood with arms folded, tapping one toe. At six-foot-two and wearing a stern expression, she looked more than a little like an iron fist herself at the moment.

"Hey, Maury might have a son. Come here and see what you think."

Fergie shrugged off the façade of any anger and grinned. She came to the couch eagerly, her long red hair swaying with each stride, and bent down to look at the picture.

———— ◆ ————

"Archie Pelligo." Maury chuckled to himself.

"What about it?" Al glanced toward the truck's passenger seat. Maury was staring out the side window at the countryside of the county going by on their way to Del Valle where they expected to find Bernie Meiyers as one of the 1,300-plus inmates in the correctional complex there.

"Can you believe it? The guy actually got by with using that as one of his aliases. Not for any of the marriages, but for at least one of his fake I.D.s. The man had a gift for making false credentials that held up enough for the two other spouses. If he had just stayed off the grid he'd be getting away with it yet."

"Do I detect admiration in your voice?"

"I'm just saying. The guy has balls of ...well, he has considerable daring." Maury looked sideways at Al. "Brass. I was going to say brass. You've got me avoiding clichés. But I meant brass."

"And a brain made of the same stuff." Al kept his eyes on the road. "Are you sure you're not dancing off after half issues instead of the big one?"

"What's that?"

"Did you just get tired on not getting gifts on Father's Day? Or do you really suddenly care about carrying your genes on to the next generation? What is it that will in all likelihood have us traipsing across half of Texas to meet Bernie's wives, women just like the ones you used to bamboozle? Tell me that."

"They don't seem the brightest peas in the patch. But let's hold off on that until we meet them. And this Bernie fellow. Don't underestimate the power of loneliness on even the most attractive of women."

"Back to you again. What has you going Captain Ahab on this?"

"Let's just say I'm curious."

"And I'm curious how you got Bonnie to forgive you for your not very silver-tongued blunder."

"What can I say? I have my charming moments."

Al shook his head. "From the noises coming from your downstairs room I thought one of you, or a cat, was caught in a weed wacker."

"Some people charm one way, others another." Maury had to look away to keep himself from laughing out loud.

The vastness and sprawling nature of the correctional complex seemed to overwhelm Maury, as it often did some first time visitors. He stared up at the towering buildings at the center as well as around at the parking lots and outer buildings covered thirty-five acres.

"Your tax dollars at work," Al muttered. He parked his truck in the visitor's lot and led the way inside. It might look like any other industrial complex, but for the razor wire coiled above the high, chain-link fence.

The harsh clang of a thick steel door on a steel frame, followed by the smell of Lysol trying to mask the odors of stale sweat and fear always made Al very glad to be a free man.

He knew the deputy behind the wire-mesh glass at the reception desk, Hancock Beatty, who went by Hank. Al had trained him once in a group learning hand-to-hand combat. Hank had wanted to be a detective like Al, but hadn't got the best grades on any of the exams. He'd been at the jail going on nine years and seemed to have settled in.

"What's on your mind, Al?" Hank's stare fixed on Maury, who he figured for a non-cop right away.

"Bernie Meiyers."

"I wish I could help you. But he got out on bail this morning."

"Bail? For bigamy?"

"It's possible. For anyone in minimum to medium custody. Funny story too." He said it without a hint of humor.

"How so?"

"One of the guards bailed him out. Rhonda Thelmsley. Been here twice as long as me. Ugly as fifty feet of dust bowl cattle fence."

"You think some sweet talking went on?"

"I think he must've tilted her head back and poured the molasses and maple syrup in."

"Do you have her address?"

"You know you have to have permission for that."

"Will Clayton's word do?" Al pulled out his cell phone.

Hank's mouth opened, then closed again. "No need to play a trump card like the sheriff on me, Al. Hell, she's in the phone book." Hank's face had blanched white there for a second, then flushed pink. He relaxed enough to share an uncertain smile.

Al had been picturing getting his former boss on the phone and having to slide it through the drawer for Hank to listen. He must have expected some smug satisfaction. Instead he felt a wave of sticky warm regret for having made a guy like Hank squirm.

"Okay. Thanks. How's your little Clara? Still in remission?"

"Yep. Yes she is. Glad to be able to say that. I'll tell her you asked after her."

Outside, on the way back to the truck, Maury asked, "How'd you know about his little girl? And will she know who you are?"

"I doubt the little tyke knows me from her Aunt Mabel's house cat. But Hank knows I was the one who started the department's collection to help with all those med bills. You should have seen the pictures of her bald when she was going through chemo."

"They must think you're a saint."

"No one thinks that. But I have my days when by sheer chance I don't piss anyone off."

Al slowed and took in Rhonda Thelmsley's house before he pulled his truck in behind the white Jeep Cherokee that could use a good washing. Handprints and smears showed in the patina of sooty grime that covered the vehicle. The house, a double-wide trailer mounted on a raised concrete slab, stood apart from its nearest neighbors by a good five or six acres of scrubby woods.

Still a dozen feet away from the front door, Al could see that the screen door was partially open, held that way by a bunched throw rug that must have once served as a welcome mat. Someone leaving in a real hurry might do that.

"Wait here." Al went back to his truck, took the Glock out of the glove box and slid it inside his pants and belt at the small of his back.

Back at the house he started up the stairs. "Don't touch anything."

Maury yanked his hand back from the black wrought iron guard rail that ran up along beside the steps.

At the door, Al knocked, then waited. He knocked again. He tilted his head, listened. Nothing. He tugged the tail of his shirt loose in front and stood close to the door so he could use it to turn the knob without smearing any existing prints too much. The unlocked door swung open. He held up a hand and eased inside, looked around to assure himself all was clear.

Before he could say anything, Maury bumped into him. He was pointing down to the floor beside the bamboo coffee table.

"I see it." Al eased closer. He leaned down, felt for a pulse, wasn't surprised when he didn't get one.

Though the body was twisted where it had fallen, Al could make out the face of Bernie Meiyers.

Maury eased away. "Al," he said. "Al," more urgently the second time. He stood where he could look into the kitchen.

"Let me guess. Rhonda Thelmsley?"

"I suppose." Maury was looking down toward the floor.

Al pushed around him, went just far enough in to confirm she had no more life in her than Bernie. He backed up and swept Maury along with one arm. "Let's get outside and stay there. We have a call to make."

———◇———

The M.E., Clive Barnes, came out the door and down the stairs, his usual much younger sidekick Teddy right behind him. She was looking around at Al's feet. "Tanner?" she asked. With her touch of autism no one could fault her for being overly chatty, but she had taken a shine to the rescue center mutt Al had brought along to a previous case and always asked about the dog. Tanner's wagging tail and raw unassuming affection had put quite a sparkle in Teddy's eyes that time.

Al shook his head. "Sorry. He stayed home."

"It's starting to look like you should have too," Clive muttered. He looked up at Al. "Those two inside are ready to go to the lab. I'll let the acting detective know what I find when I've done the autopsies."

Al stepped closer. "I'll send you a DNA sample by courier."

"Whose it supposed to match?"

"Just run it with these, if you don't mind."

"I guess I owe you one, Al. At least one."

From the top of the steps a new voice boomed down at them. "Are you still here?"

Clive nodded up at the man. "Do you know Detective Roland Washburn Fallon, Al? He'll be handling the case."

Al hadn't met the man, but he'd heard of him. He'd been recruited to the department from somewhere up around Detroit. A real hotshot, Al had heard. He had been to Quantico too, just like Al had once quite a while ago.

"So, you're the famous Al Quinn." Fallon came down the stairs and stood in front of Al. He didn't hold out a hand. Half a head taller than Al's five-eleven and with a long square jaw like the bottom of a lantern. "Best record in the sheriff's department for closing cases, I hear. But what I want to know just now is what caused you to turn up at a crimes scene where we have two murders?"

"Which I reported."

"Indeed you did. What brought you here?"

Al hesitated. What the hell? He was no P.I. on a money-paying case. "We were looking into this Bernie Meiyers. Thought he might be related somehow. Followed him from Del Valle to here. That's about it."

"You telling me you're the next of kin or something?"

"I'm not telling you anything remotely like that."

"I suppose you want to be in on this, help solve it or something."

"That's also not my intention. But I'll tell you something, and it won't cost you anything."

"What's that?"

"If I were you I'd check Rhonda Thelmsley's phone records. Bernie gets sprung from jail this morning. It came as a surprise. Nobody could have known, unless they were waiting outside and followed him, which isn't very damn likely. So he must've called someone and let them know where he was. That's what led to this." Al waved a vague hand toward the doublewide.

Fallon stared down at Al, who couldn't tell if he was mulling over what to say or if he was struck speechless. At last Fallon spun on a heel and started back up the steps toward the house. "I guess Clayton will know where we can find you if we need to talk more." He spoke without looking back. "Just stay out of my way. You hear?"

He went inside and the screen banged shut behind him, so someone must have moved the jammed welcome mat out of the way.

On the way back to the truck, Maury spoke low. "Man, you sure go about spreading that charm of yours every which way."

"I do what I can," Al said.

"Do you believe in karma?" Maury asked.

"Why?" Al pulled up to the curb behind a red Miata convertible in front of what looked like a three-bedroom red brick house whose prominent feature was a two-car garage door facing the street. It looked like the clone of the house to its left with yellow siding and the one to its right with brown shingles. Some housing developer had saved a bundle by using just one floor plan in this suburban neighborhood on the north side of Austin. Only the exteriors differed.

"You kind of accidentally step on one person and, boom, someone else is there poised to step on you."

"No one's getting stepped on. Life is clumsy. I'm just participating. And it's on your behalf, I might remind you." Al got out of the truck. A six-foot high cedar fence surrounded the back yard. The gate to the left of the closed garage doors was open. He could hear a lawn mower going in the back yard.

He headed to the open gate and looked inside. Whoever was behind the mower was out of sight to the right around the house. To his left a tool shed's door stood open, a ramp leading up into it. The mower was probably usually stored there. The shed was a good-sized one, with workbench along one wall with tools neatly hung on a peg-board. A vise, a miter saw, and a tool box with one drawer pulled open said someone spent a good deal of time here. He even saw a gun safe against the far back wall. On the other wall, a weed wacker leaned against the corner next to where the mower usually rested. Seemed like only yesterday Al had been mentioning a weed wacker. Different context, of course.

The person mowing the lawn, a young man who looked to be in his mid-twenties, came into sight, pushing a mower. He glanced left, saw Al and Maury, and let go of the handle. The motor sputtered to a stop. His frown turned into a glare. "What do you want?"

"We'd like a word or two with your mother, Allison Whitefield." Al might normally have flashed his expired badge, but he didn't want to go loggerheads with Fallon about it later. The kid's attitude supplied enough context for their official seeming visit. His face flushed an angry pink.

"No," he shouted. "Leave her alone. She's just had some bad news and needs to be by herself."

"We need to talk to her."

"No!" He stood with fists down at his sides, his forehead grew a brighter red, and spittle went flying with the word.

"Ben. Ben." The voice came from behind the closed back screen door, soft at first, then louder. "Benjamin Lee Kantor!" Different last name, which told a story.

"All right. All right, then. Have it your way." Still spraying, nearly sputtering. He left the mower where it sat, yard half finished. He stomped past Al and Maury, slammed the gate closed behind him, and in a moment they heard his car start and pull away from where it had been parked by the curb.

The screen door opened and a woman with a pale face

and long dark hair stepped out into the light. She might be in her mid to late forties but, if so, she looked much younger and fitter than that. "I'm sorry about Ben. It's been a hectic time for me and he tries to bear some of my frustration for me. Can I get you officers a lemonade or anything?"

Al didn't say anything about them not being active cops on a routine investigation. He let her assumption have its run. He nodded toward a picnic table on a flagstone patio by the back door. "All right if we sit down and talk?"

"How about water then? I can get us each a glass of that."

Al nodded. She hurried back into the house. He had learned years back to accept an offer of water or coffee because it gives the person offering something to do and made him a better acquaintance than politely saying no.

While she was away, he opened the umbrella above the table so its surface was covered in shade by the time she came back out with three glasses, two that matched and one that didn't. She handed one each to Al and Maury and they sat down.

"Did you get a call from Bernie today?" Al asked.

"Why, yes. How did you know?" She took a sip and put her glass down, tilting her head a quarter inch to the right.

"He told you he was out on bail?"

She nodded. "And where he was. He said that he would make everything right. I can't tell you, it's been a strain to pay the bills and do all that needs to be done around the house. Bernie was pretty handy that way."

Al sorted out that the bigamy charge was the bad news her son Ben had been talking about, not the murder. She still spoke of Bernie in the present tense.

"You don't seem too upset about the charges brought against him."

Her lips tightened for a moment. "Oh, I was, at first. Furious. And broken-hearted at the same time. He'd said over and over again, 'I just want to take care of you.' And he'd lived up to that, until now."

"But you pressed charges against him?"

"Well, actually Mary Jo led the charge on that, and, of course, Letitia, the first wife."

"You wouldn't have pressed charges on your own?"

She hesitated. "Well, I might have ...Oh, I don't know. I felt crushed, of course, to find he was already married, that I was his second wife. I worried about Ben most of all. What effect would this have on him? He's a sensitive young man and needs ... needed a father."

Bernie had apparently done well enough to support three families, and still had the time to have his own workshop here, live with them enough for the similitude of a regular family life. The sudden loss of support was what really made Allison a victim.

"What did Bernie do for a living?" He glanced to Maury who took a sip of water and sought to appear earnest and intense, the way a cop might look. Al had all he could do to keep from laughing.

"He was a subcontractor. A darned good one, he told me. He put together crews. Some could swoop in on development projects and slap up sheet rock. Others could do landscaping. But a lot of his work was fences and roofs. He told me he'd hate to say how many cedar fences he'd put up in his day. Well, he hadn't always done them personally, but his crews had. He was the big orchestra leader."

Al wondered for a second if Bernie's knack for making

false IDs came into play at all in his ability to quickly round up work crews. He suspected it did.

She had soft brown eyes that had warmed as she spoke. "When we had that big hailstorm a few years back he was gone most of the time for weeks putting that right with people who needed a new roof. As soon as the insurance adjustor left he'd be there and he could do a roof a day with as many as three crews going at a time on houses, with him flitting from crew to crew making sure they did it just right. You see, he said a lot of unscrupulous people take advantage of people when there's been a disaster, like tornados, hurricanes, or heavy hail. They use substandard materials and charge more than needed. He gave a fair price and used only the best thirty-year shingles. He ...he is a good man."

"Do you work as well?"

"I ...I used to. I have fibromyalgia. Bernie said I needn't work anymore. That he could carry us. That ..." She choked on what she was going to say and grabbed for her water, took a gulp. When she put her glass back down on the table she looked directly into Al's eyes. "I'd take him back, you know. Even after ... all this. I don't know what we're gonna do."

"But you didn't try to bail him out?"

"No. I don't have that kind of money. What he made was his. He hinted he had savings, but I don't even know where or how much. I was okay with that, but it leaves me in a spot now, with nothing set aside and all. I was glad he was free from jail, however he managed it. I'm looking forward to seeing him again, to being together again. He said on the phone we could. That's going to be so nice, to be a family again."

As he and Maury were climbing back into Al's truck a

few minutes later, Maury said, "You didn't tell her Bernie is dead. Why?"

"Would you?"

"No, but ..."

"It's not our place to do that. Fallon will probably be the one. We need to scramble to get to the next wife before he does."

"Why are we doing this? Why not just let him do it?"

Al started the truck, turned the AC on high. "Because you started me on this as a case, for you. It's what I do, or did. And once I'm started I don't stop very well, or quickly."

"I see." He didn't sound like he did, though.

"You still want your question answered, don't you, about whether you had a son?"

"Yes."

"Well, this is how I go about it."

———❖———

On the drive to see the next wife, all the way into neighboring Hays County, Al thought about how he might feel if he was still an active detective for the sheriff's department and some old retired duffer off the force was going around asking questions. He hadn't learned a whole lot so far, and hadn't done any real harm, but Fallon might not see it that way. When Al had been with the department he hadn't cared for private investigators thrashing around trying to make a living by often getting in the way. That was kind of what he was up to here. Ah, well.

He pulled up at row of condos far enough on the outskirts of Buda to be nearly as close to San Marcos, a town famous in his mind for Texas State University, what had once been the Aquarena Center with its glass-bottomed boats and a diving pig that swam as part of the entertainment, and one whopping big outlet mall. That showed his age since the water attraction was now called the Meadows Center. For him it would forever be the home of Ralph the swimming pig and those underwater mermaid shows, though the city had opted for a less gimmicky way to draw tourists. Al was all for nature, but he sometimes thought people will take the kitschy fun out of anything if you let them. Maybe that kind of family entertainment slipping into the past was for the best. Some days he felt more like a dinosaur than on other days.

Al pressed the doorbell, and then knocked when he got no answer. He was about to turn away when he saw a woman get out of a bronze-looking Toyota and start up the walk toward where he and Maury stood.

"Can I help you gentlemen?" She looked tall at first until she was up to Al. He realized her posture, erect and dignified, gave that illusion. Her blond hair was cut reasonably short and she wore a red suit jacket and skirt, matching shoes, with a white blouse. Al gave her points for wearing flats instead of heels. That and the outfit suggested she was just getting home from a job somewhere.

"We're here to ask you a question or two, if you don't mind."

She tilted her head. Al could hear it too. The phone was ringing inside.

"Just a minute." She stepped around Al and put a key in the lock, opened the door and rushed inside, gave them a wave to follow.

She rushed across to grab the phone hanging on the wall near the kitchen.

Al glanced out the living room window at an inner courtyard with a bird bath and a couple of white wrought iron chairs nestled close to a matching table. Someone had spent some time keeping the flowers nice.

"Oh my god." She put the phone down and turned to them. "Bernie's dead. Is that what you came to talk about?"

Al nodded. He didn't feel his nose grow or anything.

"Do you mind?" She opened the fridge, grabbed out a green bottle of Heineken beer, and used an opener to take off the cap. No mention of getting them anything. She took a deep gulp, lowered the bottle, and looked around the kitchen, dazed for a moment.

"I'm sorry," she turned back to Al and Maury, waved them toward the living room where a taupe sofa and love seat faced a blank large-screen TV on the wall.

As he went past the mantle of a fireplace that looked like it had never been used, Al took in the eight-by-ten photo in frame of her, a boy in a high school graduation cap and gown, and Bernie. It nestled between a giant pine cone on one side and a pink-throated conch shell on the other.

"You're Mary Jo Predmoore. Right? And the boy?"

"My son Kent."

"Also Predmoore."

"Yes." She'd brought the beer along and took another deep drink from the bottle before putting it down on a glass coffee table. Still no offer of a refreshment or libation for them, which was okay with Al. Years ago when he'd first become a detective he and his colleagues had played a game they called "What kind of smoke are you?" They figured they could tell a lot about a person from whether the person smoked cigars, a pipe, or cigarettes. Even the brand of cigarette mattered, and whether they were filtered or not. These days fewer people smoke. The game could go on, though, with choice of beverage as the new indicator. But he didn't feel much like games at the moment.

"What happened?" she said. "Can you tell me?"

"That's still under investigation," Al said.

"Well, it couldn't happen to a nicer man."

Maury glanced toward Al, but kept his mouth shut.

"How do you mean that?" Al asked. He'd gotten nothing from her tone, neither sincerity nor sarcasm.

"I mean I was hoping he'd rot in jail."

"No plans to bail him out?"

"Not a one."

"Did he call you when he did get out?"

"Yes, with some cockamamie story about getting back together. Fat chance."

"How did you come to marry him?"

"If you want the gritty on that I was seeing him at the time, on the side. I was married to Calvin then, a rather stuffy gentlemen on his way toward becoming a premature Lutheran elder. I didn't think he'd take well to me being pregnant, with Bernie's baby, especially since he'd gone to the bother to get a vasectomy and all. Like that's a big painful deal." She reached for her beer, finished it, and glanced toward the fridge. Still no offer to share. She probably had only one more beer in there and had marked it as her own.

"Does your son still live at home?"

"No. He's in college. Penn. A quite good school. His grades and Bernie's help at least got him that. I only hear from him when he needs money and see him on holidays."

"He helped Kent, yet you pressed the charges against Bernie, didn't you?"

"You're damned straight. Look, I work at the university. I have the respect of my peers. Bernie wasn't around as much as he should be, but I took him out to events, showed him off as arm candy when I could, such as he was. Now I have to face the looks of those people. And, oh they can give them. You have no idea how snarky the academic world can be. Kissinger once said that 'academic politics

176

are so vicious precisely because the stakes are so small.' He knew of what he spoke."

"And Bernie?"

"I'm glad he's dead." She said that with as much finality as she could.

———◆———

They had just crossed the county line back into Travis County when Al got the call he'd been expecting on his cell phone. He gave Maury a raised eyebrow as he dug it out of his pocket. When he hung up, he glanced to Maury. "That was Sheriff Clayton. For one reason or another he wants to see me. You too."

"Are we in trouble?"

"Of course we are."

"Well?"

"Let's wait and see how this plays out."

Al knew where to park. He led the way and Maury followed until a female deputy took over and led them to a conference room across the hall from Clayton's office.

They sat down at the mahogany racetrack-shaped conference table. Nice chairs. Al had spent some happier times here, and a few not so happy. Today was still a toss-up.

Clayton came in first, talking back over his shoulder to Fallon. Fallon seemed to be trying to make a case about something. His mouth clicked shut once he was in the room. He sat down across the table from Al.

The sheriff stood for a moment. He finally said, "Well, hell, Al."

Al looked up. What?"

"I'd like to say ..." Fallon started.

"You'll say nothing. Got it."

"Objection."

"Overruled. This isn't a courtroom where that sort of thing gets sustained." He took a deep breath. "Normally, I would have let this whole thing play out. This could be a teaching moment for you, Fallon. For Al, well Al is beyond teaching at this point."

"Are you saying ...?" Fallon half rose.

"I said quiet." Clayton's words had snap to them.

Fallon sat back down in his chair.

"We have a situation, and one I wish to contain. Pronto. So listen, all of you." Clayton paced slowly as he spoke. "We're going to break with protocol this once. Al likes to play his cards close to his vest. Well, he isn't going to get to this time. And normally I like my new detectives, like you Fallon, to run with a case until they have it solved. We don't have that luxury either. Turns out, Bernie Meiyers shouldn't have been let out on bail, especially by a jail employee, Rhonda Thelmsley. That's a couple of mistakes, ones that might've been rectified. But with both of them murdered we are in the deep end of the swamp here. I need to fix this, at once! You hear?" He glanced to Fallon, then Al.

"For your benefit, Al. The cause of death, according to Clive, is two shots each from a twenty-two caliber automatic." He gave his summation in a quick staccato, unlike his usual drawl. "Someone bothered to pick up the shell casings. That the person was let into the house by Bernie hints that in all probability it might be someone he knows. That's what we have on this end so far. Have you anything at all yet, Al?"

"Well, I haven't had a chance to talk yet with Letitia Joan Meiyers, the widow and first of the wives."

"That's okay," Clayton said. "Fallon has. He turned to the detective. "Give us what you can."

"Really, I barely ..."

"Don't make me give my spiel about the time issue again. Spill."

Al knew Clayton rarely pressured his deputies this way, especially the detectives, and it gave him his first measure of respect for Fallon that the man shook off anything personal about it and went into a flat delivery.

"It's not much. The couple has no children. He wanted them. They tried a lot of things. He didn't want to adopt, though. They fought about that, and the usual things, like money. But she says she loved him, even though she went along with Mary Jo Predmoore in pressing the bigamy charges. She felt he needed a lesson. Once out, he called to say he was coming back to her, although I gather he said that to the others as well. Still, she said she was looking forward to it, that she still loved him, and I believe her. Aside from having an alibi, being among several people at a book reading circle, I don't think she killed him. She was incapable. But that's just an opinion at this point, one I share reluctantly." He swallowed as he stared up at Clayton.

"That's okay. I'm going to give Al the same sort of hot foot." He gave Al only a brief glance before fixing on Fallon. "You see, not only is he the highest percentage closer of cases, he has also been the quickest on several occasions, when pressured, and I do intend to apply pressure. Al?"

"It's way too early."

"Let's just put that aside. What would you do if you wanted to do one thing to bring this to the speediest possible conclusion?"

Al frowned. He looked around at each of them, including Maury. When he got back to Clayton the sheriff nodded toward Fallon. Al told Fallon, "I'd arrest Allison Whitefield for the murder."

"You think she did it? On what do you base that? Give!"

Fallon came closer to shouting before he caught a look from Clayton.

"I didn't say she did it. I said that's the step I'd take given the sheriff's time concerns."

"Give him a bit more than that, Al," Clayton said.

"Arresting her will give you a chance to get a search warrant, go over the place. I'd especially look at the gun safe in the outside workshop. Having it out there hints she wasn't a big fan of guns herself."

"Yet you still think she shot Bernie?"

"Again, I didn't say that. She's just a domino here, Fallon."

Fallon looked to Clayton, "Well, he was right about Bernie calling the three of them. I'd have been a slow crawl wriggling my way to that."

Clayton said, "Make it happen."

Fallon stood up.

"While you're tending to that, I'll have Al and his brother here write out statements about every detail of their visits to the other wives that will go into your files, Fallon, on the case you'll get credit for solving."

"I wouldn't have it any other way," Al said.

Fallon gave him a puzzled look, but for the very first time Al thought this hard-assed guy might turn out to be a friend after all.

Four hours later Al and Maury still sat in the conference room. Glad not to be in a holding cell or interrogation room. He had to count his little blessings where they fall.

"You want to hear something funny?" Al said, only because they'd exhausted every other subject.

"What?"

"Not too long ago I came across a bit of research done

at Harvard over a seventy-five year period about what makes a man happy. The conclusion was that a person was happier and more financially successful if he was in good relationships."

"How's that work for you? You were only in the one relationship when you were married to Abbie."

"You were at least in part responsible for that marriage ending. We agreed not to talk about that."

"Okay. But what about now?"

"I have relationships, and they work well for me, however unique or peculiar they are. I'm fine with what I have with Fergie. For that matter, I have relationships with you, and with Bonnie, and even with little Tanner."

"What's your point?"

"Think on it, Maury. You're the one who started all this."

A deputy stuck his head in the door, motioned for them to follow. Al didn't know this young man. The department was changing, and the old ways and folks he knew well would soon be as distant a memory as that swimming pig in San Marcos.

They were ushered into a small room where they could look through the one-way glass. Al watched Maury, who probably expected to see Allison Whitefield across the table from Clayton and Fallon. Instead, it was her son, Benjamin Kantor. For a brief instant Al wondered if he had finished mowing the yard.

Fallon was holding up a plastic evidence bag containing what looked like a Colt Woodsman automatic pistol.

They were just in time to hear Ben shout, "How could he do this to her, to us!"

"Oh, my gosh," Maury said. "Even though he was conceived while his mother was married to someone else, that was his father, his real father. Arc you saying he killed his father?"

"Looks that way," Al said.

181

———◆———

Al gave the dog a rub on the back that went against the grain, but Tanner didn't seem to mind, just looked up at him in that way dogs can. It felt great to be at home, with no new cases in the near or distant future. He might just go fishing in the morning.

Bonnie came out of the kitchen, drying a frying pan with a towel. "Thanks for helping Maury out. I know it just about got part of you stuck in the wringer with your old boss."

Al shrugged.

"You sure got results faster than I thought you would."

"Write that off to Clayton having an agenda. When he's like that, everyone just steps along more lively. I don't personally like to leap along at that pace. But I had to this time."

"Do you think being along for the ride helped Maury any?"

"He's edging his way toward personal development. It's not fun, or easy, but he's gonna get there if it kills him. Or I do."

"And what about that notion of his, that he has some kid out there floating around like a satellite?"

"I already told him. I guess I can tell you. Bernie wasn't Maury's son. I called in a favor from my friend Clive Barnes, the M.E. He ran the DNA tests. Maury's not remotely a match. The two sons, they were both Bernie's. But Maury has nothing to do with Bernie."

"So he has no children at all, that you know of?"

"No. Sorry. Why?"

She grinned and rubbed hard at the pan. "Because I'm pregnant."

THE MOLE PEOPLE

TANNER PICKED HIS WAY THROUGH the leaf litter on the floor of the woods, pausing to sniff and gather what news he could of critter movements in the previous night. He was an old enough dog Al had to use only one finger on the leash. He rarely surged in exuberance to pull against it, except one or two times at a crime scene, and this wasn't one. Al was feeling very retired at the moment and far from his active days as a detective. Owning a dog was one concession to that status. He'd never had one in all his active years, though he'd always been a secret dog person, lavishing attention on the dogs of others, and pining inside when passing the pet rescue cages outside of pet shops along strip malls.

Fall was just starting to assert itself on the woods, which in Texas wasn't marked by the robust reds, yellows and fading greens of other states. The Sycamore leaves turned reddish and the Chinaberry tree leaves yellowish, but both quickly drop their leaves to become brown and crunchy underfoot. The Chinaberry trees kept their clusters of round yellow seed pods while the Sycamores showed their patchy white trunks and kept their bigger round brown seed balls.

"Looks like testicles hanging from those limbs." A leaf-crumpling stumble behind him marked where Maury had tripped over an exposed root that crossed their path, an

183

obstacle Al and Tanner had stepped over. Maury had been looking up at the sycamore limbs instead of down.

A scampering scuttle across the dry leaves beside them marked the hurried flight of a lizard.

Al liked the crunch of dried leaves beneath his boots, the scurrying noises, and the occasional sighting of one of the deer he sometimes fed, staying in the distance for the moment since he had Tanner and Maury along. The air was cooler, with a hint of being brisk.

He was nearly to the end of his property. Ahead he could make out the ramshackle hut of the neighbor's cabin, a tiny thing. Odd arrangement. Sometimes he saw half a dozen vehicles parked near it, but no people.

"Humpf." Maury nearly tripped again as he came to a stop beside Al. "Bonnie calls these neighbors 'the mole people.' That's to distinguish them from 'the round people' on the other side of your place."

"Bonnie's already pretty round herself. And she's going to be more so once she starts to show she's pregnant."

"She just means they're jolly people, always out in front of their house barbequing or sitting around in lawn chairs. They always wave. Real friendly folks. And, yes, eating seems to be a common group activity. You could drill three holes in any one of them and you'd have a bowling ball. But these people on this side, not so much. We've never even seen any of them."

Al had only caught brief glimpses of these neighbors from time to time and wasn't certain he was always seeing the same people. He started forward again.

Tanner saw something and made a low "whoof" as he backed from a pile of loose rocks. Al was busy ducking around a spider's web so big it crossed the path. He didn't want to break it and have web hanging to him, and possibly a spider as well.

He was about to tell Maury about the spider web when he looked up and caught a brief glimpse of a man getting out of a white pickup, closing the door, and heading for the cabin with shoulders down and face turned away. Anyone else in Texas would have stopped, turned, and waved at him. Not this guy.

"Will you look at those cars?" Maury came up beside Al, brushing spider web off his shirt. "There's a Lexus, a Jag, and if I'm not horribly mistaken, that's the bottom half of a Bentley sticking out from under that blue tarp. Yet there isn't even an established lane to it. No drive at all. They drive those in and out from there on two muddy ruts.

"Take a closer look, Maury. It's a cabin, at best, and it's not near the water, although the property goes all the way to the lake. When I'm in the boat I can't see the place."

"You can't see it from the road either," Maury said.

"Do the math, Maury. Anything odd here?"

"Not if you count five vehicles and only enough cabin for a pretty crowded two people. Maybe it's like a clown car and people pour out of there."

Al shook his head. No one came out of or went into the rustic place for a while. "We'd better get back to the house or Fergie and Bonnie will be having a yard sale of our stuff."

"I don't have a lot of stuff," Maury said. He waited on Al to start back and followed. "Maybe you noticed."

"Is that why you haven't popped the question?"

"What question?"

"Ask Bonnie to marry you."

"Al, don't even say such things."

"You'd best be thinking about it, because you know they are."

"I've never been married before."

"Why not?"

"I guess I didn't want to lose my amateur status."

Maury was in his sixties, Bonnie not quite up to her forties. It was hard for Al to tell which of them had been most surprised by the pregnancy news.

"Be honest. You were a horn dog and were always on the prowl and didn't want anything to slow you." Al didn't touch on what had happened between Maury and Al's wife, always a tender scab between them.

"If I marry Bonnie ..."

"Just because you knocked her up."

"If I did ... it would mark the end of my single days."

"Of course it would, and about time. Well, are you going to ask her?" Al caught a glimpse through the trees of his house ahead. Tanner moved out to the end of his leash and began to pull eagerly.

"We'll see. No sense in rushing these things."

"The way I see it, you have about a nine month window, or less, to decide."

"We'll see. We'll just see."

Once inside his house Al unhooked Tanner's leash and the dog shot off to get his head rubbed by Fergie and Bonnie.

Fergie sat on a chair at the dining table while Bonnie stood behind her to run a brush through Fergie's long straight red hair.

"Did she already do your hair?" Maury asked Bonnie.

"Yes."

"Rats."

"Just as well. I don't know why you find that so exotic and get so wound up from up. It's just as well you missed that."

"I think he's still wound up from a childhood of"

watching a little too much *Wonder Woman* and *Baywatch* on television." Al wasn't sure if the dates were right for that but did recall that the suspiciously long showers began at some adolescent phase in Maury's development.

Fergie held up a hand. "That's all for now, Bonnie. Thanks. I need to talk to Al."

"Uh oh. Al's in trouble." Maury could be like a kid at times.

Fergie went out the front door. Al followed, but had to scoot Tanner back inside when the dog wanted to come along too.

"You up for a short walk in the woods?" Fergie asked.

"Well, oh my. What do you have in mind?"

"Not that." She shook her head and walked up the lane toward the road.

At the road she looked both ways, waited until a pickup went by, then crossed over. "This is where the walk in the woods comes in."

Al followed as she pushed in between a sumac bush and a stand of mountain cedar. The other side of the road was sparsely wooded at first, but grew thicker the farther in and the further right they went.

They skirted the boles of two big pecan trees, a waist high stretch of prickly pear cactus, and eased up to a stand of mountain cedar. Fergie turned and held a finger to her lips.

She stepped to one side and waved for Al to come closer. He looked to the floor of the woods first and swept to one side a dry stick and some leaf litter that might have made noise with his steps. Once all the way up he eased a limb to one side.

Hard to miss the black SUV with tinted windows that sat nestled in the shadow of a limestone ridge that climbed up the side of the hill to their left. Al eased the limb back into place and turned to Fergie. She shook her head.

Without a word, they started back toward Al's house.

As soon as they were far enough away they couldn't be heard, Al stopped and turned to Fergie.

"I was driving along, saw the vehicle ease off the road and into the woods. I was still far enough away maybe they didn't think I saw them. I went by and saw tire tracks going into the woods. For chuckles I went up a ways and came back this way. By the time I got there the tire tracks were gone. Someone had done a pretty darn good job of covering them up with grass and bushes.

"We'll see about this." Al took out his cell phone and tapped in a familiar number.

At the third ring, someone picked up. "Sheriff Clayton's office."

"Betty Lou, it's Al Quinn here. Can I speak to the big guy?"

"Nope."

"What? Did I just hear you right?"

"Yep."

"Is he there?"

"Doesn't matter. Either way he's busy and can't talk to you right now."

This could have gone on for another few minutes. Al punched the "off" button. He felt warm heat running through him, up his legs and out to the ends of his fingers, which started to curl into fists before he stopped himself.

"What is it?" Fergie's wrinkled brow said she was reading his heat index right now and was ready to step back out of the way.

"Hmm. We get a black SUV with government plates parked within walking distance of my place and suddenly I'm *persona non grata* with Clayton. I've done him any number of favors, and now this. I don't like it. I don't like it at all.

⸺◆⸺

Al parked in the visitors' section of the lot at the sheriff department headquarters. He knew where Clayton parked and about what time he got done for the day.

Before he got out of his truck he took a few deep breaths. On the way here he had caught himself going faster than he should a couple of times, his agitation making his foot press down on the gas. He was going to have a hard time being patient, but something told him not to storm into the buildings the way he felt right now.

While he waited, his cell phone rang. He checked the caller I.D.: Fergie. He answered it. "What?"

"Mmm. Kind of snappy, are we?"

"What do you want?"

"Just to let you know that Maury and Bonnie were nosy and sneaked over for a peek at the black SUV. They said two guys got out for a short bathroom break and they were both wearing dark suits. In Texas!"

"Tell them to stay away from that van!"

"You tell them. He's your brother."

"I can't control him, and I certainly can't control Bonnie."

"That must drive you crazy."

He hung up without responding. He went back to fuming, and waiting.

An hour and twenty-five minutes later than he usually emerged, Clayton came lumbering out of the department offices, headed for his vehicle. Al leaned against the side of it.

The day had been a warm one for a walk in the woods, and now, after six p.m., it was getting nasty hot. A trickle of sweat ran down the middle of Al's back and Al's feet felt like they were going numb. He stood up straight.

When Clayton saw him, he slowed his steps. "Al, you know better than to bother me when you know I don't want to be bothered."

"That tells me you know something about a black SUV parked within a walk of my front door that bears government license plates and its occupants wear dark suits. I suppose the black helicopters are next."

"That information is on a 'need to know' basis."

"I need to know."

"You just think you do, being nosy. Go home and take a nap. You're retired. Remember?" Clayton tried for a smile, but didn't stick its landing.

"You ask me for favors all the time. I'm asking for a return favor."

"And I won't give it. Can't give it!"

Now they were shouting at each other.

"Why?" Al tried to keep his voice down, and failed. A deputy on the far side of the parking lot turned his head their way.

"I'm not *allowed* to tell you!" Clayton yelled, with the tone and roar of a wounded bear. "Can't you get it through your bony head that this has me every bit as pissed off as you!"

"What do you think?" Maury asked. They sat around the dining table, each with a mug of coffee.

"I'm guessing, but I'd say Secret Service," Al said. "And no, they don't just guard the president."

"Counterfeiting?" Fergie said. "Whatever are they doing way out here, then?"

"It makes no sense." Bonnie reached for the coffee

thermos to top off their mugs. "I've heard a couple of large trucks come and go in the night, wondered what that was about, but that's such a tiny little shack."

"With quite a few vehicles parked around it," Fergie said.

"And you can buy funny money, if you know the right someone." Al took a sip from his mug. "The usual price is forty-five cents on the dollar. The bill is almost always a hundred. I've heard that the Secret Service estimates one in every ten thousand is a fake. Banks can tell about most of them, but a lot of clerks in stores can't."

"What about that little pen they use to check the bills?" Bonnie asked.

"There's a way around that," Fergie said. The bills can be treated with a substance that fools those starch pens."

"But we don't really know anything," Maury said, "for sure."

"That's right. But Clayton saying nothing to me is the biggest indicator."

"Not to mention crimp on your tail bone," Fergie said.

"I just want to know you guys aren't threatened by anything going on. I can take care of myself. I'm less sure about you."

"Fergie's a former cop, and Bonnie's a crack shot with a pistol," Maury said.

"And what about you, Maury?" Al asked.

"I've got Tanner to fend off the enemy."

"Just know this isn't any kind of joke." Al felt the heat of anger rising up in a boil inside him again. He started to reach for his coffee, realized that wasn't helping, so he pushed the mug away.

"What are you going to do?" Bonnie's eyes opened wider, yet flickered with an eagerness Al wished she didn't have.

"Well, I'm not going to just sit around here knowing nothing," Al said. "I need to see what I can find out."

"Oh, dear." Fergie looked at Al over the rim of her cup, slowly lowering it back to the table.

"Is there a chance that Clayton might be using reverse psychology on you to make you charge over there in your bull-headed way?" Maury asked.

"Bull-headed?"

"Don't forget. I've seen you when a red cape is waving in your face."

"I'm not that way."

All three of the others snickered.

"Besides, Clayton was genuinely ticked off. But he's not alone. Him not being able to talk to me hints we might even be suspects as well. The Secret Service could have eyes on us!"

"Holy cow." Bonnie looked down at what she wore. "Should I dress a little more upscale while they're around?"

"I'll ask again." Fergie leaned back in her chair. She started across the table at Al. "What sane, rational thing do *you* intend to do?"

"Maury and I will take the next sniff around over that way."

"And what do we women folk do? Sit around and clean and load the weapons?" Bonnie asked.

Al sighed. "That wouldn't be an altogether bad idea."

Al Quinn's home perched on the shore of the lake, where he could look out at the calm surface or see the waves turn into ripples of orange as the sun set. But the day was early and the sun was on the other side of the canopy of trees meeting above them, so they walked in shadows.

"Why did you buy the empty lots on either side of you?" Maury whispered.

Al turned and held a finger to his lips. Maury came closer.

"I did it when I bought the house. The lots were available and the prices were a better then, though the growing property taxes on the extra lots are making that a rub. The idea was for a buffer on either side against the growing creep of civilization coming toward a lakeside retreat on this corner of Lake Travis. It seemed inevitable, even then that the growth of Austin would cause it to ooze out in his direction."

"And ooze it has," Maury agreed.

"Let's keep it quiet from here on."

"Did you bring a gun?"

"No," Al whispered. "Didn't seem a good idea. And we stay just on my property and look. Got it. And keep still."

Maury nodded, made a parody of zipping his lips.

As he moved forward, Al thought about the growing urban sprawl. He fretted at times about how long he could hold out against the reaching tentacles of a city that seemed intent on turning the whole county into parts of itself. Driving home from the city just the other day he had spotted half a dozen lots that had been chipped and prepped for building. The piles of chips were still there from where someone had cut down all the pesky mountain cedar and pulverized them in wood chippers. The live oaks still stood since they added value to the property.

When he was first a deputy in the department this whole area was back woodsy. Now it barely clung to that remote feel. He even had neighbors now, such as they were.

Maury stumbled on a tree root that bulged up from the ground. He fell forward, caught himself with both hands

193

flat on the ground, and eased himself back upright. He shrugged toward Al.

Maury wasn't the best first choice to bring out into the woods. Bonnie had grown up in the woods, plinking with firearms, and Fergie had years of experience and training as a police detective. Perhaps the twenty years they had spent not speaking was the reason. Here was a chance to do something together, a harmless reconnoiter of the edge of his property. *What could go wrong?*

As he thought that, Maury took a step into an open patch of leaf-litter covered ground. One minute he was standing upright, the next he was plunged to his armpits in the ground beneath him. "What the hell?"

He looked toward Al, his eyes big and growing bigger, with the helpless expression of a dog that had just fallen through the ice. Then he disappeared.

If he'd had time to absorb what had just happened, Al might have been amazed. One minute Maury was there. The next, *poof.* He was gone.

Al ran over, looked down into the hole in the earth that had swallowed his brother. He couldn't see a thing. He leaned close. "Maury? Are you okay? Maury?"

"Mmmpf. Mmmpf."

Wasn't a definitive cry for help, but Al took it for one. He looked around, wishing he had a rope, or a ladder, or about anything that could work.

"Mmmpf!" Hard to tell, but that sounded more urgent.

Al sat down on the edge of the hole that went into the dark and let himself slide in, feet first, the way Maury had gone in.

He fell for what felt like five or six feet, then hit something of mixed softness and hardness, slid off from that onto a hard-packed dirt floor.

The tiniest bit of light lit the area around him, along

with a beam of brighter light coming from the hole by which he and Maury had entered. Some of the light came from LEDs on what he knew to be the smallest Heidelberg Speedmaster offset printing machine. He caught just the label, but could look closer at that later.

The mumbling came from a drum of refuse paper, from which Maury's legs kicked in the air.

"Oh, good grief. How did you even manage that?" Al grabbed Maury by the waist and tugged. Maury popped out of the trash like the cork from a wine bottle, with bits of litter hanging from him and sticking out of his pockets.

Al looked either direction. So far he'd only heard the distant murmur of a voice or two. No one seemed to be running their way, carrying weapons or otherwise.

The dim light put everything past the bulky printer in shadows. What Al wanted most was a ladder, or rope, or an elevator to get up and out of here.

"When I fell I turned, trying to land cat-like on my feet." Maury dusted himself off. Loose litter of crumpled papers fell to the dirt floor.

Al held a finger to his lips, pointed in the direction from which he'd heard anything like an indication of people.

He wished he had a flashlight. As his eyes adjusted he could make out shapes, as well as form a conclusion about how Maury came to fall inside this place.

The room was probably bigger than some of the rest of what seemed interconnected tunnels. Beams of wood held up crossbeams, in the manner of mining caves, and someone had stretched plywood panels between those to hold the dirt in place. Maury had stepped onto a panel that wasn't supported as well as it should have been.

Maury bent close to Al's ear to whisper. "My gosh what an elaborate bit of digging has gone on here."

Al stayed focused on getting out. Against the dirt wall,

on the other side of the space from the printer, he could make out a large folding table. On it he could see in the dim light a paper cutter, a shredder, and a few paper trimming tools. He set the paper cutter and shredder aside and brushed the other stuff to the cave floor.

Maury's head was snapping left then right in bird-like movements until he figured out what Al was trying to do and came to help. They carried the table over to the hole where Maury had fallen through, Al glancing up and positioning it directly beneath the side of the hole nearest one of the cross beams.

Al upended the trash drum Maury had fallen into and positioned it in the center of the table. It reached almost to the hole.

They both gingerly climbed up onto the table, which wiggled beneath their movement. Al motioned for Maury to go first.

Al helped Maury go up the side of the drum and then pull himself up until he was on top of it. Al held the drum steady. Maury reached up and pulled himself upward onto the dirt above the cross beam. It held. He waved from the top of the hole.

This was going to be harder with no one to steady the drum. Al heard feet running his way for the first time. The approaching feet hit the dirt floor in hard pounding steps that beat as fast as Al's heart.

Like dogs that are too vicious to bark, whoever ran his way didn't say a word, though he did think he heard a slide work sending a bullet into a chamber. That motivated him.

He pulled himself to the top of the drum in a near frog-hop. Maury had a hand held out, but Al suspected Maury's limited strength. Instead of taking it he reached up, pulled, and dove out and up onto the forest floor, the way Maury had.

Al rolled and got to his feet, just as a shot sent a bullet their direction, missing them, but a spray of dirt sprinkled them with soil. For the first time the thought occurred to him that they were still on Al's property, even when they'd been underground.

They turned toward the house. Al saw two men in suits running through the trees, coming their way. Probably Hickey Freeman suits, unless that was just an old time FBI thing.

"Halt!" one of them yelled.

"Freeze," the other shouted.

"Should we wait on them?" Maury asked.

"You can, but I don't plan to." Al took off in a run. But Maury soon passed him, his arms waving about as he ran like an already nervous cricket on Ritalin. A waggling elbow nearly clipped Al as Maury buzzed past him.

Another shot came from back in the hole. Al glanced that way and saw the men in suits bent over the hole, giving it their full attention now.

Al pulled up to the house, panting, and a distant second to Maury. Fergie stood outside the house, though her right hand was tucked behind her, Al figured her for having her personal pistol in hand. She looked ready to use it.

Bits of the paper still stuck to Maury sprinkled down onto the ground. Al bent to retrieve a couple of the pieces. He uncrumpled one that hadn't been shredded and held it up to the light. "Fifties. They're making fifties. Why? And how did the Secret Service ever get onto that. No one checks fifties the way they do hundreds."

Al glanced around. "Where's Bonnie?"

"She got worried about you guys, got one of your guns and headed toward where you'd gone. Didn't you see her?"

"Maybe we were out of sight then," Al said.

Maury said nothing, just shook off the tired slump in his shoulders, turned, and started running again, right back toward where they had just been.

Al shoved the bills he held into his pocket and started to run after him, but realized he didn't have another hard run in him. He didn't know where Maury got his energy, unless it was concern about Bonnie.

"Well, isn't this the shits," Al said. "We lose one, who goes for the other, now the other's going back where it's dangerous for the other. It's like a revolving door of O'Henry's *Gift of the Magi*, only with spurs."

He ran inside the house, opened the drawer of his bedside table, found it empty, so he went out to his truck, got the Glock out of the glove box, and hurried back to Fergie. "She has the Sig Sauer. You'd better stay here while I go back there and see if I don't end up in a gun fight with federal agents on my own land."

He took off running.

Ahead he heard shouting, then a "Whoompf" so loud it nearly sent him to the ground.

"Maury!" he yelled.

"Whoompf!" Another explosion, this one even louder, made the ground beneath his feet tremble.

"Maury!"

Al started to run again, then slowed. He'd heard something. A muffled cry to his right, and it was moving.

"Mmmpf."

He heard it again. He spun that way and took off as fast as he had ever ran. Outreaching limbs of a Yaupon tree grabbed at his shirt. Al jerked free, losing a piece of one sleeve. He hopped over a stand of prickly pear cactus just as he caught sight of Maury. Two men were with him, one holding Maury's wrists together, the other with a hand over Maury's mouth.

Al veered to head them off. They were going toward his boat house. He regretted at once leaving the keys in the boat's ignition.

The man holding Maury's mouth turned his head and saw Al coming toward them. He let go of Maury and spun to level a pistol at Al, who heard it go off in two crisp shots as he dived and rolled under the drooping limbs of a mountain cedar.

As soon as the men took off again Al scrambled out from under the limbs, brushing dried pine needles off himself as he ran after them.

The man with the gun snapped off a couple more shots back in Al's direction, but Al figured it was nearly impossible to hit anything while shooting from a dead run.

One shot did clip a limb off a mesquite tree not all that far from Al, though.

The man holding Maury got the boat lowering for the water, and clambered in while still gripping Maury. As soon as the other fellow got in, the first one passed Maury off to him.

The boat motor started.

"Stay right there!" Al was almost to them. He held his gun out and pointed at them.

The man who held Maury now put the gun to Maury's head. "Stop! Stay Back!"

Maury's wide-open eyes screamed for help, even though he managed to keep his mouth clamped shut.

"Over here, you pinhead. Your real problem is here!" Bonnie stood on the other side of the boat house, slightly above them, with her gun pointed toward the men.

The man holding Maury spun.

"Bam." She fired.

Maury and the man who'd held him both dropped to the boat's deck.

The man holding the boat's steering wheel pulled out a gun and raised it toward Bonnie.

"Bam. Bam." She shot twice. He fell.

From the left two men in suits burst out of the woods. "Drop those guns, both of you!" one of them yelled.

To his right Al saw a boat coming toward his dock. He could see the sheriff's department decal on its side.

"What's going on?" Fergie came running from the house, a gun in her hand.

Al and Bonnie put their pistols on the ground and raised their hands. The men in suits then aimed their guns at Fergie, who put her gun down as well.

The sheriff's boat pulled up to Al's dock and a deputy hopped out to tie it fast to the dock with lines from the fore and aft. The next person off the boat was Sheriff Clayton himself, in uniform and wearing his white cowboy hat. "What the hell are you doing?" he yelled at the Secret Service men.

"Arresting these people for interfering in an investigation."

"The hell you are."

"But ..."

"See to those men in Al's boat," Clayton snapped to the deputy beside him, Pudge Smithers.

Pudge climbed into the boat, helped Maury to his knees and checked the other two. "This one's okay. The other two, not so much. They're both dead."

"Figures," Clayton grumbled. "That woman's a crack shot. Just this once I wish she'd have missed a little."

"I hope you're not going to ..." the other agent said.

"What I'm not going to do is charge you with trespassing on land Al has clearly posted with "No Trespassing" signs."

"You know we have the right to come onto anyone's land, posted or not, if it's to stop a crime."

"What crime was that? At the time you were sitting on your rumps across the road with little more than hopeful speculation, and with only a hazy and not clear enough idea of what was going on to act."

"We saw these men fall in a hole. Well, one fell and the other went in after him."

"There's no law against falling into a hole on your own property. And doesn't that make a pretty good case for them not knowing there was anything like a hole they might fall into?"

"By doing so they were interfering with our investigation."

"Which, from the sounds of it, just came to an explosive end." Clayton lifted the front of his hat up with his forefinger and looked hard at the agents. "An end which I'll just bet is going to tickle your boss pink. Now, let's go take a look at that hole Al is going to have to hire a backhoe to fill in when this is all over."

He turned to Pudge. "You'd better call in the M.E.'s crew to tend to these." He waved a hand toward the men in the boat.

"You three," he gave a wave that took in Al, Fergie and Bonnie, "you can pick up your guns, not that you'll need them. I've got cruisers out on the road in case anyone tried to get clear that way. But they tell me there's nothing left over there but a big hole in the ground and nothing's stirring in it."

Fergie didn't even try to suppress her smile as she picked up her gun.

"You two," he spoke to the agents, "Holster those guns and come along."

Clayton started to plod off in the direction of the hole. He glanced back at the agents. "Are you coming, or not?"

They hesitated.

"If your shorts are in a twist you can check with your superior, Jeb B. Stewart later. I already have." Clayton turned and started off again. "He's the one with the ramrod up his rectum who insisted I tell Al nothing, after all."

Maury, still on his knees, was looking up at Bonnie, his eyes fixed on her. His voice was a little raspy, but the words came out clear enough. "I think I'd like you to marry me."

She grinned. "Well, I think I just might."

"Now isn't that sweet," Clayton grumbled. He kept going.

———— ❖ ————

The two Secret Service agents, who had introduced themselves as Longstreet and Phillips, came along at the tail end of the group, their heads together, talking between themselves. They had lost the initiative in their case and were perhaps discussing ways to regain it.

Longstreet, tall with a rectangular face and medium-length dark brown hair, which he seemed to care for, deferred to the shorter, stouter Phillips, whose red hair was buzz-cut over his roundish frowning face. Both wore smudges of dirt and ashes on their faces and clothes.

Al eased up close to Clayton. "You were quick on the scene in a boat, and had cruisers poised to sweep in from the road. What was that about?"

"When I told you I couldn't tell you what was going on, and you can realize why now, I knew it wouldn't take long before you got your back up over your shoulders and would knock everything cockeyed out this way. And I might add you exceeded even my expectations."

They came up on a large depression in the ground. A giant rut six to seven feet deep in places dipped into the earth and ran from Al's property off across the neighboring lot and nearly to the lake. What was left of the cabin had fallen into the Grand Canyon of a ditch along with all the vehicles, which now stuck up from the ground at various angles. Al could see half a dozen deputies in uniform going down into the rut at different spots and coming back up empty-handed.

"There must have been a quarter of a mile of tunnels down there," Al said.

"Where do you think all the dirt from making it went?" Clayton asked.

"They probably eased it out into the lake by the bucket or wheelbarrow full. I've thought the water around here was unusually cloudy for quite a spell."

Longstreet and Phillips came up to stand on one side of Clayton. Fergie eased close to Al. Maury and Bonnie stood a little further off, clinging to each other like survivors from the Titanic, in spite of Maury being smudged with dirt and Bonnie holding a gun in one hand.

"The mole people," Maury said.

"What?" Clayton snapped.

"Nothing."

Al glanced at the two Secret Service agents. Even dirty, they seemed young and fit, looked like the sort who spent their free time in gyms and weighing themselves about every twenty minutes. Both their suits had tears and smudges. If Longstreet had his made by a tailor, as Al suspected, there was going to be one tailor crying like a schoolgirl when he saw the suit again.

"We don't have a single thing," Phillips said, suppressed anger showing through. He seemed to be the senior one of them, though with his buzz-cut red hair and clear skin he couldn't be older than mid-thirties. "Not a scrap of evidence and all the men dead, even the two we most wanted to talk to, who were alive until your people ..."

"Defended themselves and saved a life," Clayton said. "I hope you don't have something against that."

"We'd have traded the hostage to have those men alive to talk to," Longstreet said. Phillips gave him a glare that made him shut up.

"Who were the men in the boat who kidnapped Maury?" Clayton asked.

"The talent," Phillips said. "Santiago Lox and his son Paulo. Santiago spent time in Israel and Brazil learning his craft. Now we'll never have an idea ..." He stopped himself in mid-sentence, turned to Al. "You haven't the foggiest idea about what was going on here, do you?"

Clayton chuckled. "Why don't you take a stab at it, Al? Share your thoughts."

Al still stared at the hole in the ground. All he could see was dirt, but beneath that there was probably all kind of equipment and perhaps dead people. But it had been blown to mush. He would have crime scene people swarming around out this way for perhaps weeks. He glanced up at the others, ended on Maury and Bonnie, who held hands. The two of them had been like love birds ever since the shooting. Maybe something good came of all this. The shouts of the deputies among themselves snapped Al away from that train of thought.

He looked at Phillips, didn't blink when Phillips stared back in a glare that was intended to intimidate. "This all probably started when you got a tip from someone in a bank."

"A quicky loan joint," Longstreet said. Phillips gave him a glare again that headed off anything else he might say.

"No one does fifties. You do just as much work and

make half as much profit. So this may have been designed to sail under the radar for a while," Al said. "But one of them used some of the bills at a place he didn't think would catch on."

"Paulo, the son, had to borrow money against his truck. He paid it off in phony fifties," Phillips said.

"I'll bet that loan guy sure squawked when he found out he gets no remuneration for the bills he turned in at your field office on 8th Street here in Austin."

"We told him what we tell everyone. That he was doing the right thing."

"Must make you guys real popular." Al shook his head. Before Phillips could respond, Al said, "That gave you a name and an address. A lead to follow. I'll bet you expected at first to find he was just one of the customers buying the counterfeit bills at a discount and using them. Then you came out here and had to make sense of that clown car of a cabin. All the vehicles and too few people visible. I'll bet you had quite a moment when you figured out you might be at the mother lode, the very place where all the new fake fifties floating out into the system were being made."

Longstreet glanced toward Phillips, who stayed fixed on Al.

"This was good stuff. From the equipment I glimpsed down there they probably were capable of at least a twenty-six step process, so the bills felt right and looked right. They had the security threads, watermark, and color shifting ink, so the lower right corner of the bill could shift from copper to green. The bills had raised printing, microprinting, and the colors and the paper were right, though they probably had to use two thin sheets of low-grade paper for the correct thickness. And to make it all possible there had to be a master craftsman. Maybe two. The Loxes?"

Phillips frowned. He looked to Clayton.

"You spin a pretty fetching story for someone who claims not to be involved."

"He was my top detective," Clayton said. "I'd be disappointed if he didn't parse this out given a moment or two. I take it from all the effort your boss went to ensuring I said nothing to Al that this would have been a big feather in your hats if this had led to capturing these men."

"The counterfeiters are gone, all dead, their equipment destroyed, and we have no physical evidence now. The phony bills will stop circulating, but Stewart and his bosses will have only our word on that now. The plates these days are computer generated, and you can bet the computers are gone. Any plates on the offset printing press are more than likely destroyed in the blast as well. We have nothing, no samples, no serial numbers to match against those already circulated, nothing. No hard evidence, no credit to us. So much for the feather, even if we wore hats." Phillips glared at Al the whole time he spoke.

"I figure they brought in gasoline fueled generators so they could run some of the equipment on power they made," Al said. "That way there wouldn't be a huge spike in electricity usage at such a tiny place. A huge underground marijuana farm in the southeast was found by the DEA just that way, by following the lead of a spike in electricity usage. But with gas drums down there you guys probably shouldn't have been shooting down into that hole."

"They were shooting at us. We were only shooting back," Longstreet said.

Phillips glared at him. "The fact remains that every scrap of hard evidence we had is gone."

Clayton said, "Al, you're smirking about something. What?"

"Maury, dig into your pockets," Al said.

206

Bonnie let go of Maury's hand. For a second Maury looked as guilty as school kids caught necking in the hallway.

Maury's hands came out of his pockets and shredded paper tumbled onto the ground. But among the shreds a few crumpled bills fell out as green lumps.

Phillips bent and grabbed at those, opened one slowly. He looked over it at Al. His eyes opened wider.

Al took the ones in his pocket out and handed them to Phillips as well. "Maury did some up close accidental scouting before one of you shot down into that hole and lit up whatever fuel was stored down there to run the generator."

"Well, if that takes care of our little discussion for now, I have a crime scene to go examine," Clayton said. "I expect the media will be swarming in soon enough. I'm sure once we get any bodies out that your people will want to go over what's left of the counterfeiting equipment, though I don't expect they'll find much they can use. I'll let you boys do the talking about how you solved all this put an end to the funny paper ring."

"Uh ... thanks. Fine," Phillips managed.

"Yeah, really, you sure ..." Longstreet looked as confused as he was surprised.

Phillips jerked his head in the direction of their parked SUV. Longstreet shut up once more and followed.

"You tossed them a pretty nice bone," Al said, once the agents were out of sight.

"They're young. If they're ever going to learn the grace of separate law enforcement groups working together they might as well start now. And their boss might even take it as a lesson too about ordering others in his field around. Besides, dealing with the media isn't a treat I crave as much as they do."

"And sheriff," Bonnie said.

"Yeah?"

"Speaking of people getting along, you're invited to the wedding." She reached for Maury's hand again.

"Of course. Of course." Clayton looked at Al from under the brim of his hat, and darned if Al didn't think the grumpy old bear winked. "Wouldn't miss it for the world."

THE ANGRY BRIDE

AL PULLED HIS TRUCK UP in front of his house. He got out, but left the key in the ignition since he had promised to take Fergie out to dinner in a few minutes.

Bonnie came storming out of the house, slamming the front door behind her. She paused for just a moment to turn back and yell, "If that's the way you want it you can have the damn wedding by yourself."

She spun back and walked around Al.

"Evening, Bonnie," he said.

"Yeah. Whatever." She went around and climbed into his truck, started it up, and peeled out of his drive in a spray of gravel. He watched his truck surge out the lane, coming close to fishtailing a time or two.

Maury came out the front door and frowned.

"Any idea where she's going with my truck?" Al asked.

"Hard to tell. She's pretty pissed off, Al."

Maury stayed where he was while Al went inside his house. Fergie was making a pot of coffee, using the drip method Al preferred. She looked up. "Did you get them?"

"Yep." Al held up the book of travelers' checks from the bank. "Should make the perfect gift." Tanner heard his voice from the other room and came running in to pull up at Al's feet, look up at him with his tail wagging. Al bent to rub the dog's head. "What's up with the soon-to-be honeymoon couple?"

"Should we go with 'rift-in-the-lute' or 'trouble-in-paradise' as the appropriate cliché?"

"Isn't there always a shaky minute or two before a wedding, even when it's a planned elopement?"

"Well, Vegas may have to wait on this one a bit longer. A former girlfriend called."

"Oh?"

"On Maury's phone, while he was letting Bonnie use it."

"And she didn't roll well with that?"

"Ever see a cat get wet that didn't want to get wet? Then ramp that up to mountain lion." Fergie finished with the coffee and poured them both a mug.

They had both just sat down at the table when Maury came in with a long face. "I don't think she's coming right back."

Fergie nodded toward the kitchen land line phone on the wall. "You could always call her on your phone."

Maury crossed the room and punched in the number. He gave it a minute or two and hung up. He turned to them. "She's not answering."

"Silly girl," Fergie said. She shook her head and took a sip of coffee.

———◆———

Al and Fergie came in the door, greeting by the scurrying feet and wagging tail of Tanner, but not by Maury. He sat in the growing dark of the room, staring off at nothing.

Al flipped on a couple of lights as he went through the room. He realized then that Maury wasn't staring at nothing. He was staring at the phone.

"I see my truck's not back."

"No. Nor Bonnie."

"You haven't heard from her?"

"Nope."

"You could call your cell phone, which she has."

"Tried. No answer."

"Want me to drive out and look around at some of her favorite places?"

Maury looked up at Al with two of the saddest eyes. Before he could speak, the phone rang.

He leaped to his feet and ran to get across the room and answer it.

Maury held his hand over the phone while he talked into it. Al took the hint and went into the kitchen, where Fergie was warming up two mugs of coffee in the microwave.

Before he lifted the still-warm cup to his lips, Al heard shouting in the living room and went out in time to see Maury slam the receiver back into its rest. He was huffing, his face was red, and his hands were clenching into fists, relaxing, then clenching again.

"Are you two little love birds having a spat?" Al asked.

"That wasn't Bonnie. It was something far worse."

"What do you mean?"

"Bonnie's being held a prisoner."

A full minute seemed to tick by before Al asked. "Who?"

"Maybe I had better start at the beginning."

"If that's the best way to clear up this picture, fine." Al glanced toward Fergie, who had followed him into the room. They both sat down on the couch, holding their coffee mugs.

Maury paced back and forth across the room as he spoke. "You know that Bonnie insisted we have an engagement notice put in the paper. I couldn't even afford a ring yet, so I said okay to that."

"And?" Al nudged.

"I was letting Bonnie borrow my cell phone, the one you got me."

"And?"

"Things went South."

"How so?"

"Well, you know how I haven't exactly been practicing for the priesthood in my past."

"Vastly understated," Fergie said, "If what I've heard is even partially true."

"Most of it probably is," Maury said.

And?" Al said once again.

"One of the ladies of my past called, a pretty important one, but a kind of crazy one."

"How crazy?" Al tilted his head. Knowing Maury, he had plenty of room for speculation.

"Well, she almost married me."

"Really?"

"We were a step or two from the altar."

"What happened?"

"I ... I kind of chickened out."

"And she didn't take that well?" Fergie said.

"She took very few things well. That, not at all."

"I can see where a conversation with her might bring Bonnie's blood to a boil," Al said. "How did all this make the leap from you and Bonnie having words to this other woman holding Bonnie prisoner?"

"I don't know. I just don't know."

"Does this woman from your past have a name?" Fergie asked.

"Claudette. Her last name used to be Bertanelli. It may still be, though she can't be what you'd call young. I heard she had moved far away."

"What can you tell us about her?" Fergie glanced to Al.

"Not much."

"Try," Al said.

"Claudette had a sort of dark side."

"And yet you almost married her?"

"At the time I thought that might be what I needed."

"Dark like how?"

"She tied me up."

"Often?"

"More often than you'd think. Once for almost a week."

"How did you ..."

"She was a nurse. She took care of all that, and threw in sponge baths."

"A nurse," Fergie said. "Maybe she and Bonnie have things they can talk about."

"This isn't funny. The woman is dangerous."

"The one you almost married." Fergie glanced toward Al again.

"I'm not proud of it. She brought things out in me. We set some records. Not all my doing some of the time. I mean, when I was tied up and such. There were times, when I was chapped and raw, I screamed for my body to quit responding. But I was young, and my body was stupid."

"I can't see that you've come that far," Fergie said.

"Can we just focus? Bonnie is in real trouble here."

"Didn't I just hear you hang up on the person calling?"

"Yeah. Claudette. I guess I got angry."

"Too bad," Fergie said. "Because she could be anywhere. There's no way to find her unless we have more than we do now. Your only hope is if she calls back."

"Could we just report Al's truck stolen?"

"And have Bonnie arrested for the theft?" Fergie said.

"Can't we call the sheriff's department and have them look?"

"And tell them what?" Fergie said. "We're back to the stolen vehicle report."

"Even if someone in law enforcement found the truck, what's to guarantee something bad doesn't happen to Bonnie if she's truly being held?" Al said.

"Oh, she's being held. Claudette wouldn't lie about that. There was too much evil joy in her voice."

"What all did you do to this woman?" Fergie tilted her head.

"Let's just focus on Bonnie," Maury said.

Toward midnight, Al said, "Why don't you try again?"

Maury went to the phone and tapped in his own number. It rang and rang, but was finally picked up. He glanced toward Al and Fergie. They sat up straight on the couch.

"What do you want? What do you want me to do?"

He listened for a moment, then hung up.

"What'd she say?" Al asked.

"She asked me what time our own wedding had been planned. To expect something then."

"When was it to be?" Fergie asked.

"Noon."

"It sounds like we have until noon tomorrow. Did she sound vengeful?"

Maury nodded. "A lot."

"You'd better keep calling her."

Maury tried. But after a dozen tries, with her not answering once, he put the phone on its rest and went over to sit on the couch.

The phone started ringing at ten minutes to eight the next morning.

Al lifted his head from where it lay against the corner of the couch. Fergie, who lay against him stirred at his side. Maury's head snapped up from where he'd been slumped over against Fergie's shoulder. Tanner lifted his head from the floor at Al's feet and shook his head.

All three had tried to stay up and wait on the call, but had failed. Sleep had gotten the best of them.

"Let it ring," Al said.

"No." Maury jumped up from the couch and started to rush toward the phone.

Fergie grabbed him. But he thrashed against her grip and was about to spring free when Al stepped closer and grabbed him around the upper arms so his whipping arms could do no harm.

The phone quit ringing and the answering function played out loud.

"Oh, great. Don't answer the phone." It was Bonnie's voice. "I'm in real trouble here, you lunkhead, and it's all your fault. She's threatening to cut off parts of me, and don't even ask what she wants to cut off on you. I've been here in this dump for hours, overnight, and without even room service ..."

Someone cut off the call, and Al didn't think it had been Bonnie.

"Why? Why wouldn't you let me answer? You heard her, she's ..."

"That's not all we heard. It's why we wanted the recording. Did you hear it too, Fergie?"

She nodded.

"Why don't you call the airport and see what direction the planes are coming in for their landings."

"What the hell are you guys talking about?"

215

Al let go of Maury, who shook himself off and paced back and forth, rubbing the spots where Fergie or Al had pinched him roughly.

"South-bound today," Fergie said, when she hung up the phone.

Al nodded. He dug out a laptop, put it on the table, and got it going. Fergie went outside. She came back in with a map from her car, a city map of Austin. She spread it beside Al and got him a red Sharpie.

"What are you doing?" Maury's voice climbed an octave. "What's going on?"

Al stayed focused on the screen as it warmed up and he got the browser up. "The reason we wanted a recording and not just you talking to whoever called was to see if we could get any scrap of an idea where they are. And we did. We got lucky. In the background I heard the sound of a plane landing. They're in a low end motel near the airport. Austin-Bergstrom International Airport has two runways, one for planes taking off, the other for planes landing. From the sound of the landing plane, against the direction they have to be landing today, we have an area to start checking."

"How? How? How did you get all that?" Maury's voice was pitched high, not too far from dog whistle range.

"Bonnie let us know about the motel," Fergie said. "She called it a dump, not a house, and said it had no room service. That meant it probably wasn't a high-end motel either."

Al was peering at the screen and began making marks within a circle he had put at one end of the airport on the map.

"And those?" Maury asked.

"They're our first hope," Al said. "Motels in the right place. If we find nothing we'll have to shift to the other side of the airport, but I hope we're right because we'll be running out of time."

◆

It was going on 11 a.m. when Fergie finally drove into a motel's lot and Al said, "There it is."

He pointed toward his truck.

Fergie looked around, parked far enough away they wouldn't be spotted. Before they got out of the car, Al reached into a small black cloth bag he'd brought along and took out a stethoscope. He handed it back Maury.

"Where did you get this?"

"Well, originally from a safecracker. But more recently from my room, where I keep a few things like this."

"Why?"

"Because we can guess they're in a room near the truck, but we don't know which one, even if we knew what your Claudette's car looked like, and we don't. You get to listen, and you'd better hope for a voice. You're the only one who knows what she sounds like. I imagine, and hope, she's preaching up a storm to Bonnie right now given the time."

Once they got closer to the stretch of rooms, Maury got down on his knees and put the stethoscope's earpieces in his ears. He started crawling along the row, putting the hearing end against each door.

Al kept a watch on the motel. Fortunately, he didn't see a lot of activity at the moment. Only a handful of cars remained at the lot. One maid's cart was parked in front of an open door across the way, blocking it, but Al couldn't see her inside.

Maury froze in front of a door, bent to listen closer, then turned to give a thumbs up to Al.

Al waved him to one side.

217

Fergie stepped to the door and knocked on it. "Maid service."

"Go away."

"Yust some towels, *por favor?*"

The door opened a bare crack.

Al charged forward, gun in one hand, and kicked it open. Fregie rushed in first with her gun held ready.

She had barely taken a step into the room when an arm reached out holding a taser and pressed it against Fergie's side.

Al could hear a mumbled warning from Bonnie just as Fergie dropped twitching to the floor, her gun tumbling onto the cheap red carpet.

Al rushed in, veering to the right. He could see Claudette now, with the taser in her hand. She turned on Al, pointing the taser while ducking to scoop up Fergie's gun.

Claudette had long dark hair, swept up into a pony tail. She had been pretty once and now had a mature woman's rosy glow, but some of that could be anger given the severe, bitter scowl on her tanned lean face. A black pants suit covered a lean body that looked like it had some gym muscle to it. She might have been spending time working out, getting ready for this day. Her shin-high black leather boots glistened in the room's dim light. If the look she was going for was dominatrix, she had pretty well stuck her landing on that. Al tried for a second to picture her in white, as a bride, maybe happy and smiling, but couldn't envision anything close to that.

Maury shot in around Al and rushed to go across the room.

Claudette spun, fired a shot, missed Maury, who dropped to the floor anyway as if shot.

When he looked up, Claudette had the gun pointed

toward Bonnie, the taser in the other hand still pointed toward Al.

"You, stay put, lover boy," she said to Maury. To Al she said, "You, drop the gun. I mean it, or she gets it."

Al lowered his gun to the carpet, and she watched him closely, perhaps too closely to see Maury coil up and leap at her. She spun and zapped him hard with the taser.

Al rushed forward and knocked the pistol from one hand and backhanded the taser from the other. He spun her and put her in a headlock. She kicked at him with her boots, but he turned his body out of range. He was going to ask someone to get him the coil of rope beside Bonnie's chair, left over from tying her in place. But Fergie was still groggily barely sitting up and Maury was flopping about like a just landed fish.

He forced Claudette over to Bonnie's chair and made her bend at the same time he did to pick up the rope. He stretched her out on the floor and tied her wrists. He finished trussing her ankles, not without considerable kicking, thrashing, and general resistance to his doing it, while Fergie went over to cut Bonnie loose.

Maury slowly sat up, still twitching and looking as lit up as a pin ball machine.

A motel maid was peering in through the open door, as if trying to figure out just what was going on.

Al got on his phone to call his old friends at the sheriff's department. Fergie watched over Claudette who was struggling against her bindings like a woman possessed, and maybe she was. Al wasn't just taking Maury's word for it any longer. When Claudette tried to lash out with her bound feet Fergie calmly placed one foot on the boots at the bound ankles and held her in place, although that generated some language that would have embarrassed sailors.

While he waited to be put through, Al tried to picture Maury being intimate with this woman, ready to marry her some fifteen years ago, as he'd said. He couldn't get there, but for that matter he couldn't picture Maury as a father. He guessed he might get to see that newsreel play out. After all, anything is possible ... if a person works for it. And Maury seemed to be getting the handle on the notion that some effort was going to be required. He still trembled from the jolt of electricity that had rippled through him, but he stared at Bonnie with longing, and gratitude, and he might have even seemed a little proud, proud of her and of having played a part in her rescue.

Bonnie rushed over to lift Maury to his feet and hug him. Grizzly bears in the Rockies probably have given less vigorous hugs. Maury's eyes looked ready to pop. After a moment she pulled her head back to face him, without letting go she stared into his eyes. "I guess we all have a demon or two in our histories. I just didn't expect one of yours to scare the jeepers out of me."

"And that wedding and honeymoon in Vegas?" he asked.

"It's on. More than ever, my hero honey, it's on!"

A SPECIAL KIND OF HELL

A L WOKE TO HEAR TANNER making a low mewing sound at the foot of the bed. He lifted his head until he could see Tanner. "What's the matter? Is Timmy in the well again?"

He pushed aside the covers and slipped out of bed. But Tanner sat there, didn't rush toward the door to be let out as he usually did.

Al glanced around the room until he settled on where Tanner looked. The other side of Al's bed was empty. The sheets were rumpled and the pillow dented, but where was Fergie?

Tanner made his sound again.

Al frowned and went into the bathroom. All her stuff was gone. He came back out and looked in the closet. The side he'd cleared out for her stuff was empty. Her two suitcases were gone as well.

Tanner mewed again.

"I know just how you feel," Al said. He started to get dressed.

———◇———

As he passed through the dining area he glanced into the kitchen. Light came in through the windows that lined the wall facing the lake. Bonnie waved at him. "You want some of these eggs I'm fixing?"

He gave a curt wave and kept moving through the living room and out the front door. Fergie's car was gone.

When he climbed into his truck he didn't know where to start. Yet he turned on the engine and headed on out the drive.

He tried every place he knew she'd ever gone—her hair salon, the coffee shop, and even her favorite grocery, which was twice as far away as the one at which he usually shopped.

Traffic seemed a worse tangle than usual, with a lot of "me, me, me" self-absorbed drivers doing everything but what they should. But that could have just been a product of Al's attitude.

By six that afternoon he'd stopped just to think a half dozen times and he'd grabbed a sandwich at a gas station that tasted like sawdust before he tossed it in a trash can with only one bite gone.

He was playing back every recent moment they'd shared in the Austin area when he pulled into the Cactus Flower Motel, where they'd stayed once while on a case, and where she'd gone when she had stayed away once before. It was neither exotic nor a dump, and a nearby restaurant, Ernesto's, served up drinkable coffee and better-than-good breakfast tacos. Plus, the motel had been close enough to a pharmacy they could walk over and buy a couple of toothbrushes, since they were traveling light at that time. He saw her car pulling up in front of a ground floor room down at the far end.

For a second he hesitated. He watched her climb out of her car, the wind whipping her long red hair out behind her like a scarf. Yep. It was her.

He had absolutely no idea what he was going to say to her, this after driving around all day looking for her. He sure didn't want to go talk to the proprietor about getting a room. The last time he'd seen Eubie Lee Jonuson the guy had been rocking a mullet hairdo and had been spitting his chew into a white Styrofoam cup, not the sort of thing Al needed at this moment or time of day.

She closed her car door and started for the room. As she went to open it she turned, looked right at him. Even from across the lot it looked like she sighed.

He walked across the lot, gravel crunching under his boots.

"Is there something you want to say to me?" she asked. Her shoulders came as close to a slump as he'd ever seen.

"Yes, yes there is."

"Well?"

"I know there is, but I'll be damned if I know the words."

"You think that might be part of the problem?"

"I don't think of it as so much of a problem as a wrinkle we need to iron out."

"Well, get ironing."

"How about I buy you dinner over at Ernesto's? I know you like their tacos."

"We can't."

"Can't?"

"Because of Wacky Jackie."

"Who?"

"The afternoon cook there. Oh, she's fine when she's got her meds right. But when she doesn't ...well, you can figure it out."

"Okay. Unpredictable. It's best not to take the chance. How about Hut's?"

Traffic had tangled itself into an even worse rush-hour mess. The drive took almost an hour although 6th Street wasn't all that far from her motel. The trip seemed even longer since neither spoke in the bumper-to-bumper wait to get there.

When the waiter at last left their table with their order, for two Arnold's Best burgers and onion rings as well as fries that expressed Fergie's "what the hell" mood, Al said, "Why did you take off like that and leave without a word?"

"Ah, the oft clichéd 'words as well as deeds.' You're as remiss there as anyone, Al."

He nodded, bought a little time by unwrapping his silverware from its enfolding napkin. "What would you like to hear from me?"

"I shouldn't have to provide the script."

"How do you plan on getting along out here? I know what your pension is. Living at my place had certain perks, some of them financial."

"Some of them." She nodded a head toward where their waiter was already weaving through the tables to bring them their order. "And nice segue to a different subject, by the way."

"I'm trying. It's my nature to flounder a bit on matters like this."

The waiter put down their plates and was off through the chattering crowd like a waft of cloud.

"Look, I'll cut you a little slack," she said. "I've seen you look like you've just been pulled out of the water before, open-mouthed, flapping about on the deck like one of your fish. Having just the one marriage that ended the way it did hasn't helped you bounce back to a man of significant poise in this aspect of your life. Why don't we talk about how I expected to get by out here on my so-called lonesome."

"Fine." He repressed a really big sigh and took a large bite out of his burger.

"What have you heard about the incident on Jim Bowie Lane in Austin this week?"

He wiped a trickle of delicious from the corner of his mouth with his napkin.

"A grandmother was driving along with her three-year old granddaughter in the car. It's a narrow two-lane road and she was going slow, being careful. It apparently infuriated the driver behind her, who had honked, flashed his lights, and finally pulled around her by going halfway along through the berm at the first chance he got. That wasn't enough, because he fired three shots out his window as he went by. The bullets missed the grandmother, but not her granddaughter."

"Road rage, and a man with a loaded handgun at a bad time." Fergie had yet to touch any of the food.

"With no witnesses other than the rattled grandmother, no tire imprints on the gravel of the berm, and all she could share was that the car was brown, when they could get her to stop crying long enough for that."

He paused. "And, oh, there was a reward. Twenty thousand dollars to anyone who could help lead to the culprit's identification. That got upped to forty thousand just yesterday afternoon."

"You realize that this is the most you've spoken so far?" She reached for an onion ring.

"I'm more comfortable with this sort of thing."

"And there you have one aspect of the issue at hand."

"I thought we were going to talk about this road rage incident. I wouldn't have pictured you as the bounty hunter sort."

"I'm not. I knew the grandmother, Freddy Andrewson. We were neighbors once. She loved her kids, and I know she doted on her grandkids."

"Most grandparents do. But the money became a factor?"

"The money just happened. The minute I saw her name pop up I knew I had to help." She reached for her burger.

"But you didn't say a thing to me."

She spoke around her food while chewing. "Welcome to the club."

They were almost back to her motel when he spoke. "Why do you think you have a chance at solving this when the cops and public are going flat out on this?"

"Not so much a chance as a reason to try. Because they've got nothing so far. And the clock is ticking. You know how these things go. The more time that passes the less likely a solution is possible." She glanced toward him. "Between us, we know everything that will be going on at their procedural level. All we have to do is what they aren't doing."

"I like the sound of that 'we.' Does this mean we'll be working together on this?"

"Yep. If you're willing."

He nodded.

"We'll see how it goes and what happens after that," she said. "And for the record, I liked your liking that 'we' too."

The next day Fergie pulled her car up behind one that looked very much like the one Al used to drive as a plain clothes detective. In fact, it looked to him like the exact same one.

"How was your stay at the motel?" he said.

"You know exactly how it was, right down to the air

conditioner that sounds like a World War One plane landing all night."

"I could have hung around and comforted you."

"Hmpf." She gave him an eye roll. "Let's just focus on this for now."

They had just gotten out of her car when Victor Kahlon came out of the front door and started toward them.

Al felt his eyebrows rise. "You're a bit out of your jurisdiction, aren't you?"

"And you two aren't even official law enforcement ... anymore." He stopped in front of them.

When Al didn't respond, Victor stared hard for a moment at each of them, then smiled. He said, "I'm just here as a courtesy. We've been asked to look into this at the county level. No one knows where this guy will turn up."

"Well ..." Al let it hang.

"What?"

"I suppose city and county have taken all the normal steps. Have they?"

Victor's head rocked back a half inch. "You know what Clayton says about you, Al?"

"He probably says all manner of things."

"He says you not only think outside the box. You don't even know there *is* a box."

"I suppose he means that in a kind way."

"Your track record speaks for itself." Victor glanced toward Fergie. "But it's a big city, and county. And though it's not a first pick for many, there are a lot of brown cars out there."

"Have the police already figured that the shooter might live close to here," Fergie said, "and followed up on that notion?"

Victor nodded. "And got nowhere, which is when we were asked to pitch in, and when the reward got posted."

"Who posted the reward?"

"The city investigators. Then Clayton okayed our department chipping in another twenty when their manhunt got nowhere after a day."

"And you've gotten nowhere too?" Al said.

"There's a lot of nowhere to get on a thing like this."

"Have they thought that maybe the person doesn't live near here but is just staying near the area for a spell?"

"Let's just say it's crossed their minds." Victor glanced back toward the house. "Hard to follow up on something like that, but they're taking steps."

"If it was me," Al said, "I'd round up recent security footage from the closest gas stations and see if the vehicle popped there."

"They did that, sent copies to us. Not much to go on since we don't know make and model of the vehicle yet."

"Would it be possible for me to get a copy of those tapes?" Al asked.

"I could clear it with Clayton, have copies made and sent to your place. But they're in black and white. Hard to tell much except light and dark vehicles."

"If we find we need them, could you send the copies of the tapes to me at the Cactus Flower Motel?" Fergie asked.

Victor glanced toward Al, who shrugged. He turned back to Fergie. "Okay. Do you think you will need them?"

"We don't know yet. Al's just established where you guys think the box is on this. Now he'll bear down in his own miraculous and unique way his miracles to perform."

"And you think?" Victor asked Fergie.

"Oh, my money's always on Al. Always has been."

That gave Al a warm rush all the way to the toes of his boots. "If we run across anything, can we call you, Vic?"

"Sure. Please do. The public outcry is huge, and the

words 'cowardly act of violence' seems to be the media mantra. We'd like to solve this, and soon."

They waited until he'd gotten into his car before they walked up to the front door of a house small enough Al would call it a cottage. Fergie stepped close and rang the doorbell. After a minute or two the front door swung open.

The woman who looked up at them epitomized grandma. She was roundish, white-haired, and looked like the sort to smile a lot, although at the moment her eyes were red and puffy. "What? What can I do for you?"

"Would it be alright if we come in?" Fergie asked.

"Oh, my heavens. I didn't recognize you at first. I've been so flustered. Do come in." Freddy Andrewson turned and headed back into her small living room.

The inside of the house took Al on a time machine trip back to when people put doilies on chair arms and kept standing floor lamps around topped by fading, dusty lampshades. The cozy little house should have been filled with the smell of baking. But Freddy looked far from up to that at the moment.

"My daughter is barely speaking to me at the moment. It's just grief, the raw fresh kind, and I'm feeling it as bad or worse than her."

"I wonder if you'd be willing to help us in looking for the man who shot at your car." Fergie helped Freddy ease down into the only chair beside a lit lamp.

Al moved over beside a mantel covered with framed photos of Freddy's family. The picture in the center showed a young Freddy in a white wedding dress next to a taller young man who looked more earnest than eager. That photo had a black ribbon around its base that had gathered a layer of dust through the years. Hard to tell how long Freddy had been a widow. The other photos were all happier, filled with clusters of children, young adults, and Freddy, all at the kind of family events where he could practically hear the laughter. The small child in several of them might be the victim.

"Of course. Of course," Freddy said. "I've told the police, and even the sheriff's department now everything I can recall. But it wasn't much. I could see a vehicle behind me weaving a bit from side to side, as if eager to go around. I was focusing on being careful with my precious cargo, little granddaughter. She was only ... three." Freddy dissolved into tears and Fergie tugged a couple of facial tissues from a box on the small table beside the chair. She handed them the Freddy and patted the woman on the back. Fergie glanced toward Al.

Five long and slow minutes oozed by before Freddy looked up, dabbing at her eyes. I'm sorry. You're trying to help. I'm such a mess."

"No problem," Fergie said. "Would you mind looking at a few color samples we brought?"

"Why no. If it helps. The police didn't do anything like that."

"They might have gotten to it in time. They probably talked a lot about make and model."

Freddy nodded. "Lost on me, of course. I can't tell one kind of car from another out there on the road, unless it's those newer ones that look like shoe boxes, and I don't even know the name of them."

"Here." Fergie eased the sample sheets onto Freddy's lap and opened them to where she could take on all the shades of brown used by the automotive industry.

Freddy bent close, even scratched at one or two. Finally she looked up at them. "Nope. It was nothing like any of these."

"How so?" Al asked.

"I ...I don't know. I'm sorry."

"Try."

She frowned, thought hard. "Maybe a little redder."

Al looked to Fergie, who returned a puzzled frown.

"Can I borrow your tablet?" he asked Fergie.

She dug it out of her purse and got it going.

He took it from her when she held it out and used a search engine until he said, "Here. How about this?" He held the tablet where Freddy could see it.

She squinted a moment, leaned closer. "Yeah," she said. "That's it. That's it exactly. How did you ever ...?"

Fergie was staring at him.

He went back to the search engine, made a couple more inquiries, then closed it and handed the tablet to Fergie. "We need to go. Pronto."

"Okay." To Freddy she said, "We'll be doing everything we can and we'll let you know what we find."

Freddy looked down at her lap, then back up Fergie. Tears starting down both cheeks in earnest again. "I just want my little Abbie back."

———◆———

As soon as they were back in Fergie's car Al said, "Did you know about the child's name?"

"Of course I did. It was in all the media reports. This has nothing to do with your ex-wife, and no I didn't intend for this to pick at the scab it apparently has." She glanced his way. "Now, what did you stumble onto back there?"

"The color of the car. It wasn't brown. It was primer."

"What?"

"The car was in a pre-painting state of being completely covered in primer, a color that's more reddish brown than just brown. That's probably what made it so hard for law enforcement to make any kind of connection between make and model. The color doesn't depend on knowing a certain kind of car manufacturer that releases brown cars."

"So it could be any kind of car at all. How in the world will we ever narrow that down?"

"If you had just committed an act of violence like this, and were cooling down and wondering how to cover your tracks, what would you do?"

"Probably get that car painted, right away, any color but brown. But wouldn't the perp know we might sooner or later know that?"

"Yep. Which is why calls to every body shop in the area might not turn up a thing."

"Then how ...?"

"We have to assume he might just be an employee at such a place, someone able to do the job himself."

"I thought you didn't like assumptions in a case like this?"

"We're in a time situation here. Right now I'd ride a hunch like Paul Revere's horse."

"And just where do you intend to gallop? Is that what you were researching while I was trying to calm poor Freddy?"

"Everything we know is based on what the police and deputies don't. The guy may not live close to Freddy, but was probably staying close, enough so that his frustration at wanting to get to where he was going prompted him to such a heinous act. He probably has a record of anger, even violence elsewhere, but we have no way of establishing that until we find out who he is. He has an average-looking car that could easily get lost or overlooked on the road, but he was in the process of getting it painted, a process he should want to accelerate just now."

"So we look into nearby body shops?"

"As fast as we can."

The fifth body shop they checked seemed the most promising. It was actually the second, but no one had been there the first time they'd checked. The sign on the door said, "Out to lunch. Back in an hour." Yet the sign shared no indication of when they'd left or when they'd be back. Two hours later, when Fergie looped back to it, a crew of three was finishing up on using masking tape to cover the windows and mirrors with paper. The car on which they worked was a dark royal blue.

Al glanced at his watch. They had a few more hours before darkness would settle in over Austin and all of its body shops.

"Stay here," Fergie said. This is my case. Just remember that. Besides, I'm packing and you're almost certainly not. You're not, are you?"

He shook his head.

She walked over to the men working. The two who had just finished taping stepped back from the vehicle, out of the range of paint fumes. The third stepped in closer. His face was covered by a painting mask respirator, the kind with two large green disks on either side of its bottom that made the man look more than a little like a large insect. He held the paint gun at the end of a hose that led down to the compressor.

From the car, Al watched the three men. The noise from the compressor filled the workspace and hammered its way out to where he sat. The two men not spraying talked with Fergie when she came up to them. They shook their heads. As soon as she turned around and started back toward the car the two with whom she'd spoken waved to the man with the paint sprayer. He stepped over, turned off the compressor, and the three of them went into a huddle.

Al opened his door and got out. As she got up to her car, he nodded back to the men talking among themselves. "There's something they didn't tell you."

She turned and looked, sighed, then took out her gun from her ankle holster and started back that way.

Al hung back. It was her gig, after all.

One of the men stood up straighter when he saw her coming back. He started to say something, then looked down and saw the gun in her hand. He slapped the shoulder of the nearest man with the back of his hand. The two of them took off running, one to the left, the other to the right.

The third man, who wore a black hoodie, pulled off the respirator that hung at his neck and tossed it to the ground. He dove inside what looked to Al like a 2005 Ford Five Hundred, his hands going into the glove box.

"Fergie!" Al shouted.

But he could have saved his breath. She dropped prone to the ground and went into a shooter's stance from there. Al took off running to his right, around the side of the building toward its back. He could hear them shouting.

Al eased around the outside of the building, and reached around to the small of his back for a gun that wasn't there. He shook his head. A closed door with a glass window looked in on the port where the men had been working. He peeked through, saw the man coming out of the car with something in his hand. Al's hand tested the door. It was locked, so he stepped back and kicked it open. A spray of wooden bits flew out around the lock as the door slammed open.

Al burst through running. The man spun and Al dove across him, knocking the lifting hand away. Instead of a gun clattering to the concrete a clutter of papers flew into the air and fluttered to the garage floor.

The fellow was young. Well, youngish compared to Al, maybe in his thirties. Al had him in a head lock, from behind, a full nelson with both arms under the arms and pressing the head down. "Why don't you take a look at those papers?" Al said.

Fergie put her gun back in its holster. She picked them up, scanned them. "I've seen these kind before. They're almost good enough to pass as the real thing."

"Doesn't matter. See if there's a gun in there."

Fergie went to look inside the car.

The man squirmed in Al's grip. "Gun. I ain't got no gun. I just do paint jobs. That's why they brung me in."

"Brung you in from where?" Al asked, pressing down a bit on the man's neck as he did.

"I ain't sayin'."

Fergie climbed out of the car, shook her head. She eased closer, slid the guy's wallet out of his pocket although he tried to jerk his hip away.

"New Mexico." Fergie held up the driver's license. "You ever shoot a gun, Carl?"

"Not in my life. My uncles were hunters. Not me. I got different skills."

"Like boosting cars?" Al asked.

"You guys can't prove nothin'."

"Where were you three days ago, at about eleven in the morning?" Fergie asked.

"Hell, I was still back in Hobbs. I only got here yesterday. And now this."

"Your friends can back you up on that?"

"What friends. They just got here like me. I ain't seen none of them before."

"You know, Fergie, I believe this young man might be telling the truth."

"Course I am."

"Well, Carl, here's your chance to do some good. Do you know another shop, maybe one not listed, where this same sort of thing is going on?"

"I ain't sayin' nothin'."

"You might want to help yourself here, Carl," Fergie said. "Our jails aren't what I'd call friendly."

"Nothin'." Carl struggled again to get free. Al pressed harder. Suddenly, Carl went limp. "You think I can cut myself a break? Really?" He tilted his head to look up at Fergie.

"Can't hurt," Fergie said. "You're in some deep doo-doo here."

Carl still hesitated. "Well, there's this shop I worked at just a bit yesterday afternoon."

"And?" Al encouraged.

"I just knew it as Manny's. There was no sign or nothin'. We worked in a garage behind the house."

"And where is that house, Carl?"

"Really, you'll cut me some slack?"

The house, Carl," Fergie repeated.

'It's on Las Venture, off of Lamar a block or two. Ugly yellow house. Big garage out back, though."

Al looked up at Fergie. "Do you know anyone still in your old department who you could dump this on that would keep fairly quiet and let us keep moving? Someone to tend to this guy?"

"You're pretty sure it's not him?"

"We're looking for a guy probably with serious anger issues. This guy has issues, but the raw fiery kind it takes to grab a gun and start popping away isn't in him."

"Hey, I told you guys. I'm no shooter."

"There are a couple of guys I know. But I know just the right guy to call," Fergie said. "This can be *his* feather. He'll like that."

"Can you please get on the horn and get him over here?"

While she tapped in the number on her cell phone, she watched him. He alternately glanced at her and his watch. He could see she was thinking about something when she hung up.

"Why are you angry?" she asked.

"Because the guy who shot and killed little Abbie is probably painting away any evidence that can tie him to the crime even as we speak."

"You know, this passion you show when on the trail of someone like this, though it has a dangerous edge to it, it's not an unattractive thing, Al."

"Let's just hurry up and catch this bastard. We need to dump this and run."

"Okay. Okay."

"Why is it that I'm doing all the things that might annoy you, yet you seem to be warming up to me while I stew in my own juices of impatience."

"You'll figure it out in time ... or not." She gave him a smile that almost made it all the way up to her eyes.

"Bring me some of those plastic ties," Al said.

"You're not gonna just leave me here, are you?"

Al slid Carl over to a steel I-beam that ran up to the ceiling. He got Carl's back to it and tied his hands together with one of the clips. He used another set on Carl's legs, not that the dude was going anywhere. The plastic clips are harder to escape from than people think, at least the ones who haven't been tied up with them.

Al stood up and dusted off the garage floor grime from his jeans. "You ready to go?"

"Hey. Hey," Carl said.

Fergie went out and slid into her car. Al stood a moment, listened to the sound of a siren in the distance, coming this way. Someone hadn't wasted any time. He got in too and Fergie pulled away.

"We have a little time on the way," Al said. "Do you want to talk?"

"Why don't we just stay focused?"

"Okay with me. Now who has the issues?" he muttered.

They had a few blocks to go. He reached and turned on the radio, got a few bars of the song "Memories of Tomorrow." Worst possible selection. He flipped the radio off. Fergie glanced at him. He couldn't tell if she was smirking or a little sad, maybe both.

"What did you take away from that last little encounter?" he asked.

She glanced at him. "That someone is bringing in chop shop talent from outside, only these guys are focused on stealing and repainting cars. Someone's furnishing them paperwork for the messed up VIN numbers."

"This is organized."

"That's what I told McCarrigan, the guy who'll be putting the pinch on Carl back there. His thing is organized crime, and he loves, loves, loves him some spotlight now and again."

"They seemed to have responded quickly enough. But all of that's not our problem. We're after the one of them brought in who is a hothead, probably has a rap sheet full of priors that highlight his propensity to snap into flash anger while carrying a gun."

She kept her eyes on the road ahead. They were moving as briskly as he might hope. "And if we run this through the normal process McCarrigan and his guys will eventually backtrack to the organizer, perhaps get him, and we could get a name of this road rage hothead, maybe where he's from and get enough for a warrant, or at the least a BOLO. But he'll be repainted, rolling, and as long gone as the Dodo by then."

"Which brings us to this two-story yellow house up ahead on the left that looks like it was last painted when Truman was tromping around in the White House."

"That's some big-assed much newer garage behind it, though."

"Everything is fitting so far."

"Remember," she said, "I go in first. You hang back in case his proclivity to fire away kicks in."

"I said propensity."

"Proclivity. Propensity. Just stay in the car. Don't get shot."

She eased her car into the house's driveway, reached and got her bigger gun, the Glock, out of the glove box, and slipped out her door. She started taking slow careful steps toward the garage. Fergie was halfway to it before he realized she now had two guns and he had none.

He waited until she was pressed against the garage door listening. He got out his side and went out and all the way around the house toward the back of the garage. The neighborhood looked run down, with few back yard fences that didn't have large holes or had fallen down outright. No one in the neighborhood seemed to be on their porches or looking out of their windows.

The garage had a back door, just as he'd hoped. It had a ramp, probably for running a lawn mower down to tend to the back yard. But from the look of the yard a whole lot of tending hadn't gone on in a while. The yard was a collection of open dirt stretches marked by the litter of rusty cans and broken glass, with the green of tall prickly members of the dandelion family filling the rest. No dog either. That would have meant someone taking care of one, and little looked cared for in as many directions as Al could see.

He put a hand on the back door. Low and behold it was locked. No surprise there. No window either, so he couldn't peep in. But he could hear the front door slap against the inside garage wall as Fergie came charging in. "Freeze! Drop what you're doing. Hands in the air! I mean it."

Al could hear some scrabbling that didn't sound like compliance. He stepped back and kicked at the door. Standing a little off-balance on the ramp it took two frustrating tries before the door popped open, its locking mechanism dropping to a concrete floor in a chatter of metal falling into several parts. As he burst through to the brightly-lit inside of the garage he heard the first of the shots.

The car sat in the center of the garage, about halfway painted, one side a shiny white, the other the rusty reddish-brown of primer, the brown Freddy had seen. At least the compressor wasn't going at the moment to fill the place with its thumping loud racket.

A man holding a gun and looking the other direction crouched behind the open door of the car being painted. He wore a white plastic smock, which he tore off with his left hand while he snapped off a shot that slapped in a twang against the closed garage door, letting in a small beam of outside light.

Fergie had moved back outside the smaller open door. She called in from outside. "It's just a matter of time. You shot a three-year-old child. They're going to get you."

"Well, *you* won't." He snapped off another shot in the direction of her voice.

"You're surrounded. Lay it down!" Fergie yelled.

The guy looked back, saw Al, and fired a shot at him.

Just as the guy spun Al dove behind a fifty-gallon metal drum that served as a trash container. The bullet ricocheted off the barrel with a thud that probably left quite a dent. Sounded like a big gun to Al, maybe something like a .357. If it was the same gun, its bullet had gone through a car door before. Al didn't feel as safe behind the steel drum as he had before.

Al peeked around. The guy had the cylinder open and was shoving in more bullets. More bullets was not what Al or Fergie needed.

This was it. He sprang to his feet and charged. Fergie must have had the same idea. She stepped inside the door and slid around to one side, holding her gun with both hands, its barrel pointed at the crouched man, who had to be in her sights now, although she was in the wide open herself.

"Al. What the hell? I told you to stay in the car."

The guy glanced back. Al had his hand behind his back, so the guy wouldn't know he was unarmed. He looked back at Fergie. "Just shoot! You got a shot. Take it."

"You killed a kid. A tiny little kid. Why?"

"That was an accident."

"You were aiming for the grandmother?"

"You don't get it. The woman was a snail. I don't know. I'd had a rough day, a rough week, a rough life. I just snapped. I was going to be the rest of my life getting back to my digs."

"You're going to be the rest of your life somewhere," Fergie said.

"That's what you think." The man stood slowly, his gun hanging in his fist down at his side.

"Drop the piece! I mean it."

"Just shoot. Shoot. Shoot, damn you!" He got louder each time until he was screaming.

"You don't deserve that. Suicide by police. There's a special kind of hell for people like you. That's where you're going. But you're going to serve your stretch behind bars on the way getting there."

"That's what you think." The guy was apparently out of fresh things to say, and at the end of his playbook. He lifted his hand until the tip of his barrel pointed toward his own temple.

Al rushed forward, fast as he could go. He let his anger fuel the leap. His arm came down, slapping at the pistol.

Two shots fired, so close together they sounded like one. The Smith & Wesson .357 clattered to the concrete floor. Al would have kicked it away but that leg was consumed by a burning fire. He grabbed the guy, who was falling. They both tumbled to the ground. Al held on, though he hurt as badly as he ever had. She had shot him. Fergie had shot him. The other guy too, but Al as well.

She stood over them, slapping cuffs on the guy Al held tightly. Then Al's vision started to go and he saw black.

———◆———

His eyes fluttered open. He looked past the mask pumping oxygen into his nose and mouth. He could see red hair hanging toward him, then her face. He expected to see concern, but she was grinning. Damn her. She was grinning. Maybe laughing out loud.

He reached up and pulled off the oxygen mask with a jerk. One of the EMS guys started toward him, to put it back on. Fergie waved him away. He went back to tending the cuffed guy, who was still screaming.

Fergie leaned close. Blue and red swirling lights swept across the side of the yellow wooden house behind her. "You're probably going to be off your feet for a spell. You'll need someone to tend to you."

"Not Bonnie?"

"No. She has her hands full with Maury. I'd better move back in. Is that okay with you?'

He nodded before he thought about it. "Hey, you'd shoot me just to ..."

"Now, now," she interrupted. "You need to stay calm and get some rest. I'll come visit and take you home when you're ready."

Whatever those EMS guys had injected into him started to take hold. A pleasant wave swept through him. They must have done the same for the other guy, because he got quiet. They were loading him into the first ambulance. That meant at least he was hurt worse than Al. Good.

He looked up at Fergie, who still hovered close as he waited for his turn to be loaded. "It's not nothing," he said. "But I've been shot before, and worse than this."

"What did the doctors tell you that time?"

"To relax. That everything would be okay soon."

"Well, you just do that. You hear?"

He nodded.

This had sure been one helluva of a case. He couldn't remember when he'd known less. He knew about as much about Grandmother Freddy as he did Wacky Jackie. As for the victim, three-year old Abbie, he knew nothing. Had she liked favorite toys, certain foods? Did she have a distinctive giggle? And the hothead shooter, the epitome of the boiling rage just beneath the surface of half humanity these days, he didn't even know that guy's name, or anything about him. *Ah, well. What the hell?* The world is a tough, sad place. Maybe it's enough that some people reach and grab the smallest bit of comfort when they can. Maybe that was enough to make it all right. Or, if not right, more livable.

They closed the ambulance doors and the vehicle started to pull away.

He could see her out the back windows as she grew smaller. Just before she faded out of sight he saw her lift and hand and wave. He lifted a hand and waved back, though from this distance and with her fading from his sight, he doubted very much if she could see that. But she'd know.

OTHER BOOKS BY RUSS HALL

Thrillers
To Hell and Gone in Texas (An Al Quinn novel)
A Turtle Roars in Texas (An Al Quinn novel)
Throw the Texas Dog a Bone (An Al Quinn novel)
Island
Wildcat Did Growl
Talon's Grip
World Gone Wrong

Mysteries
The Blue-Eyed Indian
Bones of the Rain
Private Prodigy Eye (Three Sylvie
Thomas and Adam Clay novels)
South Austin Vampire
No Murder Before its Time
Black Like Blood
Goodbye, She Lied

Westerns
Bent Red Moon
Bullets in the Wind
Three-Legged Horse

Young Adult Sci Fi
Inside Jupiter

ABOUT THE AUTHOR

Russ Hall has had more than twenty books published: mysteries, thrillers, westerns, poetry, and nonfiction books, as well as numerous short stories and articles. For many years he was an editor for major publishing companies, ranging from Harper & Row, Simon & Schuster, to Pearson. Now he lives by a lake in Texas Hill Country near Austin. In 1996 he won the Nancy Pickard Mystery Fiction Award for short fiction. In 2011 he was awarded Sage Award, by The Barbara Burnett Smith Mentoring Authors Foundation--an award for the author who demonstrates an outstanding spirit of service, sharing and leading others in the mystery writing community. In 2014 he won First Place in the Austin International Poetry Festival. The Writers' League of Texas awarded the series-opening Al Quinn book *To Hell and Gone in Texas* its 2015 "Fiction Discovery Prize"